Karen King is a bestselling author of fiction for both adults and children and has also written numerous short stories for women's magazines. *The Cornish Hotel by the Sea* was an international bestseller, reaching the top one hundred in the Kindle charts in both the UK and Australia.

Karen is a member of the Romantic Novelists' Association, the Society of Authors and the Society of Women Writers and Journalists. She lives in Spain with her husband Dave and their two cats, Tizzy and Marmaduke.

By Karen King

Romance titles
I do? – or do I?
The Millionaire Plan
Never Say Forever
The Cornish Hotel by the Sea
The Bridesmaid's Dilemma
Snowy Nights at the Lonely Hearts Hotel
The Year of Starting Over
Single All the Way
One Summer in Cornwall

Thriller titles
The Stranger in My Bed

One
Summer
in
Cornwall

Karen King

ACCENT

First published in paperback in 2021 by Headline Accent
An imprint of HEADLINE PUBLISHING GROUP

1

Cataloguing in Publication Data is available from the British Library

ISBN 978 1 4722 7871 5

Typeset in 11.25/15.25 pt Bembo by Jouve (UK), Milton Keynes
Printed and bound in Great Britain by Clays Ltd, Elcograf S.p.A.

HEADLINE PUBLISHING GROUP
An Hachette UK Company
Carmelite House
50 Victoria Embankment
London
EC4Y 0DZ

www.headline.co.uk
www.hachette.co.uk

For my friends Annie and Richard whose parrot, Tipsy, is the inspiration for Buddy the parrot in this book. Xx

Chapter One

'Bloody hell! Who is it?'

Hattie Rowland froze at the voice, her finger poised on the light switch that she had been about to flick on. Someone was already in the cottage! Who could it be? A squatter? A burglar? For a moment she panicked, her breathing quick and shallow as she backed against the wall, wondering whether to run out again. Then she pulled herself together. She had every right to be here – whoever it was, they were trespassing, and she wasn't going to be intimidated by them. She took a deep, steadying breath and grabbed hold of her motorbike helmet, which she had tucked under her arm, ready to use as a weapon if necessary. The intruder would soon realise that she didn't scare easily. She pressed down the switch, gripping the helmet tightly, ready to spring into action. As the room lit up, there was a loud screech.

'Turn it off! Turn it off!'

Buddy! Hattie burst out laughing as she spotted the green parrot, perched on a thick branch running across a huge cage tucked into the corner of the living area, just before the open archway into the kitchen. The parrot's head was turned towards the door, his beady eyes fixed on her as he squawked crossly. Uncle Albert's beloved parrot. She hadn't even realised that Buddy was still alive. As the big bird glared at her from his perch, his green feathers ruffled, the yellow ring around his neck clearly visible, she was transported back to her childhood. Hattie remembered stepping into the cottage with her parents to be greeted by Buddy screeching, 'Bloody hell! Who is it?' and her mother immediately trying to cover her ears. Uncle Albert, a fisherman, was her father's much-older brother. He had never married and Buddy was his sole companion. Albert had worshipped the bird – and loved his little cottage by the sea. When he died a couple of months ago, Hattie had been surprised and touched to hear that he had left Fisherman's Rest jointly to Hattie's father, Owen, and Hattie. She had fond memories of summer holidays spent here in Port Medden with Uncle Albert when she was younger, and her parents were still together.

'Hello, Buddy. It's only me, Hattie. You probably don't remember me. It's been years since I last came down here,' she said softly. She felt guilty about that, but her parents had finally divorced, after years of acrimony, when she was twelve, and then she had barely seen her dad, who had immediately moved to France with his new girlfriend, now wife, Raina and remained there. Obviously, her mum, who now lived in Portugal with her partner Howard, hadn't wanted to spend summers with her ex-husband's brother in Cornwall, so Hattie had lost touch with Uncle Albert.

She dropped her saddlebags down onto the old brown sofa; she was sure it was the same one that had been there when she'd last visited – was it sixteen or seventeen years ago? In fact, nothing seemed to have changed, she thought, as she looked around, her mind going back to her childhood holidays. The thick grey curtains were the same, as was the now-threadbare brown patterned carpet on the floor. The TV was a more recent model than she remembered, and the fireplace was now boarded up with a gas fire in front of it. Not that she'd ever seen the fireplace in use when they'd come down in the summer, but there had always been a basketful of logs beside it, ready for the colder evenings. The old wooden rocking chair was still in the corner by the fire, but there was now a thick cushion on the seat. The dark wooden dresser, full of ornaments and decorative plates, still stood against the wall by the window. Over the fireplace was a stunning painting of fishermen tending their boats in the harbour. She didn't remember that, but the rest of the downstairs of the cottage was almost exactly as she remembered, except it no longer looked exciting and welcoming but dusty, faded, old.

Her eyes flitted back to the rocking chair where Uncle Albert had often sat, smoking his pipe and telling them stories of his fishing escapades. He'd been a broad, larger-than-life man, who had always made them welcome, cooking them hearty breakfasts, taking them out on his boat, joining them for a drink at the local pub where everyone had seemed to know him. And now he was gone. And he'd only been in his late seventies, no age nowadays. She felt sad that she had lost touch with him over the years. She wondered if her dad had kept in contact.

She walked over to the cage, which sat on a wooden wheeled trolley. Buddy immediately ruffled his feathers and eyed her warily from his perch. 'Bugger off!' he screeched.

'Charming!' Hattie thought with a smile. Had the parrot been here on his own ever since Uncle Albert was taken to hospital, over two months ago? she wondered. Uncle Albert had died within a couple of days of being admitted. Surely Buddy hadn't been here alone all that time?

The cage was clean, the water seemed fresh and was half full. Buddy appeared cared for, if irritable. There were several things to keep him amused: a thick rope, a mirror, ladders, even a swing. Someone was obviously looking after him. Who? Maybe one of the neighbours had a key.

'Bugger off! Go to bed!' Buddy shouted, obviously wanting his sleep, too.

She grinned. From what she remembered of Buddy, he was cantankerous and prone to cursing! There had been no mention of any arrangements for the parrot in her uncle's will, but she was happy to look after him. She owed Uncle Albert that much. It had been so generous of him to leave her half of his cottage, especially now when she desperately needed a haven. Not that this was a permanent move: Hattie and her father had agreed to sell the cottage and split the money, but at least it was a roof over her head until they found a buyer, giving her breathing space to decide what to do next.

'I think I will. Goodnight, Buddy,' she said.

She took her toiletry bag out of one of the saddlebags – she'd unpack the rest in the morning – then walked through the arch into the galley kitchen and put it on the table while she searched the dark wooden cupboards for a glass. Letting the tap run for a while to clear out the pipes, she poured herself a drink of water and leant back against the sink, surveying the kitchen as she drank the cool liquid. It didn't seem to have changed much in here, either: the same wooden table with a red, checked, plastic tablecloth over it, the same old cooker – how could it still be working? A washing machine – surely that had been replaced – and, amazingly, a silver microwave. And even an electric kettle!

She yawned. She was weary after the motorbike ride down from Bristol. It had been a long day and was now almost midnight. She really needed her bed. She'd wheeled her bike into the front garden – which was nothing more than a small, tiled patio – and parked it against the wall, taking off the top box containing her necessary clothes and possessions and leaving it in the hallway until morning. Hattie toyed with the idea of wheeling her bike into the more secure back yard but it seemed too much effort.

She'd packed the rest of her belongings and left them with her best friend Mali, who'd promised to bring them with her when she drove down next week, with her six-year-old daughter Lou, for the end of May half-term holiday. Mali was a teacher, and luckily her holidays coincided with her daughter's so they could get away together. Hattie had planned to travel down next week too. She, Mali and Lou had been going to spend a few days at the cottage, tidying it up a bit, but then Hattie had been made redundant and homeless within a couple of days, so had decided to come down earlier.

She finished her water, picked up her toiletry bag, flicked off the light and headed off for the stairs at the end of the hall. She'd forgotten how narrow and steep the staircase was, and held tightly to the wooden rail as she climbed up, the dim bulb above not helping much to light the way. How had Uncle Albert managed? He was twenty years older than her dad,

5

which was one of the reasons they hadn't been particularly close. Uncle Albert's dad had died when he was a young boy, and his mother had remarried again years later then Owen, Hattie's father, had been born, so Uncle Albert was actually his half-brother.

After stopping off at the dated bathroom to go to the loo and clean her teeth, Hattie continued up the other flight of equally steep stairs to the attic bedroom where she and her parents had always used to sleep – it didn't feel right to sleep in what had been Uncle Albert's bedroom. She pushed open the creaky door and groaned in dismay when she saw that both the double bed, and the single bed by the window that used to be hers, had only a mattress on them. Of course they wouldn't be made up! She cursed her impetuousness in coming down tonight. Why hadn't she waited until the morning when it would be light? She could have stayed with Mali.

There hadn't seemed much point in waiting, though. There was nothing left for her in Bristol. Once the keys had been handed over to her landlord, who had decided he was going to let his recently separated daughter live in the flat that had been Hattie's home for the last three years, she had set off. Originally, Hattie had intended to sit out her month's notice and look for another flat, but when she lost her job, too, she decided that getting away from it all and going to Cornwall while she sorted out her life was the best thing to do. The flat had been furnished, so she hadn't had much stuff to pack up, and Mali had been happy to take the few boxes of items Hattie couldn't fit on her bike and then bring them down to her. The landlord had been so grateful – his daughter and baby were temporarily staying with him and his wife – he'd returned her deposit immediately and let her off with that month's rent. So, here she was. Jobless, homeless – well, once Uncle Albert's cottage was sold – and boyfriend-less, since her lying, no good ex, Adam, had cheated on her a few months ago and she'd told him where to go.

It can only get better, she thought, determined to remain positive. *Now, where did Uncle Albert keep the bedding?* She was so tired, she felt as though she could fall asleep on the spot. She glanced around, then spotted the huge dark-wood wardrobe across the far wall. She vaguely remembered her mother getting bedclothes from there. She walked over to check inside, but the doors wouldn't budge. There was no sign of a lock, so she tugged hard. Still they wouldn't budge. She held the handle with both hands and tugged again. The door sprang open with such force she fell back onto the wooden floor. *Ouch!* Scrambling back up and rubbing her tender – and probably bruised – bum, she checked out the wardrobe, and to her relief, folded on the bottom, was some bedding. *Thank goodness!* She pulled a clean pillowcase onto the feather pillow, threw a sheet over the bed, and a bedspread over that – nothing as modern as a duvet for Uncle Albert! – then pulled off her motorbike leathers, draping them over a chair, and got into bed naked: she hated wearing pyjamas, they always seemed to tangle around her in the night. She was so exhausted, her eyes closed as soon as her head hit the pillow.

Chapter Two

Sunlight streaming through her window woke Hattie up the next morning. And it sounded as though the seagulls were having a party on the roof. She sat up for a moment, hugging her knees, thinking how drastically her life had changed in the past few days. On Monday, she'd had a home and a job, now, five days later, she had neither. She shook her head. She wasn't thinking about that now – this was a chance for her to sort out her life, and she was going to grab it with both hands.

Throwing back the sheet she ran over to the window and looked out, just as she used to do when she was a child on holiday here, eager to see the shimmering ribbon of sea over the rooftops. The cottage was just a few minutes' walk from the picturesque harbour, and when she was younger she had often opened the window and inhaled the sea air, with her mother anxiously warning her not to lean out. She wasn't going to do that now, not until she was dressed, anyway, so contented herself with kneeling down, so only her head was visible, and peering at the sparkling turquoise ocean just a stone's throw away. She couldn't wait to walk along the beach and have a paddle. She almost felt as though she was on holiday! *I'm going to take a few days to relax and have a good look around*, she decided, *then I'll start tidying up the house*. She and her father had agreed to put the cottage on the market as soon as they could, so she would probably only be here for the summer, but at least it gave her some time to sort out the shambles that her life had become.

First, though, she needed a cup of milky coffee to wake her up. She'd put a box of three-in-one sachets in her right saddle-bag, in case there were no supplies in the house. Carefully negotiating the first set of narrow stairs to stop off at the bathroom to go to the loo and splash some water on her face, she cautiously descended the other staircase to the kitchen.

'Who is it? Who is it?' Buddy screeched as she walked in.

'Morning, Buddy. It's me, Hattie!' she called. She filled up the electric kettle, glad that the old stove kettle she remembered, with the high-pitched whistle that let you know when the water had boiled, had been replaced. The almost-new silver kettle and matching microwave looked a bit out of place in the dated kitchen, but she was grateful for them. She took a clean mug out of the cupboard, then froze as she heard the back door open and someone stride in, whistling cheerfully. Horrified, she spun around and stared at the sun-tanned stranger, dressed in low slung grey surfer shorts that skimmed his hips, his long fair hair tied back in a ponytail revealing a tiny silver cross earring dangling from his right ear, a large tattoo on each upper arm, his body taut and toned. Then his hazel eyes widened as they flitted to her naked body. *Shit!* She'd forgot she was starkers! They both stared at each other, dumbstruck for a second, then Buddy's screech of 'Bloody Hell!' brought Hattie to her senses.

Two quick steps and she'd whisked the checked tablecloth

9

off the table and quickly wrapped it around herself. She glared at the man. 'Who the hell are you? And how dare you walk in like this!'

'More to the point, who are *you*?' the man demanded. 'I'm Marcus, from next door. I'm here to feed Buddy. I've been looking after him.'

Damn! She remembered thinking yesterday that Buddy looked well fed and cared for, so a neighbour must be popping in to feed him. Why the hell hadn't she pulled her dressing gown on this morning? Because it was still in her saddlebag and she was half asleep and hadn't expected someone to walk into her kitchen this early in the morning, that's why. It was barely eight o'clock!

'I'm Hattie, Albert's niece. He left this cottage to me and my dad in his will.' She held the tablecloth tighter around herself, the plastic feeling sticky and uncomfortable against her skin. 'I came down last night. I'm staying here until the cottage is sold.'

A look of disdain crossed Marcus's suntanned face and his hazel eyes narrowed. 'I thought you were coming down *next* weekend. You obviously couldn't wait to claim your inheritance. Shame you didn't see fit to visit your uncle when he was alive and lonely.'

Ouch! Well he had obviously got her earmarked as a gold-digger who didn't give a damn about her uncle. She opened her mouth to explain, but then anger set in. How dare he judge her when he didn't even know her?

'You don't know a thing about me, so keep your high-handed moralistic opinions to yourself!' She lifted her chin defiantly, then, clasping the tablecloth tightly with one hand to

10

ensure it didn't slip down, she held out the other. 'And I'll have the key to *my* cottage back, thank you. I don't want strangers walking in on me any time they like. Thank you for looking after Buddy,' she added stiffly. 'But I'll take care of him now.'

Marcus's eyes flashed sparks of anger and his mouth was set in a grim line, but he put his hand in the pocket of his shorts and pulled out a key. 'Be my guest.' He threw the key down on the table, then turned, revealing a large eagle tattoo with wings outspread across his back, and walked out.

'Bugger off, then,' Buddy screeched loudly as Marcus slammed the door behind him.

Hattie giggled at the parrot's outburst; she couldn't have put it better herself! What a horrible man! He might look hot with his lean, sun-kissed body and surfer-boy hair, but he didn't appeal to her one little bit. He was so up himself and bad-mannered, he hadn't even apologised for walking in on her. Just her luck that he lived next door. Well, she intended to avoid him as much as she could. She hoped the neighbour on the other side of her wasn't so unpleasant.

Well done, Marcus, you not only walked in on the poor woman naked, but you also didn't even stop to check that she knew how to look after Buddy properly. Parrots aren't as easy to care for as most people think, and Buddy had been pining since poor old Albert died. It was only seeing Marcus's familiar face first thing in the morning and last thing at night that seemed to cheer him up. He needed to be let out to exercise his wings, too . . . would – what was her name? – *Hattie* even think of that? And if she did, would she think to close the windows to make sure Buddy didn't fly

11

out? And would she be able to get the parrot back in the cage again? Buddy could be pretty stubborn. Like his owner.

It's not my problem anymore.

He'd promised Albert when he was taken into hospital that he would look after Buddy, and he'd kept that promise even after Albert had died. At first, he'd taken Buddy back to Curlew Cottage with him, thinking it would be best not to leave him on his own, but Mr Tibbs, his tomcat, had taken an instant dislike to the parrot, spending his time either staring into the cage or climbing onto it, and poor Buddy had got really agitated and stressed so, after a couple of weeks, Marcus had taken Buddy back home again and since then had popped in to see him every morning and evening. Buddy was happier back in Fisherman's Rest, but he missed Albert. Marcus did too. He'd befriended the old man when he'd moved next door, into Curlew Cottage, seven years ago, and although Albert had been independent right up until the day he'd caught the flu which had turned into the pneumonia that had killed him, he'd been happy to accept the meals that Marcus had brought around for him. Marcus had even bought Albert an electric kettle and microwave one Christmas a couple of years ago, so he could warm the meals up. He'd admired the old man very much and spent many an hour in the evening after work sharing a dram of whisky with him and listening to Albert's seafaring tales.

You shouldn't have been so rude to his niece, he told himself. *Your cottage was inherited too, from your grandparents.* Yes, but he'd loved and looked after his grandparents, and the cottage had been left to him, his mother and his sister. He had bought them both out – okay, at a discounted price, but even so it hadn't been a complete gift. This Hattie hadn't been down to see Albert once

12

in all the time Marcus had lived next door. She was obviously a spoilt townie, eager to put the cottage on the market and get her share of cash so she could buy a bigger house, faster car, or whatever she wanted to spend the money on. *As for her dad, don't get me started on him.* Owen Rowland had flown over for the funeral, spent a couple of hours in the cottage, and flown back the same day. Marcus had returned from work just as Owen had been leaving, so hadn't even had time to tell him that he was looking after Albert's parrot for him. Fat lot he seemed to care about his brother.

Albert, however, had been proud of his younger brother, often telling Marcus what a go-getter Owen was, how he had his own business over in France. A five-star B&B. There were twenty years between them so they weren't close, Albert had said, but they kept in touch. Sometimes, when he and Albert were chatting over a whisky in the winter evenings after Marcus had finished his shift at work, the old man had talked about his niece Hattie, showed Marcus photos of her – a blonde, vivacious-looking child – related how she used to come down on holiday until her parents split up. Marcus could see that he missed them all and had tried to persuade him to get in touch with them, but all Albert said was that 'folks have their lives to live'. And now he'd left them the cottage. There had been no one else to leave it to, of course, but Marcus resented – on Albert's behalf – the fact that his family hadn't eased the loneliness of his later years, but then couldn't wait to come down and sell his home.

Even so, he had walked in on Hattie unannounced and ... the image of her sensual naked body flashed across his mind: full breasts, tiny waist, a cute stars and crescent moon tattoo on the top of her right arm and looong legs. Tousled white-blond hair cut into a shaggy bob and those summer-blue eyes flashing with anger as she tore a strip off him, looking ridiculously cute wrapped in that red, checked, plastic tablecloth. Not to mention the enchanting slight lilt to her voice – he'd certainly noticed a lot in those couple of minutes that they had stared at each other! He was impressed that she hadn't screamed or blushed but had held her ground. She seemed like a tough cookie. He should have apologised for walking in on her like that, and he *would* if he bumped into her again. Apart from that, he wasn't wasting any more time thinking about a spoilt little townie, even if she was gorgeous. He was going surfing, as he did every morning, then he intended to do some painting – he had a commission to finish – and then he was working tonight. It suited him to be chef for the evening shift, it left him with the days free to surf and paint, whilst Shanise was happy to do the lunchtime meals as then she had the evenings free with her partner and children.

He changed into his wetsuit, leaving the top half to dangle from his waist until he got to the beach, picked up his surfboard, a bag with his rash vest, wetsuit boots, surf gloves and a towel, and set off down the hill. An hour or so riding the waves was all he needed to regain his equilibrium.

Chapter Three

An hour later, showered and changed into denim shorts and a black vest top, Hattie took her camera bag which held her Nikon D810 and her tripod camera equipment out of her top box and slung the camera around her neck,. Then she moved her motorbike around to the back yard and parked it by the side of the shed before heading off down to the harbour, hoping she would find a café open and be able to grab some breakfast. She probably should have headed uphill for the corner shop instead, and stocked up on a few supplies, but she was ridiculously eager to see the beach and take some photographs. Photography was a hobby of hers, bringing her in a small, part-time income, and was one of the ways she chilled out. She specialised in 'people photography' and loved to capture people in spontaneous, relaxed moments, especially action shots. It wasn't ten o'clock, so she doubted if the beach would be very busy this early on a Saturday morning, but she thought she might catch a few fishing boats, and early bird tourists, and then she could head to Medden Beach where the local surfers went to ride the waves.

To her surprise, there were a few families strolling along the harbour front, and to her relief, the café was open. Hattie headed straight for it and ordered a cup of coffee and two slices of toast off the pleasant lady serving, then sat down at a table facing the harbour, where she could see a couple of boats bobbing about in the distance.

'Here you are, dear. Down for a holiday, are you?' The wait-ress came over with Hattie's breakfast and placed it down on the table in front of her.

'I'm living here temporarily,' Hattie replied. 'I didn't expect it to be so busy this early in the morning.'

'It's half-term week; some of the families came down last night, wanting to make the most of the week off.' The waitress flashed her a smile. 'Enjoy.' Then she went to serve the next customer.

Hattie sat nibbling her toast, gazing out at the harbour, reliv-ing the events of the last week. Firstly Brian, her landlord, had called around on Tuesday evening to give her notice to leave as he needed the flat for his daughter. Then yesterday, George, her boss, had come into work looking grim, called a meeting and told them all that unfortunately the Bridgnorth branch of Mil-ton and Banner Insurance was closing that day and everyone was being made redundant – bar himself, who would be mov-ing to manage another office. Hattie had been shocked and panicked. Okay, she didn't look on Milton and Banner as her forever job, but she worked with a lovely crowd and she needed the wage. Now, she was jobless and homeless. How could her life change so drastically so suddenly?

Trying to keep positive, she had reminded herself that she had her share of the money from Uncle Albert's cottage, when

16

it was sold, and also her redundancy money when it came through. She'd been working for Milton and Banner for five years so the redundancy money was enough to tide her over for a few months whilst she tried to turn her passion for photography into a full-time business. And she could live in Uncle Albert's cottage until it was sold, which would save her rent money. She'd phoned her dad to check that he didn't object and he'd agreed, asking her if she could tidy the cottage up a bit while she was there and also reminding her that the house would be harder to sell with a 'tenant' so she had to tell the estate agent that she was just 'looking after it' and it would definitely be sold vacant. *Great, thanks for being concerned that I've lost my job and my house, Dad*, she'd thought as she'd ended the call. She'd texted her mother who was on a Caribbean cruise with her stepfather, to let her know her change of address and circumstances, but hadn't received a reply yet. Not that she expected one. Both her parents were so wrapped up in their own lives with new partners and families, they didn't have time for their eldest child, the only one they shared together. Well, she was twenty-eight, which was plenty old enough to take care of herself, and it wasn't as if she was penniless, was it? She knew that if she was really in need, both her parents would help her out like a shot.

George had let them all go after telling them the redundancy news, so they'd congregated in the coffee bar around the corner, all commiserating with one another, cheering each other up, promising to keep in touch. Hattie had phoned Brian to tell him she would be moving out that day, then had headed home, phoned Mali, who had immediately come over after school to cheer her up and help her pack, then Hattie had set off for Cornwall.

Last night, she had wondered if she'd done the right thing, but now, sitting here looking out at the boats bobbing about on the endless blue sea, she was sure she had. A summer in Cornwall, tidying up the cottage ready to sell and setting up her photography business, was just what she needed. It was a shame about her hostile neighbour – especially when he was so undeniably easy on the eye – but she would avoid him as much as she could. This was a new chapter in her life, and she was going to seize it with both hands.

When she'd finished her breakfast and taken a few shots of the harbour, Hattie decided to take a stroll to Medden Beach, hoping there would still be some surfers there so she could get some photos of them in action. She wanted to update her Facebook business page to attract more customers, and knew that photos of surfers, the beach and quaint seaside towns were very appealing. She was in luck, there were half a dozen surfers already riding the waves. One of them, a tall man, clad in a black wetsuit, caught her eye. He was standing, knees bent, poised to ride a huge wave that was crashing towards him. She watched as he expertly rode right over the wall of white foam, held her breath as his surfboard disappeared underneath him, then let it out again as somehow he landed right on top of it, steadied it and got ready for the next wave. He was good, she thought in admiration. She managed to get some brilliant action shots of him. Surfing looked exhilarating and she wondered whether to have a go herself. There was a notice on the nearby beach hut offering surfing lessons, as well as wetsuits and surfboards for hire. Not today, but maybe in a week or two, she decided. She was a good swimmer and loved doing physical activities.

She picked up the camera again as the surfer in the black suit came walking out of the sea, a white surfboard with a blue tip tucked under his arm. Something about him looked a bit familiar but it wasn't until he turned and glared at her that she realised who it was. Marcus.

'Did I give you permission to photograph me?' he demanded.

Jeez, what is this guy's problem? 'I was just taking some shots of the beach and the surfers,' she said. 'It's not a crime. This is a public place.'

'And I am a private person. I don't want photos of me surfing on your Facebook page.'

He really is an arse, isn't he? 'I'm a photographer, I'm always taking photos,' she informed him. *Well she was, even if it had only been a hobby up until now.* 'But don't worry. I don't want a photo of you anyway and certainly wouldn't dream of putting it on my Facebook page.' She selected the photos she had taken of him on her camera and deleted them all. 'There, deleted. Want to check?' She held out her camera.

'I'll take your word for it,' he said stiffly.

'Nice of you. And you can be sure I won't be taking any more photos of you.' She walked off, dangling her sandals from her fingers, inwardly seething. Why did she have to have this obnoxious man for her neighbour?

Putting on her sandals as soon she left the beach she set off back home. As she approached the row of three cottages, with Fisherman's Rest in the middle and Mr Obnoxious on the left, she wondered who lived on the right of her. She hoped they weren't as unpleasant as Mr Obnoxious; one shirty neighbour was enough to contend with. The small front gardens were all surrounded by a low wall with a gate, but that was where their similarity ended. The front garden at Fisherman's Rest was paved and bare apart from a paint-chipped bench underneath the window and the name plaque of the cottage on the wall. Mr Obnoxious on the left had a lawn on one side of the path and a flower bed on the other, whereas the garden on the right – Primrose Cottage, the name plaque said – was paved, but there were lots of hanging baskets and colourful pots. It looked cared for, so someone must be living there.

When Hattie had taken her bike around the back before she went to the beach, she'd noticed that all the back yards had a high, shoulder-height wall and padlocked gate. The back yard of Fisherman's Rest was completely paved, with a shed on the left, and a rusting small table and two chairs on the right. She could soon pretty it up with some colourful pots, she thought, and maybe she could sand the table and chairs down and give them a coat of paint.

She unlocked the front door and was greeted by a loud 'Bloody Hell!' from Buddy when she walked into the lounge.

'Charming!' she told him, smiling at the way he was glaring at her, as though he was annoyed that she'd disturbed his sleep. *He doesn't remember you*, she reminded herself, wondering how often Marcus had come in to look after him. She guessed the poor parrot must have been on his own a lot since Uncle Albert died.

'I bet you miss your owner, don't you, boy?' she said softly, going over to the cage.

The green parrot cocked his head to one side and stared banefully at her with his beady eyes: orange ringed by a circle of black then white. She glanced at his food dish; he had hardly touched the pellets. Maybe he liked to eat later in the day. There must be a supply of food somewhere – she'd top up his food this afternoon and give him some fresh water. She had to admit she was a bit nervous about opening the cage door to do it, in case the parrot either attacked her or escaped. *I'll just have to be careful and make sure all the windows and doors are closed*, she thought.

She made herself another coffee, using one of the sachets she had brought with her, then decided to have a good look around the cottage. She had arrived too late last night to take anything in. She wanted to take some photos to send to her dad, too; he'd asked her to let him know if she thought the cottage could be sold as it was, once it had had a tidy up, or whether it needed some refurbishment. It seemed strange to have so much contact with her dad, when she had hardly seen or spoken to him since the divorce. Her teenage self had resented him going straight off to France to live with Raina, his new love, and her son, Nick.

The one time she had gone over to spend the summer with her father, she had felt odd, out of place, and Nick had made it clear that he didn't want her there either. Raina had tried to be welcoming, but the more she had tried the more Hattie had resented her for coming along and splitting up her family. She felt that to be friendly to Raina would be being disloyal to her mum. Then when baby Lacey had come along a couple of years later, Hattie had really felt an outsider; her father and Raina had a new child together, a new family. She'd avoided going over to visit again, not wanting to desert her mother, so her father had come over once a year for an awkward long weekend with Raina, Nick and Lacey and they'd all met for a polite lunch and that was it. By the time Hattie had gone to college to study photography, her contact with her father was reduced to phone calls on her birthday and Christmas. Hattie's mother, Caroline, had met her partner Howard a few years ago and gone to live in the Algarve, so that was both her parents living abroad. Hattie didn't really mind; she had a busy life and at least both her parents were happy now.

Armed with her iPad – far easier to send quick photos to her father that way – and a notebook, she moved from room to room, assessing what needed doing. The kitchen was functional but dated, the dark cupboards making it look rather dingy; the white paint covering the stone walls in both the kitchen and the lounge area needed refreshing, and maybe a new bright carpet, the existing brown patterned one being stained and worn. An hour later, she had completed her tour and jotted down a page of suggestions. Uncle Albert didn't seem to have done much to the cottage in all the years he'd lived there, but she didn't think they should modernise it too much; part of its charm was that it was so traditional. She was sure her dad wouldn't want to spend too much money on it either.

She tried to log onto the wi-fi to send the notes and photos over to her dad, but the only wi-fi connection available was secured and she couldn't find a router anywhere to get the password. There was a phone but it was disconnected. She should have realised that Uncle Albert wouldn't have wi-fi – why would he? She sighed. Well, at least she had an unlimited mobile-data package, so she could just use her phone or iPad for the Internet. It would be a waste of time getting wi-fi installed now, as she would only be here a couple of months and you usually had to sign up for a twelve-month contract.

She zapped the photos over to her dad, had another cup of coffee and decided to draft a poster to put in local shop windows to see if she could drum up some photography work.

Then she went into the back yard to check on her bike, wondering if she should put the cover over it. There were a lot of seagulls about.

She heard a *miaow* and saw a big black cat perched on the top of the wall, its intense amber gaze fixed on her.

'Hello, puss,' she said, walking over towards it.

The cat glared at her, then scrambled back over the wall as soon as Hattie got closer. She wondered if it was Marcus's cat. It didn't look very friendly and that stare could terrify the birds in the trees. Maybe that's why he had kept Buddy in Uncle Albert's cottage and come around to feed him rather than taking him home with him.

Walking over to the bike, parked up by the shed, she looked with dismay at the white splodges on the black leather seat. The bike cover was definitely a good idea. Hearing the gate open next door, she glanced over and saw Marcus walk in, hair wet and tousled, carrying his surfboard. His eyes met hers over the shoulder-high wall, then flicked to the motorbike. She saw the surprise on his face, then he looked away, placed his surfboard against the wall and went indoors. Just her luck to have such a disapproving, up-himself neighbour!

Chapter Four

Hattie wiped the bike seat and put the bike cover over, then went inside to take her printer out of the top box in the hall. Placing it on the kitchen table, she booted up her laptop. The lack of Internet was a problem, as her printer usually worked via wi-fi, but luckily she had brought the cable with her so could use that to link the printer to the laptop. Half an hour later, she had half a dozen A5 sized posters printed out with a link to her business Facebook page which featured some of the photos she'd taken. They looked pretty impressive, she thought as she read over one of them. She'd try the corner shop first, she needed some food supplies anyway and didn't fancy riding out anywhere to get a big shop in yet. She wanted to explore the little town of Port Medden after lunch. So, she popped the posters into a cotton shopping bag then grabbed her shoulder bag and set off up the hill.

The lady in the corner shop was very friendly. 'Of course you can put your poster in the window. How long do you want it in there for?'

'Would three months be okay?' *It would take that long to sell the cottage, surely?* 'I need to try and get some photography work to keep me afloat and I'm guessing the summer months are the best time for that.'

'It certainly is. Have you just moved into Port Medden, then?' the woman asked.

'Yes, I'm here for the summer.' Hattie sensed that the woman would've liked to ask her more, but there was a queue behind her so she had to move onto the next customer. That was a close shave, she had purposely not told her where she was staying as she didn't want to upset anyone else who thought she'd neglected her elderly uncle and now couldn't wait to get her hands on his cottage.

'Excuse me?'

Hattie turned around. A middle-aged woman with bleached-blond, chin-length hair, and lips coated in bright-red lipstick, was standing behind her. She smiled, her blue, heavily mascaraed eyes looking warm and friendly. 'I couldn't help overhearing that you're a photographer. I'm Mandy. I work on the reception at Gwel Teg, the hotel up the hill. We've got a wedding booked there next Saturday and the photographer has just had to pull out because of a family emergency. Would you be able to cover it?'

Wow! Her first commission and she'd only just put the poster in the window. It wouldn't be the first time she'd covered a wedding, either; she'd been asked by a couple of friends to do the photos for theirs – mates' rates, of course – and they'd been delighted with the results. Thank goodness she had some of the photos on her Facebook business page.

'That's such a shame and so close to the wedding too,' she said, sympathetically. Exactly a week today! She bet the bride was panicking. 'I'd love to take the photographs. Would you like to see some samples of my work? I have some on my Facebook page and could also show you some print samples.' Luckily, she'd brought her sample album with her.

'Fabulous. I'll check out your page first. I'm guessing the details are on your poster.' Mandy smiled. 'Sue, the manager of the hotel will want to meet you and see samples so it would be good if you could bring some prints then. It's Sue's daughter, Ellie, who's getting married, to Reece, the co-owner of the hotel.'

'Of course. When would you like me to meet her?'

'I'm on the afternoon shift today, so how about you pop in about two thirty? Bring your photos to show Sue and we'll take it from there. Does that sound okay?'

'Perfect.' Hattie felt a flutter of excitement. If she got this commission it would look great on her profile and be a big boost for her photography business.

She went back to Fisherman's Rest feeling much happier. Things were really looking up.

'Bloody hell. Who is it?' Buddy squealed as she walked in. That seemed to be his favourite phrase!

'It's me, Hattie,' she replied, putting down her shopping and going over to him. He still didn't seem to have touched his food, she noticed. Well Mr Obnoxious had been looking after him so she was sure he'd had plenty to eat yesterday. 'Hello, Buddy,' she said. 'Do you remember me? Can you say Hattie? Hello, Hattie.'

Buddy glared at her. 'Bugger off,' he replied, then turned his back as if to emphasise that he meant it.

He was a real ray of sunshine, wasn't he? Hattie thought with a smile. She remembered that Uncle Albert used to let Buddy out sometimes to fly around, and the parrot would perch on his plate and try to eat his food then the old man would swipe him away saying, 'Bugger off!' She guessed that's where Buddy got his language from. He must miss the old man. Maybe she ought to let him out to fly around, but she was worried she wouldn't get him back in the cage again. If only Marcus wasn't such a grouch she would pop around and ask him, but the less she saw of that man, the better.

I'll spend some time with Buddy tonight, she decided. *I'll give him some fresh water and food and have a chat to him.* He might perk up with a bit of company. She'd do a google on what parrots liked to eat, too; it must be boring for Buddy to eat pellets all the time, and she was worried that they hadn't even been touched today. Right now, though, she wanted to sort out her portfolio of photos ready to take to Gwel Teg that afternoon.

By the time Hattie had sorted out her photos and had a bite to eat it was almost time to leave for her appointment at the hotel. She changed into a pair of loose black-and-yellow-print cotton trousers and a yellow cap-sleeved T-shirt and added a touch of make-up to her face, wanting to look casual but professional. Then she googled the directions to Gwel Teg – and, out of curiosity, the meaning of the name, which was 'Beautiful View' – and set off for the short walk.

The hotel was situated halfway up the hill, on the corner. It was very pretty and quaint with its white pebble-dash exterior, colourful window boxes, prime location near to the beach and the glorious view to the sea. *What a beautiful place to get married in*, she thought. She'd read on the hotel website that Gwel Teg did the whole wedding package, with a dedicated room for the ceremony and reception. How wonderful that the manager's daughter was getting married there.

She went inside and spotted Mandy on reception straight

away. 'Hello, Hattie!' She waved. 'Take a seat, lovey, Sue will be here in a few minutes.'

'Thanks.' Hattie sat down on the comfy-but-smart long blue sofa and looked around. The reception was clean, bright and modern. There had obviously been some money spent on the hotel in the last couple of years. The wedding package was new, too, she'd noticed; it was something they'd started this Easter. It was a really good idea, she thought; couples could book into the hotel for the wedding, and have their honeymoon here too. She was sure that would be very popular. It was a beautiful part of the country to get married in.

'Hello, Hattie. I'm Sue Truman, the hotel manager.'

Hattie looked up at the small, dark-haired woman standing in front of her, holding out her hand. She'd been so deep in thought she hadn't noticed her approach. 'Pleased to meet you.'

They shook hands, then Sue sat down beside her. 'Mandy said you're a professional photographer and are free next Saturday, so you can take the photos for my daughter, Ellie's, wedding? I can't tell you what a relief that is. The other photographer only cancelled this morning – distressing circumstances, so it couldn't be helped – and I really didn't want to break the news to Ellie and her fiancé Reece at such short notice.'

'Yes, I'm free and I'd love to do it.' Hattie paused; she didn't want to mislead the woman. 'I'm only a part-time photographer at the moment but am hoping to expand my business to full time. I completed a photography course at college and have been taking photographs for years now, but I had a day job and took photos in my spare time. I have had my photographs published in several magazines, and I've photographed several weddings too so I am very experienced.'

'Well, that all sounds very promising. Have you got some samples of your work with you?'

'Yes.' Hattie opened her portfolio at the wedding-photo pages and showed them to Sue, who seemed very impressed. 'Do you mind if I look at some of the other photos as well?' she asked.

'Of course not,' Hattie told her.

She watched the expression on Sue's face as she turned over the other pages, photos of young babies, children, family groups then stunning sunsets, moonlit lakes, magical woodlands and forests. 'These photos are wonderful.' Sue closed the album and handed it back to Hattie. 'I would love you to take the photos for my daughter's wedding, but the final decision will be Ellie and Reece's. They are coming tomorrow morning; they want to spend the week here, having a relax and getting the hotel ready for the wedding. Could you pop in and meet them tomorrow afternoon? I'm sure they will be as impressed with your photos as I am.'

'Of course. What time do you want me to come?'

'About three thirty?' suggested Sue.

'Perfect,' Hattie replied. She just hoped that Sue's daughter and fiancé would be as impressed with her photos as Sue was.

'Do you live in Port Medden?' Sue asked.

'Not permanently. I'm here for the summer. My uncle recently died and left his cottage to me and my dad in his will.'

'Albert's cottage? Fisherman's Rest?'

'Yes.' Hattie replied anxiously, wishing she hadn't mentioned it now. What if Sue thought she was a selfish money-grabber, as Marcus did, and didn't want to employ her?

'Ah, then you live next door to Marcus, our chef. He's a

29

lovely man. You'll meet him at the wedding – he and Shanise are doing the food.'

A lovely man! Well, that's not how she would have described Marcus and she certainly hoped that she didn't bump into him at the wedding reception. As far as she was concerned, the less she saw of him, the better.

Chapter Five

Hattie spent the rest of the afternoon reacquainting herself with Port Medden, which hadn't changed very much in the years since she'd last visited. Such a lot had happened since then. Hattie had left home as soon as she started work in the insurance office, renting a flat and intending to build up her photography business so that she could eventually leave her job. Then she had met Adam who had moved into her flat a few months later, and there had been little time for her photography, as they set up home together, worked full time and had a busy social life. She really had thought Adam was the one, and it had devastated her when, after three years of living together, she'd discovered that he'd cheated on her. She told him where to go in no uncertain terms and decided from then on, she was going to live her life for herself. That's when she'd started to build up her photography business again. Now, thanks to her redundancy money, she might be able to do it full time, and thanks to Uncle Albert, she might be able to rent a studio and put a deposit down on a little flat. Things were looking up, especially after this morning. She couldn't believe that she'd got her first professional photography job in Port Medden. Well, she hoped she had – she still had to meet the bride- and groom-to-be and get their approval.

When Hattie arrived back home she was greeted by the usual 'Bugger off' from Buddy as soon as she walked in.

'Well, you're a pleasant soul, aren't you?' she said, walking over to the cage to see if he had eaten anything yet. The pellets seemed untouched. 'What's the matter with you? Do you fancy something tastier?' she asked.

Buddy gave her a scornful look and turned his back on her.

He really was a character, Hattie thought, remembering that she still hadn't googled what parrots liked to eat. She grabbed her phone and pulled up a search on feeding parrots. *Ah!* They liked fresh fruit, veg, cooked eggs, chicken and turkey. She'd get him some broccoli, a good source of vitamin D. And a corn on the cob to peck at. That should cheer him up. As soon as she'd had a bite to eat, she'd clean out the fridge and then go to the local supermarket for a shop. She wanted to spend tomorrow morning cleaning and sorting out the two bedrooms and bathroom, before going to Gwel Teg to meet Sue's daughter and fiancé. Then she planned on taking a walk along the beach. She was going to make the most of the glorious late-May weather and beautiful location. The day after, Monday, she would take a trip to Truro and leave a poster in some of the shops there too.

It was still warm, too warm to traipse around the supermarket in her bike leathers, so she changed into crops and a T-shirt, then took the cover off the bike and wheeled it out of the back yard – just as the gate to next door opened and Marcus came out. His gaze went to the bike, then back to her. She guessed he was surprised that she rode a motorbike instead of driving a car;

a lot of people were. She loved motorbikes: the feel of the wind against her face, the convenience of being able to weave in and out of the traffic, of not having a problem parking. She fastened her helmet and straddled the bike, giving him a smile and a wave before she zoomed off.

Marcus watched her ride away. It was a nice bike, an electric-blue Harley, and she had good control of it although he thought she was pretty stupid to ride without her leathers, even if it was hot. Marcus could see why people liked motorbikes; he'd had one himself when he was younger, although he preferred his Volkswagen camper now, so he had somewhere to put his surfboard and other gear. Plus, it was far warmer than a motorbike in the cold and rain. He often took off in his camper van for the weekend if he wasn't working, and liked not having to worry about booking accommodation.

He watched as Hattie turned the corner, her crops showing off an enticing expanse of tanned legs. She really was gorgeous.

He swatted his last thought away. Looks weren't everything. Kaylee had taught him that. He would never again be turned by a pretty face and a hot body. It was personality, character, and loyalty that mattered. And this Hattie seemed to be lacking all three.

He wondered how Buddy was doing. He must wonder why Marcus wasn't coming around anymore, and who Hattie was. He hoped she had remembered to give the parrot some fresh water and food, and to clean out the cage. Buddy hated a messy cage, so Marcus always changed the paper in the bottom every day, and gave the whole cage a good clean every week. He'd mention it to Hattie next time he saw her – if he could manage to get a few words out without them arguing, that was! He'd tell her the treats Buddy liked, too. She would probably think he was interfering, but he had a responsibility to Buddy – he'd promised Albert he'd look after his beloved bird.

Right now, though, he had to go to work. He enjoyed his evening shifts at Gwel Teg, it gave him time to paint during the day and meant he earned a living doing his two favourite things: cooking and painting. Most people assumed that he was waiting for his big break so that he could quit his job and spend his days painting instead, but he didn't want to give up his job. Painting could be a solitary occupation, and Marcus enjoyed company far too much to be on his own every day. Also, not having to earn his living by painting meant he didn't have any pressure to paint. If he didn't feel like painting one day, fine, he would go surfing, or out for a ride in his camper. Unless he had a commission, like now. He frowned. This current job paid well but it wasn't really his cup of tea; he'd be glad to be finished it. Lady Felicity Thornwell was nice enough, but her daughter Estelle made no bones about the fact that she had designs on Marcus, which made the job difficult. How did you turn down a client's daughter without upsetting her and without losing the work?

Hattie parked her bike in the supermarket car park then grabbed a trolley and went inside, taking the short list she'd scribbled out of her back pocket. She'd love to get a treat for Buddy but – as she'd thought – there wasn't much of a pet-food section, so she got him some fresh fruit and vegetables.

She finished her shopping and went home, preparing herself for Buddy's usual greeting as she walked through the door. To her surprise, not a peep came from the parrot's cage. Putting her shopping down on the table she walked over. 'Hello, Buddy, how are you?' she asked. The parrot glared at her, but didn't reply. Hattie glanced in the cage. It didn't look as though he'd touched any of his food, and his water dish was still half full. That was worrying. 'I've got some tasty treats for you. I just need to unpack first. I won't be long.'

She hurriedly put her shopping away, then took the corn on the cob over to the parrot's cage. She was a bit worried that Buddy might fly out when she opened the cage and that she wouldn't be able to get him back in again, so she opened the door very warily. 'Here you are, Buddy.' Buddy watched her from his perch, but didn't move. Hattie opened the door a little wider so she could get the corn on the cob inside. She placed it carefully on the floor of the cage. 'You'll like this, Buddy,' she said. 'Very tasty.'

Buddy flew down to the corn on the cob and sniffed it. Hattie watched him with relief. Thank goodness, now he was going to start eating – but suddenly she yelled as Buddy climbed up the cage bars and pecked her hand.

'Ouch!' she yelled, instinctively letting go of the door, and then Buddy was out.

'Oh no! Buddy, come back!' Hattie shouted in panic as the parrot flew across the room and perched on the dresser. She looked around frantically to see if any windows were open. *No, thank goodness*. So at least Buddy was confined to the cottage. Now all she had to do was coax him back into the cage again – which she was pretty sure wasn't going to be easy. The only way she could think of doing it was to tempt him by putting some food in the cage, which wasn't going to be simple as he didn't seem to be interested in the corn on the cob. If only she knew what his favourite treat was! Well, she'd have to hope that the broccoli would entice him. She washed a chunk and pushed the stalk through the bars of the cage, near the perch.

'Here you are, Buddy. Come and get a tasty treat,' she called.

Buddy looked down from the top of the dresser but didn't move.

Then Hattie remembered that Uncle Albert used to let the parrot out of his cage in the evenings and that Buddy would run along the top of the sofa screeching – and sometimes pecking the hair of anyone who was sitting on the sofa. She couldn't remember how Uncle Albert got Buddy back in the cage again, but every morning when she came down for breakfast he was back inside, so she guessed he went in when he was ready. Providing she didn't open any doors and windows, he ought to be safe enough. She didn't want him getting out, or that black cat getting in and chasing him. *Perhaps that's what's the matter with him*, she thought. Maybe he was fed up of being locked in the cage. If she left him out for a while, he might go back in by himself and start eating.

She made herself a cup of coffee and sat down on the sofa with her laptop. A couple of hours passed as she sorted out photographs to add to her Facebook page then used her phone to reply to emails. When she'd finished, she sent a message to Mali. Lou was with her father, Ricki, at the moment but she would be back home on Tuesday, so they were coming down then – only three days away - and going back Friday evening, travelling after dinner so Mali could avoid the heaviest traffic.

Hattie was looking forward to seeing her friend again and having some company. Maybe she would be able to persuade Mali and Lou to come and stay with her for the six-week summer holidays, she thought.

Suddenly aware that she hadn't heard a sound from Buddy for a while, she looked over at the cage, hoping he had flown inside. No sign of him. She got up and looked around. 'Buddy? Where are you?' she called, looking around in panic.

Oh no, the kitchen door was ajar, she realised in panic. Had Buddy flown upstairs? Suddenly remembering that she had left the attic window open to air the room, and that she wasn't sure she'd closed the bedroom door, she raced up the stairs.

Please don't let Buddy have flown out!

As she hurried past Uncle Albert's bedroom, she heard a familiar squark. 'Get up, lazy sod. Get up!'

Buddy? She stopped. The door to the bedroom was open so she looked inside. 'Buddy!' she called, walking into the room. Uncle Albert's bed looked as if he had just got out of it, the bedspread thrown back, a dent in the pillow. Buddy was hopping along the pillow, squawking. 'Get up, lazy sod.'

Hattie swallowed the lump in her throat. He was looking for Uncle Albert.

She walked as softly as she could over to the bed. 'He isn't here, Buddy,' she said gently. 'I'm looking after you now.'

Buddy tipped his head on to one side and eyed her quizzically. 'Bugger off!' he screeched and flew to the top of the wardrobe, where he perched, staring at her with disdain.

Now what am I going to do?

'He's got to eat,' she told herself. 'He'll come down when he's hungry.' She left the bedroom door ajar, went up and closed the attic window and door, then went back downstairs. She cooked a lasagne, leaving the door open so that the smell would waft up the stairs, but Buddy remained where he was. No amount of coaxing and cajoling would persuade him to come down, and eventually Hattie had to go to bed and leave him there. She left the lounge door open, hoping he would come down in the night and eat the broccoli or corn on the cob that she had left in the cage to entice him. And she prayed that he wouldn't injure himself in any way. She could just imagine Marcus's reaction if any harm came to Buddy.

Chapter Six

When Hattie got up the following morning, she found Buddy was fast asleep on the pillow of Uncle Albert's bed. As soon as she stepped into the room, he squawked 'Bugger off!' and flew to the top of the wardrobe again.

Hattie sighed. There was nothing else for it. She would have to enlist Marcus's help. Apart from the fact that she was worried about Buddy not eating, Mali and Lou were coming Tuesday night – just two days away – and would have to sleep in Uncle Albert's room, so Hattie needed to change the sheets, freshen it up, and clean out all the parrot poo Buddy was leaving everywhere.

She frowned. She certainly wasn't relishing the idea of asking for his help. It had to be done though. She'd have a shower and breakfast first, then go and see him.

Marcus opened the door, still towelling his hair dry, and stared in surprise at Hattie standing on the doorstep. He'd just stepped out of the shower when the doorbell rang, so had hastily pulled his shorts on.

'Sorry to bother you,' she said, looking awkward. 'It's just that Buddy has escaped from his cage and—'

'What? How has he got out? You didn't have a window open, did you?' Marcus jumped in, annoyance and alarm in his voice.

'No, of course not!' she snapped. 'I was putting some fresh food in his cage and he bit me, then flew out.' Hattie showed him the red mark on her hand. 'The – er – door was open a bit and he flew up the stairs into Uncle Albert's room. He's been there all night and won't come out. I've tried to tempt him with broccoli and corn on the cob but he won't budge. Actually, he doesn't seem to be eating or drinking,' she confessed. 'I was wondering—'

'He's upset, that's why. You're a complete stranger to him, and all of his routine is shattered.' He knew that the parrot was still grieving for Albert, and he was probably also wondering where Marcus had gone and what the hell a strange woman was doing in his house, and that's why he wasn't eating.

Her eyes sparkled with anger. 'I realise that. I'm doing my best here. I came to ask if you could help me get him back into his cage. Sorry I troubled you.' She turned and started to walk away.

He felt a bit bad for snapping at her like that. It wasn't her fault. Buddy was really crafty and had managed to sneak out of the cage a few times when Marcus had been cleaning him out.

'Look, he's done that a couple of times with me. He's missing Albert,' he said, softening his tone. 'That's why I left the sheets on Albert's bed. I usually let him out for a bit so he can go into Albert's old room. He can smell Albert on the bedding and it comforts him a bit. He usually flies back to his cage in the night though; he's always there when I check on him in the morning. So, maybe if you leave it a little while, he'll fly back.'

'The thing is, I really need him out of there. I've got a friend and her daughter coming to stay in a couple of days, so I need to change the bedding and clean the room for them.' She pushed a lock of white-blond hair out of her eyes. 'And I'm really worried that Buddy's not eating.'

Just as he'd thought: she wanted rid of the parrot. Well, it was only what he'd expected. He'd have to offer to take Buddy off her hands, and make sure he put him somewhere safe, away from Mr Tibbs. Maybe he could keep him in his studio in the attic and make sure the door was always closed. 'Give me a few minutes to put a top on and comb my hair, and I'll come and get him,' he said. 'I'll bring my carry cage. I bought it when Albert was ill because he wanted Buddy to keep him company and it was easier to take him upstairs in a little cage.' Marcus had let Buddy out for an hour to keep the old man company in the evening, then come back after his shift to coax the bird back inside again and take him downstairs for the night so Albert could sleep in peace.

'Thanks. Can you come around the back? I'll leave the gate and back door unlocked.'

Hattie walked away and Marcus went upstairs to grab a T-shirt and give his hair a quick comb, then went into the spare bedroom for the small carry cage. He would bring the big cage around, too, later on; this one didn't have enough room for Buddy to fly around. On the way out, he grabbed a banana from the fruit bowl, and his keys, then pulled the door shut behind him and went round to next door.

'Only me!' he called as he let himself in, closing the door behind him. Hattie walked through from the lounge, her eyes resting on the smaller cage and then flitting to the banana.

41

'We'll get him in this, then move him to the big cage.' Marcus held up the banana. 'Buddy's favourite treat,' he explained.

She looked disappointed. 'I got him broccoli and corn on the cob,' she said. 'I did an Internet search and that's what it said parrot's like.'

'Buddy likes carrots and apples, but he's really mad for bananas.'

'Ah, I've got a couple in the fruit bowl. They're one of my favourite snacks,' Hattie said. 'I'll show you the way.' She set off up the hall to the staircase as if she thought that Marcus didn't know the way, whereas he had climbed these stairs many a time, often with a hot meal in his hands when Albert had been bed-ridden with the flu.

Marcus tried not to notice Hattie's cute bum in those clinging denim shorts and her long, long legs as she went up the narrow staircase ahead of him – he was way past the stage where looks were the most important thing to him – although, yes, he was a red-blooded male and a pretty face and gorgeous figure were appealing, but personality was what mattered most to him, and he wasn't impressed with what he'd seen of Hattie's character so far.

'He's in there.' Hattie pushed the door of Albert's bedroom right open, and Marcus stepped inside. He had to swallow and compose himself for a couple of minutes, as the memory of the old man lying desperately ill in bed came flooding back to him. Albert had been so weak and helpless and had had no one to depend on but him. Marcus's anger at Albert's selfish, absent, vulture family came flooding back.

'Are you all right?'

Hattie's question jerked him back to the present. He turned

42

to her and, to his surprise, saw genuine concern in her brilliant-blue eyes.

'Yes. It's just . . . being in this room reminds me of when your uncle was ill,' he said gruffly.

'You used to come up here, you mean? Was he ill in bed and you looked after him?'

'Yep. Too ill to do anything for himself. It was me who called the doctor in to him. I tried to look after him, but he got worse and had to go into hospital. He never came out.' Marcus knew that he sounded abrupt and cold, but he was actually fighting back the tears that sprang to his eyes as he remembered how ill and alone the old man had been.

'I'm sorry. I didn't know.' Hattie's voice was a whisper.

He didn't dare look at her face. He was just about holding it together as it was. 'You would have, if you'd have bothered to keep in touch with him!' He snapped the words out, then glanced at her and felt a twinge of remorse at the hurt look on her face. The quicker he got Buddy and himself both out of there, the better. His anger at how callously Albert had been treated, and how quickly his family had turned up to claim their inheritance as soon as he had died, was eating into him and he felt that, any minute now, it would erupt into a furious outburst.

He put the travel cage down on the bed and opened the door.

'Where've you been?' Buddy screeched, peering down at Marcus from the top of the wardrobe.

'Hello, mate,' Marcus said. 'Look what I've got for you.' He sat down on the bed and unpeeled the banana. Then he took a bite out of the top of it.

43

There was a flutter of wings and then Buddy was on his shoulder, biting into the banana too. Marcus let Buddy nibble it for a while, then casually tossed the last piece of banana into the cage. Buddy squawked and flew in after it. Marcus closed the cage triumphantly.

'Hey, well done!' Hattie said, clapping. 'I'm so pleased to see him eating.'

'I'm used to looking after him. I know what he likes. And he's used to me. I guess he's been missing me.' Marcus picked up the cage and carried it down the stairs, leaving Hattie to follow him.

'Thanks so much,' she said as they both reached the bottom of the stairs.

'No problem. I was going to come around later to ask you if you wanted me to take Buddy anyway. I thought he might be too much for you.' Marcus strode up the hall towards the front door, the cage cradled in his arms so that he didn't unsettle Buddy too much. 'If you wouldn't mind opening the door for me,' he called over his shoulder. He heard hurried steps behind him, then suddenly Hattie was standing in front of him, barring the door.

'What do you think you're doing?' she demanded.

He stared at her. 'Taking Buddy home, of course.'

'You are not! *This* is Buddy's home. I asked you to help me catch him, not to take him away.'

Marcus shifted the weight of the cage in his arms. 'You're telling me that you want me to leave him *here*? That *you* want to look after him?'

Hattie had her hands on her hips now and looked furious. 'Yes, I am. How dare you assume that I wanted rid of him?'

'Well, you couldn't be bothered to visit your uncle, even

44

when he was dying, so I presumed you wouldn't want to look after his parrot!'

She tossed her head back and jutted out her chin. 'Before you jump to conclusions and judge people, you should check your facts.' Her eyes glittered and her cheeks glowed. 'I lost touch with Uncle Albert because my parents divorced when I was twelve and my dad went to live in France with his new partner. Obviously, my mother didn't want to come down and visit her brother-in-law and I wasn't going to come down by myself, was I, when I barely knew him and was already trying to cope with the fallout from the divorce, as well as a new neighbourhood, new school and absent father. Yes, we lost touch, but Uncle Albert didn't contact me to ask how I was, either. Communication works both ways!' She grabbed the cage out of his arms. 'I am very grateful to Uncle Albert for leaving me and my dad his cottage, and have every intention of looking after his parrot. So, if you wouldn't mind letting your-self out!' She stormed off into the lounge and slammed the door shut behind her with her foot.

Chapter Seven

Hattie was shaking with anger. That man was pig-headed, sanctimonious, judgemental and downright infuriating. And the less she saw of him the better. How dare he judge her like that without even knowing the facts? It's not as if she even lived in the same area as Uncle Albert; she lived hundreds of miles away and he hadn't been in touch with her once since her parents had split. No phone call, Christmas card, birthday card, zilch.

'Bloody hell!' Buddy squawked as Hattie clumsily dropped the cage down on the table. *It was heavy!*

'Sorry, Buddy!' She sank down into a chair, resting her head on her hands. She was exhausted already and had no idea how she was going to get Buddy back into the bigger cage and give this smaller one back to Marcus. She looked over at the couple of bananas in the fruit bowl by the fridge. Perhaps she could open the door of the big cage, put a banana inside it, carry this smaller one over to it, open the door, and then Buddy would hop from one cage to the other.

Or fly away again. That would be just her luck.

She closed her eyes, the turmoil of the past few days washing over her. She had lost her job and her home, then come down here on impulse, grasping at the chance to make a fresh start, but had she done the right thing? Should she have stopped in her flat until the month was up, and signed up with an agency to get office work? She'd already made an enemy, the cottage needed a lot of cleaning up, and the parrot was a nightmare. What if she made a mess of the wedding photography next Saturday, too?

If she got the job, that was. She had only ever photographed friends' weddings before. Mandy had said that Ellie was the manager's daughter and her husband-to-be, Reece, the hotel co-owner. They would be expecting professional photographs. What if hers weren't good enough?

There was a knock on the lounge door, and she looked around as it slowly opened.

'Is it safe to come in?' Marcus asked, poking his head around the door.

God, is he still here?

'If you're waiting for your cage back, I'll leave it in your yard later,' she said wearily.

'I thought you might need help to get Buddy back in his big cage.'

Marcus was looking at her hesitantly, as though wondering whether she might throw something at him – it would be no more than he deserved if she did! She wanted to tell him to get lost, that she was quite capable of getting Buddy into the big cage by herself, but she knew that she probably couldn't, and she didn't want to risk losing him again.

'That might be a good idea. Then you can take your cage

47

back with you,' she said. 'Do you need another banana? I've got a couple.'

'Yes. And . . .'

She eyed him suspiciously. 'Yes?'

'Well, I guess I owe you an apology. I don't really know your circumstances so shouldn't judge but, in my defence, it was hard seeing your uncle so ill and no family bothering to get in touch or visit him.'

'We didn't know he was ill. Dad never said – I don't think he even knew.'

'Albert was a proud man. I guess he didn't want to bother anyone.' Marcus nodded at the cage on the table. 'Are you sure you don't want me to take Buddy? He's used to me and I don't mind looking after him. I did have him at mine for a bit, but he's nervous of my cat, Mr Tibbs.'

She guessed that was the black cat she'd seen on the wall. She didn't blame Buddy; the cat's eyes were a bit mesmerising. 'I can manage.' She pushed her chair back and stood up. 'Let's get him in the big cage, shall we? And I'll be more careful next time I feed him.'

'Albert used to let him out every evening for a fly around,' Marcus told her. 'To be honest, I think he was out of the cage more than he was in it, when Albert was home, which was a lot, in the later years. He adored that bird.'

'Which is one of the reasons I'm going to keep him. No matter what you think, I'm grateful to Uncle Albert for leaving me a share of this cottage, and I'm going to look after Buddy for him. It's the least I can do.'

Marcus's hazel eyes flitted to her face then he nodded. 'Fine. Well, if you need any help or advice with him, ask me and I

48

promise not to bite your head off. And if you change your mind and want me to have him, then let me know. It's not a problem. I can keep Mr Tibbs away from him. I could put his cage in the attic, he'd be safe there.'

'Thanks.' She picked up the cage. 'Shall we do this?'

Another banana and a few minutes later, Buddy was back in his cage. His retort of 'Bloody hell!' when the cage door was closed on him made Hattie giggle. 'My mum used to cover my ears whenever he swore when we used to holiday here.'

'And when was the last time you were here?' Marcus asked. He held up his hands, palms outwards. 'Genuine question.'

'The summer before my parents split. I was eleven, so seventeen years.'

'Ah, so that's why I've never seen you. Your uncle talked about you, though, showed me some photos of when you were little.'

'Really?' She was touched that her uncle had talked about her to Marcus. Suddenly she wanted to know more about Uncle Albert. 'Look, I'm going to have a coffee, do you fancy one?'

She saw his slight hesitation. 'I'd love to, but I'm running late. Can we do it another time?'

'Of course.' She wondered if he was meeting a girlfriend; a guy like him was bound to be hooked up with someone. Or if he simply didn't want to spend any more time with her than he had to. He might have apologised, but it was evident she still didn't rate very highly in his opinions, which was fine as she didn't think much of him either. He had obviously cared a lot about Uncle Albert though, and been really kind to him. And he was her neighbour, so it was best if they could at least be polite to each other.

★   ★   ★

He'd been tempted to stop for a coffee; he felt a bit of a heel for how he'd accused her of not caring about her uncle, and he could understand now why she hadn't been down to see him, a distant older brother of her father and someone she had only met a few times as a child. He wasn't normally so quick to judge, but poor Albert had been so lonely and struggled so much. Hattie had said that none of them had known, and he believed her. Albert had been as stubborn as a mule – obviously a family trait, he thought with a wry smile, remembering how Hattie had insisted she would look after Buddy, although he was sure the parrot would be too much for her. Buddy was as cantankerous as his owner had been. He just hoped that Hattie would accept defeat before the bird pined away. Or escaped out of an open window. Maybe now they had made some kind of truce he could pop by occasionally and ask how Buddy was doing. That way he could keep an eye on him.

Meanwhile, now he really *did* have to go. He had to get over to Thomwell Manor, on the outskirts of Truro, and finish the painting Lady Felicity Thomwell had commissioned him to do for her husband's sixty-fifth birthday.

Felicity was friendly, but kept a professional distance. Not like her daughter, Estelle, who had just returned from Paris for the painting – which was of the Manor, with Felicity and Estelle dressed in crinolines and holding parasols, picnicking on the lawn – and had made no secret of the fact that she would like to get to know Marcus better. *Much* better. It was tempting; she was older than him, early forties he'd guess, beautiful, outrageous, and used to wrapping men around her little finger, but he had a firm rule to never get involved with a client or a member of their family. However, the more Marcus kept his distance, the more outrageous Estelle became. He wouldn't be surprised if one week she didn't walk into the room Felicity had set aside for him to use completely naked and offer to pose for him! Male artists often had an unfair reputation of being womanisers, when the truth was, it was often the clients who did the chasing – there was something about an artist they seemed to find irresistible. He had the same rule about getting involved with holidaymakers. He'd only broken that rule once, and that had been a big mistake that he would never repeat.

He changed into a T-shirt and jeans, grabbed his phone and a bottle of water, and set off. His painting materials were already in his van.

Thomwell Manor was a beautiful old house surrounded by colourful, well-looked-after gardens. Marcus knew that Felicity and Rupert Thomwell often entertained, and ran many high-profile charity events, and he had been delighted when she had approached him to do a special painting for Lord Rupert's sixty-fifth birthday. Marcus had spent hours on the painting – usually on Sunday afternoons when Lord Rupert was out golfing – but really needed to make more progress as it was Lord Rupert's birthday in two weeks' time. Marcus would miss coming to the Manor, it was beautiful and peaceful, and Lady Felicity kept him supplied with snacks and drinks, whilst Estelle was entertaining company. She was tempting too, if he was honest, but even though he was single and could do what he liked, she wasn't tempting enough to risk all the trouble a relationship with her would bring. And to be honest, apart from the obvious, she wasn't the kind of woman he was attracted to.

Whereas Hattie . . .

He shut the thought down right away. Hattie might not be

as selfish as he'd first thought her to be, and was undeniably gorgeous, but she wasn't the sort of girl he'd get involved with either. He'd bet high odds that she'd have the cottage on the market within a month. She was definitely not a little-seaside-town girl.

Pushing all thoughts of Hattie out of his mind, he set up his easel outside and got to work, and was soon absorbed in recreating the house in front of him in oils on the paper. It was coming on well, he'd be adding the two women to the painting soon, their position on the lawn already pencilled in.

'Fancy a drink?'

He turned to see Estelle, clad in the skimpiest of bikinis, holding out an enticing-looking cocktail. 'Don't worry, it's a mocktail. I know you don't drink alcohol when you're working. Which is a bit boring, if you ask me. I thought artists were all a bit wild and spent most of their time out of their head.'

'We wouldn't get much painting done, if we did,' he told her wryly. He put the palette and brush down and took the ice-cold drink off her. 'Thanks.'

'It looks good,' she told him. 'You're very talented.'

'Thank you.'

'I was hoping you might do me a favour.' She sipped her drink slowly through her straw, her eyes meeting his. 'Don't look so worried, you'll enjoy it. I promise.'

Chapter Eight

Hattie spent the morning cleaning up Uncle Albert's bedroom ready for Mali and Lou to sleep in when they came down the day after tomorrow, then made herself a sandwich for lunch, got changed and went to Gwel Teg to meet Ellie and Reece.

She'd been a bit nervous about meeting them, but she needn't have worried – they were both very warm and friendly and loved the photographs that she showed them.

'We want our wedding to be relaxed and informal. That's why we are having it here, at Gwel Teg,' Ellie said. 'I'll feel like my dad is watching over me here, as if he's part of it too.'

'Your dad died here?' Hattie asked softly. Ellie didn't seem much older than herself; her dad must have died young.

'Yes, just over four years ago,' Ellie told her. 'It was totally unexpected, a heart attack.'

'I'm so sorry.' Hattie wasn't particularly close to her dad but she would hate it if he died. *Maybe I should make more of an effort with my dad*, she thought. He seemed to be trying harder to keep in touch with her now, phoning her quite regularly since they'd learnt the contents of Uncle Albert's will, but still Hattie kept it short, never discussing anything personal.

Reece left Ellie to discuss the photos with Hattie whilst he checked on various things to do with the hotel. 'Whatever Ellie wants is fine with me,' he said.

'Let me take you around first, show you the room where the ceremony and reception are taking place, and the grounds where we want the photos taken,' Ellie suggested.

'That would be really helpful, thank you.'

Ellie led her down a hallway to the back of the hotel. 'We had an extension built last year so that we could host weddings and business conferences,' she said. 'It was Reece's idea, and it's proved really successful.' Ellie pushed open some double doors and they both stepped into a long dining room, with a wooden tiled floor and large windows that let in a lot of light. There was a stage to the left immediately as they walked in, and on the far side were some chairs and a table stacked against the wall.

Hattie followed Ellie through the folding doors in the middle of the room. 'We close these doors to make the area for the wedding ceremony smaller, more personal, and then after the ceremony the doors are opened to give more space for the reception and evening entertainment.' Ellie closed the doors behind them to illustrate.

Hattie's gaze flitted around the now-smaller room, then over to the closed folding doors. 'So, you open the doors after the ceremony and go through for the wedding breakfast?'

'Yes. Then we move the tables to the side for the entertainment in the evening.'

Hattie nodded. 'That sounds ideal. I presume there will be chairs placed in rows for the guests to sit here?'

'Yes, we have covers for the chairs and tables – the theme is white and gold. There will be two rows of chairs and a table, covered and decorated, where the registrar will conduct the ceremony. I'll walk in then, under an arch decorated with flowers, and follow the red carpet to the front of the room where Reece will be standing. Mum will be giving me away.' She smiled. 'Mandy's made our wedding cake, it's a hobby of hers, and we're using a local florist.' Her face lit up as she explained the ceremony to Hattie.

She looked so happy and in love, Hattie thought, imagining Reece standing at the front and Ellie walking up the aisle towards him, their guests watching. The room was so light and airy, she would be able to take some beautiful photos. 'Perfect. And what about outside photos?'

'We've got a pergola at the bottom of the garden, and the beach is right below. That's where the usual photographer takes most of the photos. Come outside and I'll show you.'

Hattie followed her outside to a surprisingly big garden with immaculate lawns and colourful flower beds. At the bottom of the garden was a wooden domed pergola, the sparkling ocean a spectacular backdrop behind it. The perfect setting for some stunning photos. 'How gorgeous!' she said. 'It's the perfect setting for a wedding.'

'Thank you, we think so too.' Ellie smiled. 'Now, if you're happy to take the job, let's go inside and discuss terms over a cool drink.'

'I'd be delighted to accept the job,' Hattie told her.

Half an hour later, an agreement had been signed, with a very lucrative fee, to Hattie's delight.

'Mum said that you've just moved down to Port Medden,'

Ellie said after she had shown Hattie the Silver Room on the second floor where she and the bridesmaids would be getting ready, telling her that she would like some photos of the pre-wedding preparations too. They were now both sitting in the private quarters sipping an iced tea.

'Yes, my uncle – someone I haven't seen for years – died and left his cottage between me and my father, so I came down to spruce it up ready to sell. My father and stepmother run a B&B in France and he can't get away yet.' Ellie was a good listener and Hattie found herself confiding in her about the split with Adam, losing her flat, and then her job. 'It seemed a good opportunity to reassess my life.'

'It seems a wise choice to me. And your photos are lovely, I'm sure you'll have no problem getting work down here. We're hoping to hold weddings regularly at the hotel, so would be happy to recommend you to other couples who want to get married here.'

'You haven't seen your wedding photos yet,' Hattie quipped.

'They'll be gorgeous, I know they will,' Ellie told her.

Ellie's kindness and confidence in her made Hattie determined not to let her down.

Reece and Sue came in to join them, and after a little more chit-chat about the specific photos they wanted Hattie said goodbye and walked home feeling a lot more confident than when she'd set out. Ellie had been full of ideas about how Hattie could promote and extend her photography business, and both she and Reece had taken one of Hattie's flyers and promised to recommend her to people.

It's so kind of them. I'd better not stuff up their wedding photographs, Hattie thought as she walked down the hill to Fisherman's Rest.

She unlocked the door and walked in, expecting to be greeted by Buddy's familiar cursing, but to her surprise the parrot didn't make a sound. Hattie made her way over to the cage and peered inside. Buddy was hunched listlessly on the perch, and a couple of feathers were lying on the bottom of the cage. She looked at them worriedly. Was he moulting because he was hot? Was it something to be concerned about? He still wasn't eating any pellets and she was sure the level in the water bottle hadn't gone down either.

'Are you okay, Buddy? Are you missing Uncle Albert?'

The parrot stared at her miserably but still didn't utter a sound.

'You don't have to worry, I'll look after you,' she said, wanting to reassure the bird even though she doubted if he could understand anything she was saying.

Buddy looked away and started pecking at a feather on his wing.

Was that normal? Hattie wondered. She was worried about Buddy, and wished that she hadn't been so stubborn and had accepted Marcus's offer to look after him. The poor bird must wonder what the hell was happening, he'd had so many changes in his life. He probably would have been better off with Marcus, who he seemed to have a bond with, she thought, remembering how Buddy had nibbled the banana in Marcus's hand. Then she remembered the big black cat, and how Marcus had said Buddy was nervous of it.

You can do this, you just have to earn Buddy's trust, she told herself.

She'd spend some time talking to Buddy when she got back from the beach, she decided. He probably just needed some

57

company. Meanwhile, she'd leave the radio on; her mum used to do that when she had to go out all day and leave Timmy, their cat, alone. It might take a little while, but Buddy would soon get used to her. She didn't need Marcus to rescue her. She could handle a parrot.

Chapter Nine

Hattie was on her way back from the beach when a sleek white convertible raced past her, a glamorous woman with short blond hair and wearing designer shades was driving and Marcus, looking very smart in what seemed to be a dinner suit, sitting beside her. Well, she'd got the impression he was a bit of a hippie, surfing in the daytime and doing evening shifts at the hotel, yet here he was all togged up and with someone who looked like they'd be more at home sailing across the sea in a yacht than surfing on it.

Not that it was any of her business.

She let herself back into the cottage and headed straight over to Buddy's cage. The parrot eyed her warily. He didn't seem to have plucked out any more of his feathers, she noticed with relief. Maybe leaving the radio on had been a good idea. It didn't look like he'd eaten any of his pellets though, or touched the corn on the cob she'd left him. 'Hello, Buddy. Do you want some more banana?' she asked him.

He stared at her, but didn't reply.

She picked up a banana and peeled it, broke half off, and

then opened the cage very cautiously and slipped it inside, then closed the cage door again. Buddy squeaked and scrambled down the bars to grab it, then climbed back up onto the perch and sat eating it. She'd love to let him out and have him share the banana with her, as Marcus had done, but knew she had to take it slowly. At least he seemed to be getting used to her. She'd spend a bit of time talking to him tonight, and she'd clean out the cage and give him some fresh food and water. Hopefully he wouldn't escape again.

Hattie went over and put the kettle on. She was pleased with how today had gone, Ellie was really warm and friendly, like her mum. And Reece was very nice too. She felt honoured to be photographing their wedding and was determined to do them proud.

She'd just made her coffee when her phone rang. It was Mali. 'How's it going?' she asked. 'Are you all ready for me and Lou to descend on you Tuesday?'

'I will be.' Hattie carried her cup of coffee over to the sofa and curled up, knees underneath her, to talk to her best friend. She couldn't wait for Mali and Lou to come down. Mali was such a lively, fun character and Lou was a sweetie. It would be good to have other people here to liven up the place. It might do Buddy good too. She glanced over at the cage and saw that the parrot was now nibbling at the corn on the cob. She smiled. She was worrying over nothing; he'd soon get used to her. 'I'd better warn you about Buddy, you might need to cover up Lou's ears,' she said.

'Buddy? Who's Buddy? That was quick work, you've only been there a couple of days.'

Hattie giggled at the surprise in Mali's voice and settled down for a long conversation.

She felt a lot happier when she and Mali had finally finished talking – with a brief interruption from Lou extracting a promise from Hattie to build a big sandcastle with her.

Maybe being made redundant and having to leave her flat had been the push she needed to make a new start. Her job in the insurance office was okay but it wasn't what she really wanted to do with her life, just like her relationship with Adam hadn't been what she really wanted, they'd drifted into it if she was honest.

'You never stop to ask yourself what you want, Hattie. You go along with the flow,' Mali had told her more than once. Which was true. It made life easier. It seemed to be a pattern that had started when her parents were married and anything could provoke an argument. After the divorce, she had accepted without question that she would live with her mother and had gone along with her mum's excuses as to why she shouldn't visit her father and *that woman* after the disastrous first visit. Not that she had wanted to; her dad had betrayed them, made a new life for himself and left Hattie and her mother behind. Except, now he was back in her life, wanting to airbrush the past as if it never happened.

Almost on cue her phone rang again and it was her dad. She hesitated, wondering whether to answer it; she knew he'd try and chat to her while she preferred to keep their exchanges to texts or emails, such a distance had grown between them over the years that she didn't feel close enough to him to chat. Then Hattie remembered how Ellie's eyes had filled up when she talked about her father dying, and how she'd promised herself that she'd make more effort with her own father. So she slid her finger across the screen to answer the call.

61

'Hello, Dad.'

'Hello, Hattie. How are you settling in down there?'

'Okay. I've got a wedding photography commission for next Saturday.'

'Brilliant. Where?' He sounded genuinely interested.

She briefly filled him in on the details, then the conversation turned to the cottage, which was obviously the real reason he had phoned, not to ask how she was.

'How long do you think it will take to get ready to put on the market?' he asked.

Hattie wondered what Marcus would make of her dad's eagerness to sell the cottage; he'd already got them both down as gold-diggers. 'I don't know Dad; you saw the photos. It needs painting and updating and maybe even rewiring. The pipes make a lot of noise whenever I turn on the taps, and the bath is cracked.'

'Maybe you could get an estate agent in to give you a rough idea of what needs fixing in order to sell it? It might not be a good idea to update it too much. A lot of people like the fishermen's cottages to look authentic, especially if they want to rent them out. An estate agent could give you a general idea what it would sell for too.'

Hattie's mum had suggested that they rent the cottage out to bring themselves in an income but Hattie felt it should be a family home and her dad wanted a quick sale and a clean break.

'I'll get someone in this week and let you know,' she promised. It probably was best to get things moving. The quicker the cottage was sold, the quicker she would have the money to get on with her life.

She decided to stay in that evening, keep Buddy company

and tidy up downstairs a bit. Tomorrow, she was going into Truro to try and drum up more business by putting her posters into some shops, and also to see if she could find a local photographic, printing and framing service rather than an online one, as it would be easier and more convenient for her to pick up her prints. Then she planned to tidy up Uncle Albert's room for Mali and Lou. Not a job she fancied doing.

The next morning, she woke up bright and early feeling really refreshed. She jumped out of bed and threw open the curtains. It was a glorious day! She looked down into the back yard where she could see her bike parked against the shed, the rusty table and chairs, and the clothes line stretching from one side of the wall to the other. She ought to tidy it up a bit and also put some pots out the front, to make it look pretty and welcoming.

She could see over into Marcus's yard too, which was bare apart from a small wooden table and two chairs. Suddenly the back door opened and the woman she'd seen in the car yesterday stepped out, with Marcus behind her, barefoot and wearing just a pair of shorts slung low on his hips. He really did have a toned body and those tattoos on the top of his arms made them look even more muscular.

Hattie pulled back so that they couldn't see her, as the woman flung her arms around Marcus's neck and snogged him.

'Sorry, I have to dash, darling. See you later.'

Then she was off, her heels clicking on the cobbled path.

So they were an item then. Well, Marcus obviously went for the older woman with money, and he had practically called Hattie a gold-digger! What a cheek!

They might genuinely love each other, she reminded herself. Anyway, it was his life, nothing to do with her.

She pulled on what was becoming her regular attire of shorts and a T-shirt, and went downstairs to check on Buddy, who was nibbling away at the corn cob on the bottom of his cage. *Thank goodness*, she thought in relief. He seemed to be getting used to her being here now. 'Morning, Buddy,' she said, walking over to his cage. 'Say morning to Hattie. Morning, Hattie.'

Buddy looked up from the corn cob then turned his back dismissively and carried on eating.

Well, at least he hadn't sworn at her. It was a start.

After coffee and breakfast, she left the radio on for Buddy and went upstairs to set about stripping Uncle Albert's bed and putting the bedclothes on a wash, opening the window wide to let in some fresh air. She wanted it to smell fresh and clean for Mali and Lou to sleep in tomorrow. She did wonder if she should offer Mali the attic room, after all there was a double and single bed up there, but she knew that Mali would be happy to share with her little daughter, and Hattie wouldn't feel right sleeping in Uncle Albert's room. She felt at home in the attic, even a little nostalgic, remembering the holidays with her parents.

She vacuumed the bedroom, cleaning the top of the wardrobe too to make sure there were no parrot feathers or droppings, and left the bed to air. Then she hung the washing out to dry on the line running across the back yard, had a shower and set off on her Harley for Truro.

She parked the bike up in the council car park and then had a walk around the pedestrianised shopping centre. It was a beautiful city, the gothic-looking spires of the cathedral dominating the skyline. She remembered coming shopping here with her parents before they split up, visiting the cathedral, stopping for a coffee in the upstairs restaurant of one of the bookstores, which didn't seem to be there anymore. Truro was an eclectic mix of the larger stores on the main street with smaller, independent stores. She browsed around for a while, enjoying the bustling atmosphere. Her mother had always insisted on coming here at least once when they were visiting Uncle Albert and, whilst Hattie had been bored with the shops back then, preferring to spend her time on the beach, she could understand why, now.

She left her flyer in a stationery shop, and a couple of photography shops. Then she browsed the albums, wondering which one Ellie and Reece would like most. The best thing to do, she decided, would be to look online, then send them the link, so they could choose the one they preferred.

When she arrived home, she felt in a reflective mood. She hadn't thought about her childhood or her parents for a long time but staying in Fisherman's Rest brought a lot of memories back to her. And not all good ones. She had to admit to herself that although her parents had tried not to argue when they were on holiday, she had always sensed an atmosphere between them, and had always been trying to please them, anxious to avoid anything that heightened the tension.

They hadn't been happy together, she had known that even though she hadn't expected them to divorce, because as a child you don't really think about that. You accept your parents' relationship. Now, looking back, she could see that it had only been a matter of time. Yes, Dad had been the one who had cut the tie, walked out and made a new life with someone else, but she and Mum had been happier afterwards, there had been a better atmosphere in the house. And Dad was obviously happier too, so happy he almost forgot about them.

65

She thought back to her own relationship with Adam. He hadn't wanted to get married, which had suited Hattie as she had no plans to marry either. Not that she was completely against marriage but she would need to be really, really sure that this was the guy she wanted to spend the rest of her life with because she didn't want to go through a divorce. And she hadn't met anyone she felt that sure about. And maybe she never would, in which case she would be perfectly happy living her life as she chose. She didn't see marriage or having a partner as the be-all and end-all of life. She was comfortable with her own company and happy to tread her own path. Relationships always meant compromising, and right now she had had enough of compromising. Now, she wanted to live her life for *her*, no one else.

Chapter Ten

'I love it!' Mali exclaimed, her eyes widening in appreciation as she stepped into the lounge.

The cottage suddenly seemed more colourful and alive; Hattie wasn't sure if it was because of the orange top and print trousers her friend was wearing, or because Mali's character was so vibrant. Lou was a mini version of her mother, her dark hair worn in braids adorned with pretty beads, like Mali, but she was dressed in a bright-pink T-shirt and shorts. Her eyes were dark and serious, like her father Ricki's, and she had his nose, but her personality was pure Mali. She was staring at Buddy wide-eyed. 'Mummy, it's a parrot!' she said in a half-whisper.

Mali was too busy gazing around in awe to hear her. 'This is amazing, Hattie. It's got so much character. Look at those stone walls, and the beams across the ceiling. It's incredible. There's so many of the original features here. I reckon this will be snapped up.'

It was interesting to see the cottage through someone else's eyes. To Hattie, it was simply Uncle Albert's cottage, a bit small, dingy and old-fashioned but, yes, quaint too. 'I hope so, but it's a bit tired and dated, don't you think? We're getting an estate agent in to give us a quote and tell us what to do to get the best price.'

'As little as possible, I'd say,' Mali told her. 'A coat of paint, of course, and maybe a new carpet.' She walked into the kitchen area and pulled back a corner of the red checked tablecloth. 'This table will come up great with a bit of a sanding down and a fresh coat of paint.'

After staring at Buddy for a few minutes, Lou plucked up the courage to go over to his cage. She stood at a safe distance from him. 'Hello,' she said.

'Bugger off!' Buddy said loudly.

Lou giggled. 'Mummy, that parrot swore.'

'That's Buddy and I'm afraid he swears a lot. You'll have to cover your ears up,' Hattie said conspiratorially. She threw an apologetic glance at Mali. 'I did tell you what he was like.'

'Oh, we don't mind him, do we, Lou? We like character. And this place has plenty of it. How long did your uncle live here? Did he never get married?'

'No. That's why he left the cottage to me and Dad.'

'Lucky you. Aren't you tempted to live here?' Mali asked.

'I can't if I wanted to, it's half Dad's cottage too and he wants to sell. There's no way I could afford to buy him out,' Hattie replied. 'Besides, it's a bit out of the way down here. There's no wi-fi by the way. I hope you're okay using mobile data '

'No problem. We've come on holiday not to be glued to our phones and iPads.' Mali wrinkled her nose. 'Bit of a bummer for you though. Can't you get some in?

'Not worth it for the couple of months I'm here. Besides I've got unlimited mobile data so I can manage.'

'Can we go to the beach?' Lou begged. 'I want to see the sea and build a sandcastle and have an ice cream.'

Mali smiled. 'She's been looking forward to this all week. How do you feel about a stroll on the beach? We can go by ourselves if you're too busy.'

'No way, you're only here for a few days so I want to spend as much time with you as I can. I can do anything that needs doing when you've gone back home.'

Lou smiled and clapped her hands, her dark bunches bobbing up and down. 'Hooray! Remember to unpack my bucket and spade, Mummy.'

'It's in the boot, we'll get it as we go out,' Mali told her. She turned to Hattie. 'I've parked on the wasteland over the back. Will my car be okay there or do I need to move it?'

'It's fine, that's where most of the people who live in these cottages park. It's difficult to find a place in the summer, though, every spare bit of land is grabbed by the holidaymakers. Luckily, my bike can be parked in the back yard.'

'Shall we get your stuff out of my car first? I worry about leaving it there,' Mali suggested. 'I don't want anyone breaking in and taking it.'

'I'm hoping we don't have as many break-ins here,' Hattie told her. Her old flat had been in one of the suburbs in Bristol, where Mali still lived, and there had been a spate of break-ins over recent months. 'But yes, let's get my stuff.'

They were both carrying a big box, with Lou following them, holding a bulging carrier bag with both hands, when Marcus pulled up in his camper van.

'Hi. Need a hand?' he asked as he opened the driver's door.

'No thanks, we've got this,' Hattie told him.

He jumped down. 'How's Buddy.'

'I think he's going to be okay. He ate some corn on the cob this morning. And he's started swearing again.'

'He's really naughty,' Lou added.

'I know, but you'll have to excuse him, he doesn't understand what he's saying,' Marcus told her.

'Oh, I think he does!' Mali said, grinning broadly.

Marcus's gaze flickered over her in interest, and Hattie was sure he was noticing how gorgeous Mali looked in the orange top and colourful trousers that contrasted so vibrantly with her dark skin, and the beaded braids emphasising her soft brown eyes. Mali was so pretty she always turned heads, but her nature was as beautiful as her looks so it was impossible not to like her. If you upset her, though, you knew it. She didn't suffer fools gladly. Actually, she didn't suffer anyone gladly, which is why she and Ricki had split up. Ricki was a bit of a lad and Mali said she had one child to look after and didn't need another, bigger one. Ricki adored Lou, though, and willingly shared parenting. In fact, as Lou said herself, she and Ricki were better as friends than as partners.

'You might be right, he's a clever old bird.' Marcus grinned back at Mali. 'Are you down for a visit?'

'Yep, making the most of half term.' Mali shifted the box a little in her hands. 'I'm Mali, and this is my daughter Lou. I couldn't come down earlier because Lou's been staying at her dad's.'

She fancies him, Hattie thought with a smile, admiring how neatly Mali had slipped into the conversation that she was single. And from the way Marcus was looking at her, he fancied her too. Hattie wondered if his lady friend knew what a flirt he was.

70

'Pleased to meet you, Mali and –' he bent down face level with Lou – 'Lou. Enjoy your stay.'

Mali watched admiringly as Marcus walked over to his back gate, opened it and went in. Then she let out a low whistle. 'He's your neighbour? Another reason you should think about staying here. He's so hot he's on fire.'

'He's easy on the eye but he's not so easy to get on with,' Hattie told her as they walked across to her gate, which they'd left open. 'I've had a couple of run-ins with him.' She stood back to let Mali and Lou in first.

'What about?'

Hattie kicked the gate shut behind her. She'd lock it in a minute. 'He thought I was a money-grabbing gold-digger. I'll explain it all to you at the beach.'

'Can't wait. Shame hunky neighbour isn't coming to the beach too.'

'You might see him there one of the days, he surfs.' Hattie put her box down and opened the back door.

'Now that I would like to see,' Mali told her.

Lou gave her a stern look. 'No more boyfriends, remember?'

Mali giggled. '*She* thinks she's *my* mother.'

Lou raised her eyebrows. 'She's man-mad but she never likes any of them after a couple of weeks.'

Lou was worldly for a six-year-old, and she certainly had her mum's number, Hattie thought with a smile. This was going to be an entertaining few days. Mali and Lou were just what she needed to cheer herself up.

Later, as they sat on the beach, keeping an eye on Lou who was collecting shells, Hattie told Mali all about her spats with Marcus. Mali grinned widely when Hattie confessed that the first time they'd met, Marcus had walked in on her naked in the kitchen.

'Now that's the way to make a first impression!' she remarked.

'Well, I don't think it impressed him, and he certainly didn't impress me,' Hattie retorted. 'We've called a sort of truce now.'

'I can't believe you don't fancy him,' Mali said. 'How can you not?'

'Yeah, he's a looker, but he's also a player. You should see the woman who stopped over the other night. Talk about a cougar. And he was making eyes at you. I had enough of all that with Adam. If I do get with a guy again – and right now I'm happy on my own, thanks – then I want someone who's got a good heart more than good looks.'

Mali winked. 'See now me, I want both!'

They both laughed. It was good to have Mali here, Hattie thought. She was her oldest friend and was always so full of life.

Apart from the dark days when Mali had just had Lou and suffered from post-natal depression. Hattie had barely recognised her fun-loving friend then, and knew that it had put a terrible strain on her relationship with Ricki. Still, she had bounced back, thank goodness.

A lot of people kept their struggles to themselves, she and Mali were like that, and she had an idea Uncle Albert had been too. He had never reached out to contact his family; if he had, he wouldn't have been left to spend his final years alone.

He'd had Marcus, she reminded herself. No matter how much the man annoyed her, she was grateful that he had looked after her uncle.

Chapter Eleven

When Hattie got up the next morning, Lou was sitting at the table drawing a picture of Buddy, who was climbing up the bars of the cage squawking at her.

'I think Buddy wants to come out of the cage,' Lou said, looking up at Hattie.

'He probably does, but I'm scared he'll fly off.' Hattie looked around. There was no sign of Mali but the back door was slightly open. 'Where's your Mum?'

'Hanging out the washing.' Lou nibbled at the end of her pencil as she studied Buddy.

Hanging out the washing? It was barely eight o'clock – and they'd only arrived yesterday, what washing could they have?

'Have you been up long?' Hattie asked.

'Ages. The seagulls woke us. They're really noisy.' Lou had started drawing again now.

Hattie padded over, barefoot, to the back door and peered out. The costumes and towels they'd used on the beach yesterday were hanging on the line and Mali was standing by the wall, looking gorgeous in white shorts and a bright-lemon top, talking to Marcus, who was wearing his wetsuit, pulled up to his waist, revealing his tanned chest. Hattie refused to stare at him or to feel self-conscious about the old denim shorts and a black vest top she had pulled on when she got up, or the fact that she hadn't combed her hair.

'Ah, there you are, Hattie. Marcus was just telling me about his paintings. You didn't tell me he was an artist.'

That's because I didn't know, Hattie thought, wondering what Mali had divulged about Hattie. Mali was a people person, she'd strike up conversations with strangers in the shops, at bus stops, anywhere. Whilst she would never divulge anything confidential about her friends, anything else was considered conversation material and no doubt Marcus had now heard a few tales about her and Hattie's s exploits

'He said we can use his wi-fi too, he's given us his password.' Mali held up a piece of paper. 'We can pick it up here, I've checked.'

Hattie felt her cheek's flush. Trust Mali! 'Thank you, that's really kind of you but there's no need ...'

'It's no problem. Please use it, it doesn't cost me any extra.' Marcus's eyes met hers and held them for a minute then he turned to Mali 'Well, I'm off, I want to catch the surf a bit before I start work, so see you both later.' He picked up his surfboard and walked out of the gate.

'He seems very nice. I think you two just got off on the wrong foot. You should give each other another chance; I reckon you'd get on really well.' Mali turned around. 'He's gorgeous and super fit. Did you get an eyeful of that body? And those tattoos?'

How could I not? 'He's okay, I guess,' Hattie admitted grudgingly, refusing to acknowledge how much that eye-gaze he'd given her had melted her insides. 'But I don't think we're ever going to be bezzie mates, so don't bother trying to matchmake. If that's what you're doing? Or do you fancy him for yourself?' She shot her friend a questioning look.

'Just being friendly, hunny. I've already got someone on the back-burner at home.' Mali winked and turned back to the washing. 'These will be dry in a couple of hours. Shall I fix some breakfast?'

'You're my guests, I'll do it,' Hattie said, about to go back inside.

'I've come down to look after you,' Mali told her. 'Go grab a shower and I'll make us some eggs Benedict.'

Mali's eggs Benedict were to die for. 'Done. I'll be ten minutes,' Hattie agreed. 'And later, when Lou is playing or asleep, you can tell me about your "back-burner guy". I can't believe you haven't mentioned it.'

Mali grinned. 'That's because it's only just happened. It's someone I met at the gym. He asked me for a date last week but I'm still thinking about it.' She looked over her shoulder as Lou came out into the garden.

Mali had started going to the gym a few years ago to get rid of her 'baby belly' which still clung to her when Lou was a toddler. She loved it, and her body was now toned and fit. She had tried to persuade Hattie to go a few times but Hattie's preferred exercise was swimming. She was hoping to have some early morning swims in the sea while she was living in Cornwall.

As she showered, Hattie's mind drifted to what Mali had told her about Marcus being an artist. Mandy had said he was one of the chefs at the hotel, so Hattie guessed that meant he did his painting in his spare time, as she had done with her photography. She wondered what he painted. *Mali will soon find out*, she thought with a smile as she turned off the shower and reached for her towel. By the time Mali went home on Friday, she would probably know all Marcus's life story. She had the knack of talking to people and extracting information from them. It was Mali's bubbly personality that had attracted Hattie to her at high school. An only child, Hattie was quieter and more reserved, whereas Mali came from a big family. It had been a few years before Hattie had realised that behind that friendly face and big smile, Mali was dealing with her own issues and that big families had their problems too.

It was lovely having Mali and Lou here, she was really looking forward to the next few days.

She glanced at her phone as a text pinged in: *Breakfast is done*.

His conversation with Mali, Hattie's friend, had been interesting, Marcus thought as he drove over to Thornwell Manor. Mali was lively and fun. He liked her, and the conversation had flowed easily – until Hattie had come out. It was a shame that he and Hattie had got off on the wrong foot and there was the awkwardness between them. From what Mali had said, she'd had a bit of a double whammy – losing her job and her home – and Albert's inheritance had come just in time. He wished he'd been a bit kinder to her. He was always too impulsive when forming an opinion, his father had always told him that. 'Don't be so quick to judge, son,' he'd said when Marcus had spouted off about something, but Marcus was like his mother, hot-headed, impetuous, and fiercely loyal. It was his loyalty to Albert, that had made him attack Hattie. She wasn't a pushover though, and had held her ground, managing to look feisty and forceful even when she was completely naked. An image of her gorgeous curvy body flashed into his mind. She hadn't freaked out about him walking in on her like that either, just grabbed the table-cloth and wrapped it around herself before laying into him. She really was something. She had an edge to her, too, with that tattoo on her arm and the fact she rode a motorbike. He sensed a bit of a wild side to her and it intrigued him.

He pulled up outside the manor gates and was about to press the intercom button to announce his arrival when they started to open. Estelle must have been looking out for him. He sighed. He'd got himself into a bit of a mess with Estelle. He never should have gone out with her the other night, or at least not let her drive him there, which then led to her dropping him back, them having a couple of drinks, then her staying over. He always avoided getting involved with clients, but Estelle was strong-minded, beautiful and hard to resist. Still, he'd almost finished the painting now and then she would hopefully go back to Paris.

Estelle was waiting on the front steps for him. 'Good morn-ing.' She walked up to him and kissed him on the cheek. 'Mum and I will be ready on the lawn in a few minutes.' Then she leant closer and whispered in his ear. 'Thanks for the other night. I hope you enjoyed it as much as I did.'

Marcus had to smile at the innuendo in her voice. She really was a terrible flirt. It had been very tempting when she'd come on to him on Sunday night but he had resisted, showing her the spare room instead and saying apologetically, 'You're gorgeous, Estelle, I'm flattered but I never mix business with pleasure.'

'Oh, you're such a bore,' she'd told him, leaning in to snog him, her hand moving down to his crotch. For a brief moment, he'd been tempted again but he'd pulled away reluctantly. 'And you are very tempting, so I'm going to bed now – alone – while I can still say no.'

He'd learnt that it always paid to let women down gently, especially rich, successful women like Estelle who were used to getting what they wanted. And maybe if she wasn't his client's daughter, he would have been tempted, but he'd learnt to his cost that there were always complications if you mixed business with pleasures. It took a long time to build a good professional reputation, but it could be destroyed in no time by someone with a grudge, and he sensed that Estelle would want more than a 'one-off' and would want to be the one to call the shots. He didn't want to be on call for anyone. He wanted to be free. He'd agreed to her appeal to come along to a dinner dance as her plus one, when the friend who was going to partner her had suddenly come down with a stomach bug, because she had pleaded, saying she didn't want to go alone and it was too late to ask anyone else. It had been a fun evening but it wasn't a partnership he wanted to continue. Being a rich woman's play-thing didn't appeal to him at all, although he could imagine what some of his mates at the Old Salt pub would say. They'd tell him to 'get in there' but it wasn't his style. Those days were behind him. He preferred to spend his time painting and surfing, and yes, now and again he was tempted to spend the night with someone but it was always no strings attached and although that is exactly what Estelle had promised, he didn't trust her to keep to that. He had a plan for his life and didn't want anyone interfering with that.

'Sorry to keep you waiting.' Felicity rushed over. Both women were dressed in crinoline dresses and carrying parasols, as in the manner of Victorian women. Felicity looked elegant and Estelle looked sensational, but then Estelle would look sensational in anything. Felicity handed Marcus a blanket. 'Spread this over the grass, will you, dear?'

When Marcus had spread out the blanket, the two women sat down on it, smoothing the skirts of their dresses out, and Marcus continued with his painting. He had to admit that Estelle's idea of having her and her mother picnicking on the lawn in front of the house, dressed as Victorian ladies of the manor was a good one, much better than just the house, as Felicity had originally suggested, although it meant extra work for him to meet the already-tight deadline he'd been given. The painting was almost complete now, thank goodness, and he was hoping Estelle would return to Paris then, which would get her out of his life without him having to hurt her feelings.

Chapter Twelve

After breakfast, Hattie, Mali and Lou decided to go for a walk around Port Medden. Hattie glanced at the cottage next door as they passed; there was still no sign of life. 'I haven't seen my other neighbour yet,' she told Mali. 'I was wondering if the cottage was a holiday let, but it seems lived-in to me.'

'Someone called Winnie lives there. She's a widow and has gone away for a couple of weeks to look after her sister who's been in hospital. Marcus told me; he's watering the plants for her,' Mali added, obviously seeing Hattie's surprised expression. 'He's a nice guy, you two just got off on the wrong foot.'

Hattie snorted. 'You can say that again. He was downright rude.' He'd apologised though, hadn't he? And if they were living next door to each other, she didn't want to be at loggerheads with him. It had been kind of him to offer her the use of his wi-fi though, and Mali was right, he was easy on the eye. An image of Marcus's super-fit torso flashed across her mind. She batted it away. It took more than a sexy body to attract her. Not that she wanted to be attracted to anyone. Especially Marcus. She wanted to get her life straight, not mess it up.

They were passing an estate agency now, so paused to take a look at the prices of the cottages. Mali gasped and pointed to a picture of a cottage very similar to Fisherman's Rest. 'Look at how much they're asking for this! I didn't realise the cottages were worth that much.'

Hattie stared at the property in the window in surprise. 'Neither did I!' Mind, this cottage was a lot tidier and more modern than Fisherman's Rest, but even so, it looked like her half of the sale money would give her a big deposit for a house. Or, if she put it with her redundancy money, maybe she could actually buy a small flat.

What would she live on, then? She'd need to get a job and bang would go her dream of being a full-time photographer. She'd have little or no mortgage though, so it was worth thinking about.

'We'd have to tidy it up a lot to get that sort of money,' she said.

'Maybe not as much as you think. Let's find out.' Mali was already pushing open the door to the estate agency.

'Can I help you?' A smartly dressed dark-haired man in about his mid-thirties, looked up from the computer screen. 'Jonathan Connolly' said the gold-letters-on-black sign on his desk.

'Yes, we'd like you to give us a valuation for Hattie's cottage please,' Mali said, before Hattie could open her mouth.

Jonathan smiled at Hattie. 'I'm presuming you're Hattie?'

She nodded. 'My uncle left his cottage – Fisherman's Rest – to me and my dad when he died recently. It's one of the old fishermen's cottages around the corner from the harbour. We want to sell it, but it does need tidying up a bit. Well, quite a lot, actually.'

She could see the interest on his face 'I'd be delighted to take a look. There's a lot of call for those cottages. Do sit down, all of you, while I take down some details.'

Hattie sat in the chair opposite him, whilst Mali sat next to her, pulling Lou onto her lap.

'Would you like another chair for your little girl?' Jonathan asked.

'No, thank you, she's fine,' Mali assured him.

'How about a drink? Would you like some coffee? Tea? Juice for the little girl?'

Hattie shook her head before Mali could reply. 'We're fine, thank you. We've just had a drink.'

'Then let's get on with business, shall we?' Jonathan flashed a mega-watt smile at Hattie and produced a form. 'Can we start with your name and telephone number, please?'

Half an hour later, Jonathan had all the details and had promised to visit Fisherman's Rest that afternoon at about two o'clock to do a valuation, as he was doing one on a house around the corner. 'We'll need your father's permission, of course, to put it on the market, but I can email him a form to sign. Once a sale has been agreed he will have to come over to sign the papers, though.'

'That won't be a problem,' Hattie told him. She and her dad had discussed this and he'd promised to come over as soon as he could get away, and hopefully help Hattie sort out any work that needed to be done.

Jonathan seemed excited to have the cottage on his books,

82

assuring Hattie that there would be no problem selling it, no matter what the condition. 'We have a waiting list of buyers for these cottages. They make ideal holiday lets,' he told her.

Hattie felt a bit sad that the cottage Uncle Albert had lived in for most of his life would be inhabited by a succession of holidaymakers instead of being a much-loved home. *Don't be silly*, she told herself, *it's good that so many people will get to enjoy the cottage.*

'Well, that's what I call a success! He was almost snatching your hand off. I bet you won't have to do much to the cottage at all,' Mali said. 'It sounds like it will be snapped up. What are your plans once it's sold? Where are you going to live? Will you be moving back to Bristol?'

'I've no idea.' Hattie hadn't thought any further ahead than coming down to Cornwall for the summer. 'I guess I will.'

'Well, you can come and stay with us while you're looking for somewhere. You know that.'

She did know that; Mali was her lifeline. And Hattie was hers. 'Thank you.'

'I want to see the boats,' Lou said, tugging at her mother's hand.

'Okay, Sunshine, we'll take a walk down by the harbour, and maybe stop for an ice cream. Is that okay with you, Hattie?'

'Sure.' Hattie loved walking along by the harbour. 'Mind the seagulls, though, they'll swoop down and snatch the ice cream out of your hands if you aren't careful.'

'No, they won't. I'll shoo them away if they do,' Lou said determinedly.

Hattie grinned. 'She's just like you,' she told Mali.

Mali shook her head. 'No, she's going to be stronger than

me. There's a couple of seagulls I should have shooed away sooner!'

Hattie grinned, knowing that Mali was referring to a couple of bad relationships she'd had. 'It's all good now, though. Right?'

'You bet it is.' Mali's face broke into a smile as she looked at Lou, who was now peering over the railings at the boats in the harbour, fascinated. 'This is such a gorgeous place, Hattie. You're so lucky to have been left the cottage – well, part of it, anyway. I reckon it will sell in no time. Shame, really, me and Lou could have had some nice holidays down here.'

Port Medden was beautiful, Hattie thought as she looked out over the picturesque harbour with its strip of golden sand. The sun had come out now and the morning chill was lifting. She glanced over at the row of shops opposite the harbour: gift shops, surf-wear, pottery, an artist's gallery and the little café. Soon, the streets would be teeming with holidaymakers, as they had been when she'd come down for holidays with her parents. She had loved the weeks she'd spent here, and often thought how lucky her uncle was to live in such a beautiful place.

It's bound to take a few months to sell the cottage, she thought, *so I'm going to make the most of the time I'm here. I'm going to use this summer to relax, build up my photography business and sort out my life.*

'Mummy, there's the ice cream shop!' Lou shouted, running back to her mother and then pointing over the road to a shop with an ice-cream-cornet-shaped sign. 'Can I have one, please?'

'Sure you can.' Mali took hold of her hand. 'Let's go and see what flavour you want today.'

★   ★   ★

84

Marcus pushed open the gate and paused as he heard a man's voice in next door's back yard.

'I think I can safely say that this place will be sold by the time summer is over, Hattie.'

He recognised that voice – it was Jonathan from the estate agent's. Hattie couldn't wait to get rid of the place, could she? He felt a surge of disappointment, then reminded himself what Mali had told him, that she had lost her home and her job. And she only had a share in the house, so the decision wasn't completely hers.

'Are you sure I shouldn't do it up first? Give the walls a coat of paint at least?'

'You could give it a general tidy round and declutter a bit but there's no need to redecorate. Whoever buys this place will want to put their own stamp on it. As I said, it will probably be used as a holiday let and that could go two ways, either the new owners will want to keep everything as traditional as possible, or they'll want to strip it out and modernise it. You don't want to alienate either buyer, so best to leave it as it is as much as possible and give them the option.'

Holiday let. Marcus was seething with anger. Now he would have to put up with people coming and going at all hours of the night, and so would poor Winnie in Primrose Cottage. What a shock the news would be for her when she came back from visiting her sister. What did Hattie and her father care, though, as long as they got their money?

'Well, that's a relief. I thought I'd have to do a lot of work to it before we could put it on the market.' Hattie sounded pleased. 'I'll talk to my dad tonight and tell him that you're emailing the consent form to him. Will you be sending a photographer?'

'Yes, I can send one tomorrow, if that's okay with you. If your father agrees, I can get the cottage on the market by the end of the week. No need to put a "For Sale" sign up, as I said, I have a list of prospective buyers so let's go with them first.'

Marcus walked over to the wall. 'Remember to tell them the difference in sale price if they sell the house in the state it's in rather than do it up first.

Jonathan spun around. 'Ah, Marcus. Good to see you again.' The look Jonathan threw him suggested that he wasn't happy to see him at all. There hadn't been any love lost between them since Jonathan had pulled a couple of sneaky stunts to try and persuade Winnie to sell her house, pretending it was in more of a state of disrepair than it was. Fortunately, Marcus had got wind of it and had managed to sort the work out for her at a reasonable price meaning she didn't need to sell.

Hattie looked over at him, her expression worried. 'Will there be that much difference in price?' she asked.

'At least twenty-five thousand, I'd say. Whereas you could do it up for about five,' Marcus told her.

'Well, I'm not sure that's accurate . . .'

'But it will be a significant drop?' Hattie asked.

'Obviously, the selling price will reflect the work the potential buyers will need to do on the property, but I thought you wanted a quick sale? And do you really want to do all that work?

Hattie looked hesitant. 'I'll have to talk to my dad. He wants to sell quickly so I'm not sure which action he'd prefer to take.'

'That's fine. I'll email you the form and a quote later and then you can talk it over with your father and let me know.'

'Thanks so much, Jonathan. You've been really helpful.'

Marcus watched as Jonathan reached out and touched her

arm. 'It's my pleasure. Now, if you have any questions at all, please contact me. Any time.'

'I will. Thanks again.'

He turned to Marcus, who was still standing by the wall. 'And do let me know if you ever intend to sell your property. I can give you an excellent deal.'

'That will never happen,' Marcus told him. Then he went inside before he said anything he regretted. Hattie had every right to sell the cottage but he wished she hadn't gone to Jonathan, who was always interested in buying up properties for holiday lets. More and more cottages were being sold for holiday rentals, or as second homes, and it was ruining the economy in Port Medden and other Cornish towns. Once summer was over, many of the towns and villages were dead, with hardly any shops open. Port Medden wasn't like that yet, thank goodness; although it was quieter in the winter, there was still a strong community, but townies like Hattie didn't help.

'What did I tell you?' Mali said after Jonathan had gone. 'Do you want me to make a start on the decluttering and painting while I'm here? I can help.'

It was tempting – the thought of sorting through all of Uncle Albert's stuff was overwhelming – but she wanted Mali and Lou to have a holiday, not spend the few days of their break working. 'Thanks but no. I'll do it after the wedding on Saturday. I'll need something to keep me busy. And I need to talk to dad, too. That's a lot of money to lose.'

It was tempting to sell the cottage as it was. Jonathan seemed to think he could do it within weeks, which meant she'd be out of here by the end of the summer and could start planning a new life for herself.

Yet, somehow, even though she had only been here a couple of days, she had started to love Port Medden and the people in it. Part of her didn't want to move.

Chapter Thirteen

'It's a lot of money to lose, Hattie and ideally I'd prefer to do the place up and get the extra twenty-five grand or so, but I don't have the time or the money to do that. I need to put the cottage on the market as soon as possible. Let's stick to our original plan and just give it a quick tidy up,' her father told her. He'd sent her a message asking to speak to her while she'd been at the beach with Mali and Lou later that afternoon, so Hattie had left them making a big sandcastle and called him.

Surely he could hang on a bit whilst she gave the downstairs a coat of paint, at least. 'Just give me a couple of weeks to see what I can do,' Hattie told him. 'I can use my redundancy money, it'll be through soon. You could pay me back out of the sale of the house.'

'That would take us to almost the end of June.' Her father hesitated. 'Okay, I can hold off that long if it means a quicker sale. Don't do too much though, just cosmetic stuff. And just paint the walls white, that's more appealing to buyers.'

'That's what Jonathan said, but I'd like to put a new bathroom suite in too, that bath is cracked, and maybe a new carpet in the lounge. It's worth it to get a bit extra money, surely?'

'As long as it isn't too much work for you. I know how cluttered that cottage is. I wish I could come over and help you but I can't spare the time right now. I feel terrible leaving all this to you.'

'It's fine, honestly. It's helped me out of a corner being here, and I am living rent free,' she reminded him. 'There is one thing, though.'

'Go on ...' Owen said, obviously noticing the hesitation in her voice.

'Well, I would really like to sell Fisherman's Rest to a family rather than someone wanting to let it out as a holiday rental. Uncle Albert loved this cottage, and it would be lovely to think a family was enjoying his home.' She'd been thinking about that last night, ever since Jonathan had told her he had lots of clients waiting to snap up the old fishermen's cottages to turn into holiday homes. She had no objection to holidaymakers, she'd loved her own holidays down in Port Medden, but this cottage had character, and she wanted to retain that, not have it gutted for a holiday home.

'So would I, love, but we can't afford to be choosy. We need to go for the highest bidder. We don't want this dragging on through the winter. Besides, you need to sort yourself out somewhere to permanently to live and a job, don't you?'

'Yes I do but it's only the beginning of June, there will be lots of interest in the summer months, surely? And I don't mind staying here for the summer and sorting it all out.' Actually, she was looking forward to it.

She heard her father draw in his breath. 'Look, I've got to be upfront with you, love. We needed urgent repairs done to the B&B in time for our summer guests,' he told her. 'So, as soon as

I heard Albert had left us the cottage, I took out a short-term loan for six months at a good rate, but if I go over that time the interest rates go up drastically. I really need to have the money from the cottage within the next three months, otherwise me and Raina could lose this place. We're just about breaking even.'

She had never considered her dad short of money. It had seemed to her that he'd walked out on them, hopped on a ferry, and started a fantastic new life. She'd never been to the B&B; he and Raina had bought that after they'd got married a few years later, but it sounded idyllic.

'What if Uncle Albert hadn't died and left us the cottage, what would you have done then?' she asked.

She could hear his sigh down the phone. 'We'd have had to sell up, Hattie. We'd already prepared ourselves for that.'

She was silent. Had things really been that bad? Perhaps her dad's life wasn't as charmed as they all thought.

'What about you? What would you have done?' he asked.

'Moved in with Mali, I guess, until I could sort myself out,' she replied. She was being selfish, and just looking for an excuse to stay longer she realised. The cottage provided her with a much-need home and chance to have a go at setting up her photography business. Well, it belonged to her dad too, and he needed the money. Even so, they couldn't afford to turn down a few extra grand for the sake of a bit of work.

'I promise that I'll have the house on the market by the middle of June. I'll start tidying up as soon as Mali and Lou go home,' she told him. 'And we'll accept the highest bid.'

'Thanks, love.' They discussed the cottage a bit more, then Owen asked, 'What about Buddy? What will you do with him?'

He'd been surprised when Hattie had told him about Uncle Albert's parrot still being alive and in residence. Hattie hadn't told him about the problems she'd had with Buddy, and actually, the parrot had livened up since Mali and Lou had arrived and was eating fine now.

'I'll take him with me. I'd like to keep him, for Uncle Albert's sake.'

'If you're sure.' There was a pause on the other end of the phone. 'And Hattie ...'

'Yes?'

'You can always come here for a few months when the cottage is sold, if you want to. There's plenty of room at the B&B in the winter months and, if you like it, well, property is cheaper here than in the UK. It might be a fresh start for you.'

His offer stunned her. She had never thought of moving over to France, or to Portugal, where her mother and Howard lived, although her mother hadn't asked her to. It was lovely of him to offer. 'Thanks, Dad. I really don't know what I want to do yet. I need a couple of weeks to sort out my head. But thank you, I do appreciate it.'

'You're my daughter and I love you. I know we've got a bit estranged, but I'd like to put that right. So you're welcome, any time, and for as long as you want.'

Hattie was really taken aback. After they'd finished talking she sat, hugging her knees, deep in thought. There seemed so many directions her life could take and she didn't know which one to choose.

'What's up?' Mali plonked down on the sand beside her. The sandcastle was finished now and Lou was carrying buckets of water from the sea to fill up the moat they'd dug all around it.

'Dad's just offered me a room at his place until I get sorted out when the cottage is sold,' she told her.

'Wow! That's great. Do you think you'll go?'

Hattie shook her head. 'I doubt it, but I'm gobsmacked he offered, and even more gobsmacked that I'm considering it.'

'You know, I think your Uncle Albert knew what he was doing leaving his cottage to you both. This is the most you two have talked to each other for years. I reckon he wanted to bring you together.'

'Mum! The handle's broken on my bucket!' Lou shouted.

'Back in a mo!' Mali got to her feet and went over to help her daughter.

Hattie thought over her friend's words. Even if Uncle Albert hadn't intended it, it's what was happening. She was seeing her father in a new light, and he seemed to be doing the same with her. Perhaps he regretted the lost years as much as she did. Was it too late for them both to reconnect?

Chapter Fourteen

Hattie phoned Jonathan the next morning and told him what she and her father had decided. 'I'll need a couple of weeks to tidy up the cottage and paint the walls, so can we say you'll send a photographer around a week on Monday and have the cottage on the market by the end of that week?' she said.

'Don't go to a lot of effort. I've got buyers waiting who don't care what condition the cottage is in. We could sell it exactly as it is, you can declutter while the sale is going through,' Jonathan sounded disappointed. And a bit pushy.

'I know, but we don't want to throw a considerable sum of money away just for the sake of a bit of hard work and TLC,' she told him firmly.

'Want me to help you tidy up a bit? Or go out for the day so you can get on with it?' Mali asked.

'Definitely not. You're going home tomorrow, and I want to spend as much time as I can with you both.' Hattie filled the kettle and switched it on. 'I thought we could go out for the day after breakfast. How do you fancy a trip to Marazion? We could walk over the causeway to St Michael's Mount – or take the boat, if the tide is in?'

'Oh yes, can we, Mum?' Lou was almost jumping up and down with excitement.

'That sounds a brilliant idea,' Mali agreed.

So, a little later, they had all piled into Mali's car and set off. When they arrived, they were delighted to discover that the tide was out, so walked along the causeway to the iconic Mount.

'I remember coming here as a child. Dad told me all about the legend of how the castle was built by a giant called Cormoran. He used to paddle to the shore and snatch animals like sheep and cows to take back to the island with him for food,' Hattie said. 'The villagers were terrified of him.'

'That's horrible!' Lou's eyes were as wide as saucers. 'What a nasty giant!'

'He really was. The farmers were scared of the giant and wanted to stop him from stealing their animals, so they offered a big reward to anyone who killed him. Then a young boy named Jack managed to trick the giant and kill him. Everyone was really happy.'

'That's a bit like *Jack and the Beanstalk*,' Lou replied. 'Jack was very brave. How did he kill the giant?'

'According to the legend, Jack dug a deep hole in one side of the Mount, then early the next morning when the sun was rising, he blew on a horn to wake the giant. The giant heard the horn and ran down the mountain to see what was happening, but he was blinded by the sun and fell into the hole. Jack quickly filled up the hole and buried the giant.'

'Clever Jack. Can we see the hole?' asked Lou.

'No, but there is a heart-shaped stone which is supposed to

be the giant's heart,' Hattie told her. 'I'll show it to you when we go up the Mount. The legend says that if you stand on the stone, you can sometimes hear the giant's heart beating.'

Lou's eyes widened. 'You mean that the giant is still alive and buried in the mountain?'

'Who knows?' Mali grinned.

'Wow! I can't wait to see that!' Lou was almost jumping up and down with excitement.

They stepped off the causeway onto the island. 'It looks so magical,' Mali said, gazing around.

'Shall we have a bit of a look around the village first? Then we can go up to the castle,' Hattie suggested.

'People live here?' asked Lou, astonished. 'Do the children go to school?'

'Oh, yes. There used to be a primary school, I'm not sure if it's still there. I know the older children go over the causeway to school on the mainland. If the weather's bad and the boats can't go out to sea, then the children have to stay at home.'

'That's cool! I bet they have lots of days off in the winter,' Lou said.

'I'm sure the school provides them with homework to do if the weather's bad,' Mali told her.

Hattie grinned at Lou's excitement; it reminded her of her first visit here when she was about the same age as the little girl. They'd spent a week with Uncle Albert in Cornwall every summer until her parents had split up, it was such a shame they'd lost touch with him.

Circumstances change, she reminded herself; we are all just adjusting to our new lives. Including her father. Their conversation last night had opened her eyes to how much her father had

96

had to adapt, too, to his new life in France. Yes, he had made the decision to walk out, and she had hated him for that for years, but now she was an adult, she could understand how relationships broke down, and looking back she knew her parents hadn't been happy. Maybe if she had been younger, like Lou, instead of an awkward preteen she might have handled it better. Lou seemed to have accepted her parents' break-up and had adapted to living with her mum but sharing weekends and holidays with both parents.

They had a walk along the harbour front, stopping at the Island Café for a drink and snack, then going on a guided tour of the village before climbing the cobbled causeway up to the island's summit.

'I think the heart-shaped stone is here somewhere,' said the guide. 'Can you see it?'

Lou looked around then clapped her hands and squealed, almost jumping up and down in excitement. 'There it is!' She ran over to the stone and knelt down, then put her ear to it. 'I can hear it! I can hear the giant's heart beating!'

Hattie, Mali and the guide all exchanged a smile at the excitement on the little girl's face. Hattie couldn't resist taking a photo of her, her face was so alive. She showed it to Mali, who smiled. 'You're such a brilliant photographer.'

The guide looked at it too, nodding in agreement. 'You should do that professionally,' she said. 'You've got the knack.'

'Thank you, it is a hobby of mine, but I hope to make it a full-time business,' Hattie told her, pleased with the guide's praise.

When they got to the castle, Hattie took a deep breath and looked down at the sea below. The view was breathtaking.

Cornwall was working its magic on her, and she wasn't sure that she wanted to leave.

Well, you have no choice, you can't afford to stay here, she told herself. *Besides, you'd be bored in the winter. You're just in holiday mode, that's all. No one ever wants to go back home when they're on holiday.*

'I hear your new neighbour has come to the rescue with the wedding photographs,' Shanise said as Marcus walked into the kitchen of Gwel Teg, ready to start his evening shift.

Marcus looked at her, puzzled. 'Who? Hattie?'

'I don't know her name. I just heard Sue and Mandy talking. The photographer they booked has had to let them down so your neighbour has stepped in.'

'Really, when did this happen?' No one had mentioned it to him and the wedding was only two days away. Ellie and Reece must have been in a right panic. How had Hattie found out about the original photographer cancelling. She hadn't even been here a week!

'The photographer pulled out last week – a family tragedy – then Mandy met your neighbour in the corner shop last weekend and found out that she was a photographer.'

Hattie really was a photographer!

'She came to see Sue first, then Ellie and Reece,' Shanise continued. 'They're all very taken with her and her work apparently.' She shot Marcus a curious look. 'You seem a bit surprised. Haven't you met Hattie yet?'

'Yes.' *And had a few clashes* – but he wasn't about to tell Shanise that. 'I had no idea she was taking Ellie and Reece's wedding photographs though.'

'Well, she's saved the day – they were in a right panic about it.'

How had he missed this? *Probably because you've been pre-occupied with the Thornwell painting and how to deal with Estelle.* Estelle had been all over him this afternoon, teasing, pouting, innuendos. At first, it had amused him, and yes he'd found her appealing and her attention flattering, but now it annoyed him. Thank goodness the painting was almost finished and then hopefully he wouldn't have to deal with her again. He could see that she was getting really annoyed that he wasn't responding to her advances, she obviously wasn't used to being turned down.

'So, what do you think of this Hattie, then?' Shanise asked.

He shrugged. 'She seems okay, and if she's managed to rescue Ellie and Reece's wedding day, that's great.' He put on his apron and cap. 'See you on Saturday, then. It's the first time we've worked a shift together for a while.'

'Just remember that I'm the boss.' Shanise threw back her head and laughed.

Marcus grinned. Shanise would no doubt be bossing everyone about, but she was such a bubbly, friendly character no one minded. He was looking forward to doing the wedding food. And to the wedding itself. He'd been invited to join the wedding reception once the food for the buffet had all been prepared, and he had thought he'd go straight home, but now he thought he might stay a while. Especially if Hattie was there. As they were neighbours, he should make the effort to get on with her.

Chapter Fifteen

After his early morning surf, a shower and breakfast the next morning, Marcus decided to go down to the beach for a stroll. He was feeling a bit uneasy about going to the Manor today, especially as he'd received an early morning text from Estelle, with a rather saucy picture of her in risqué underwear. The situation was escalating, and he wasn't sure how to handle it without upsetting everyone.

The painting had to be finished today as it was Lord Thomwell's birthday on Sunday and Lady Thomwell wanted to present him with the painting then. Marcus had hoped that Estelle would be going back to Paris after her father's birthday but the photo and message she had sent him that morning made him doubt that. He had an uneasy feeling that once the commission was finished, Estelle would think that there was nothing to keep them apart and would up her game.

He should never have gone to that do as her plus one. That had definitely given her the wrong impression. And he should have pretended that he had a girlfriend that night when she'd made a pass at him, instead of telling her he didn't mix business with pleasure. He was such an idiot. Why hadn't he handled this better?

It always made him feel calmer to gaze out at the sea, so he planned on sitting outside the café with a cup of coffee and watching the world go by for a bit before he had to head into work. He grabbed a coffee and sat down at a table at the front, gazing out at the harbour.

'There's Marcus!' He looked up to see Lou waving at him. Hattie and Mali were with her, obviously heading for the café. 'Hello, Marcus!' Lou shouted.

He waved back and she dashed over to his table. 'We're having a drink too. I'm having a milkshake. Can we share your table?'

From the look on Hattie's face, she didn't want that any more than he did, but how could he say no? Especially as Lou had already scrambled onto the chair next to him and Mali was about to follow suit. 'Er, of course,' he said.

'I'll go and get the drinks, you two sit down,' Hattie said, obviously eager to make an excuse to get away.

'Frappé for me please, and chocolate milkshake for Lou,' Mali told her, seating herself beside Lou, leaving the seat by Marcus free for Hattie.

Awkward.

'We're going home tonight,' Lou told him. 'I wish we could stay longer.'

'I've got things to do before school on Monday, Lou, and Hattie is working tomorrow,' Mali reminded her.

'Yes, I heard that she was taking the photos for Ellie and Reece's wedding. I'm doing the food,' Marcus remarked, feeling that he should talk to them. Besides, he liked Mali, she was warm and friendly. Unlike Hattie.

Whose fault is that? It's thanks to you that you both got off on the wrong foot.

'So, you'll probably bump into each other, then?' Mali asked.

'I expect so. Have you both enjoyed your stay here?' he replied, changing the subject.

'It's been brill. I'll miss it so much, especially Buddy, but he's naughty. He swears a lot.' Lou told him from across the table.

Marcus grinned. 'I know. That's because his owner was a fisherman and he swore a lot too.'

Lou nodded. 'Hattie told me all about it. She used to come down here when she was little. She showed me the bucket and spade she used to build sandcastles on the beach with. And the wetsuit she used to wear. They were in Uncle Albert's shed.'

'I can't believe he kept them all this time,' Hattie said, coming over with a tray of drinks. She put the tray down on the table and, after a slight hesitation, she sat in the empty seat which was next to Marcus. 'There's loads of things in that shed. I'm going to have to look through it all.'

'Albert was a bit of a hoarder.' Marcus took a sip of his coffee. 'How's Buddy doing? Has he settled down now?'

'He's perked up a lot. He's eating okay, although he still pulls out his feathers now and again,' Hattie replied.

Marcus was concerned to hear that. 'Keep an eye on that – pulling out his feathers is a sign that he's stressed. He's probably pining a bit too, for Albert and possibly me. I used to pop around a couple of times a day when Albert had ... gone. Buddy's a very social bird, he's used to being with Albert all day, so he might start stressing again when your visitors have gone back and he's on his own a lot.'

'I'll keep him company as much as I can, but I do have to work.' Hattie sounded defensive.

'I know, I'm just saying—'

'Perhaps you could still pop around, just until he gets used to Hattie. It's a shame if he's pining,' Mali butted in quickly.

Marcus saw the warning look that Hattie shot at her. 'I'd be happy to do that but I don't want to impose.'

'Oh, it's no imposition, is it, Hattie?'

'Well, I guess Buddy would like to see you, and then you can check that he's okay. I'm doing my best.'

'I've no doubt that you are. Look, I'm off to work in a while, but I'll be home about ten thirty this evening. I could pop in then, but if that's too late, then tomorrow morning? Whatever suits you.'

She thought about this for a moment, then said, 'Tonight will be fine. I'll still be up and about.'

'See you later, then.' Marcus finished his drink and stood up, glancing at Mali and Lou. 'Bye, you two. Nice to meet you.'

'See you next time we're down,' Mali said cheerily.

'Honestly, did you have to do that?' Hattie demanded as soon as Marcus was out of earshot. 'It was so obvious that you were trying to matchmake, it was embarrassing. He probably thought I'd put you up to it and I fancy him.'

'What, with the look you gave me? It's a wonder he agreed to come after that. But be fair, Hattie, that parrot probably does miss Marcus and would love to see him. What harm will it do? You can leave him to talk to Buddy and busy yourself with something. You don't have to entertain him.'

103

She was right, Hattie acknowledged. Buddy had already lost one person he loved, it wasn't fair to cut Marcus out of his life too. Besides, she was sure that Marcus didn't want to spend any more time with her than she did him – he had left more or less as soon as she'd sat down. She had to stop thinking how awkward it would be and put Buddy first. Uncle Albert had adored that parrot and she was determined to look after him the best she could.

'I guess not.' She looked at Lou. 'I'm going to miss you. And your mum. Fisherman's Rest is going to seem very quiet without you two.'

'I wish you didn't have to sell it, then we could come down every holiday,' Lou said, sipping her milkshake noisily through the paper straw.

'Me too.' It was daft, but she was actually getting fond of the cottage, and she had already fallen in love with Port Medden. 'I'd love to live here,' she said with a sigh.

'Really? I mean it is beautiful, and quaint, but wouldn't you miss the city?' asked Mali.

Hattie gazed out at the harbour. 'I don't think I would. I feel so at home here. I'm sort of sad that I have to sell the cottage.' She turned her gaze back to the table. 'Maybe I could rent a place and stay here for a bit longer once it's sold.'

'It might be worth a try; you've already had a few enquiries for photographs this week while we've been here,' Mali reminded her. 'Perhaps you could rent for six months and see how it goes. You do seem happy here.'

She was. Even though her whole life felt so up in the air at the moment there was something about Port Medden that drew her in. Living by the sea was so calming. She guessed that's why Uncle Albert had lived here all his life.

'I'll think about it,' she said.

After they had finished their drinks, they walked along past the shops on the harbour front so that Mali and Lou could buy some souvenirs. Lou bought a cap with a seagull on the front for her dad, and some seashells for herself. Hattie bought Lou a dolphin necklace, and some fudge for Mali. Then they had some fish and chips before returning to Fisherman's Rest.

This time, when Hattie opened the door, Buddy shouted, 'Hello! Hello!'

'He's pleased to see us!' Lou said in delight. She ran over to the cage, where the parrot was hopping along his branch. 'Hello, Buddy,' she said.

'Hello!' Buddy cocked his head to one side. Then he squawked 'Bugger off!'

Lou giggled. 'I'm going to miss Buddy,' she said.

'I'll FaceTime you over the weekend, and you can see him then,' Hattie promised her.

She wished that Mali and Lou weren't going; the cottage would seem so empty without them. She did have a lot to do, though. She was taking the wedding photos tomorrow, and she had to tidy up the cottage and give the rooms a coat of paint. It was going to be a hectic couple of weeks.

'Can we come down in the summer holidays?' Lou asked as she and Mali gathered their things together.

'If Hattie is still here, and she doesn't mind,' Mali told her.

'I'm sure I will be still here, and I'd love you to come. I'm really going to miss you both.' She held out her hands. 'Group hug?' Mali and Lou both wrapped their arms around her, and she them. She wished she had a daughter. If only . . . She pushed the memory from her mind. Her baby was gone, its short life ended almost as soon as it had started to form in her womb. Yet, although it had been a shock to discover that a bout of sickness had caused her mini pill not to work, in that brief time while it was growing inside her she had loved her baby and been devastated at the loss. Adam though, had been barely able to hide his relief.

'You're welcome down here anytime you want,' she assured them. 'Now, let me help you out with your things, and be sure that you text me as soon as you're home.'

'I will!' Mali gave her another hug, then they picked up their suitcases and bags and set off for the wasteland at the back where their car was parked. Hattie stood waving until they had disappeared around the corner, then she went back into Fisherman's Rest.

As she stepped into the lounge and closed the door behind her, she felt a sudden wave of loneliness. Is that how Uncle Albert had felt, sitting here every day on his own? she thought, feeling a stab of guilt. *You didn't know*, she reminded herself, *you hardly knew him*. If only he had reached out, though, she was sure the family would have made an effort to see him. At least he'd had Marcus, and she was grateful for that. So grateful that she decided that when Marcus popped in on the way home from work tonight to see how Buddy was, she would make an extra-special effort to be friendly to him.

Chapter Sixteen

It took Marcus all afternoon, but he finally finished the painting. It would have to be framed, but at least it was finished and had time to dry before the party on Sunday. He was so relieved that he didn't mind that he'd had to stop longer than he'd wanted and go straight onto his shift at Gwel Teg.

When he'd arrived, Estelle had greeted him with a triumphant look and he had merely smiled and been his usual polite self, with no mention at all of the picture she had sent him, although she would know that he'd received it because the message would show the two blue ticks that indicated it had been read.

She had flirted consistently throughout the day, even stroking his arm and patting his backside at one point, but he'd remained polite and professional, knowing that if he responded with any kind of friendliness, she would take it as a sign he was interested in her.

He stood back as Lady Felicity and Estelle both studied the painting.

'The paint is still a bit tacky, so it's best not to touch it,' he warned them.

'I love it. And so will my husband,' Lady Felicity said approvingly. 'And I must say, we really look the part, don't we, Estelle?'

Estelle flashed Marcus a dazzling smile. 'We certainly do. Although, I'm very pleased that I don't live in those times. Women were so restricted. I like to be free.' She gave Marcus a knowing look.

'I think that was only on the surface, dear. Victorian women weren't as strait-laced as everyone thinks. Especially the higher classes. It was accepted that you would marry someone with money to keep the property within the family, provide an heir and then you were free to satisfy your own desires – and both partners often did.'

'I think that's still pretty much what goes on today,' Estelle said.

'Well, it certainly wasn't in our case, I can assure you,' Lady Felicity retorted. 'Now, let me settle up with you for this, Marcus. And you will come along to Rupert's birthday party on Sunday, won't you? I know he'll want to meet the artist who painted this wonderful picture. It will be good networking for you too; I think this will gain you a few commissions.'

There was nothing he wanted to do less. Marcus had been planning on spending the day surfing. He was working at Gwel Teg all day Saturday because of the wedding and was looking forward to a complete day off on Sunday. Hobnobbing with the Thomwells was definitely not his idea of fun. And it would mean socialising with Estelle without having the excuse of working for her father to turn down her advances.

'Well . . .'

'Of course you must come. I'll come and pick you up. We

108

don't want you arriving in that ghastly camper van. And do dress up smart, this is a special occasion,' Estelle said firmly.

He definitely didn't want Estelle picking him up, but perhaps he ought to go. Lady Thomwell was right, it could get him some important commissions. He intended to make his own way there, though, and definitely didn't want to accompany Estelle. Neither did he want her telling him how to dress.

'Nonsense, darling, Marcus can dress as he chooses – his hippiness is part of his charm,' Lady Felicity said. 'The party is starting at three. Don't be late, will you?' This last remark was directed at Marcus. 'I'll just go and get my chequebook,' she said, walking off.

'Ignore Mother, she thinks it's trendy to befriend a bohemian artist. You have to look the part if you want to get the right kind of business. If you arrive in your surfer clothes, no one will take you seriously. You really need to make the right impression.'

'I know you mean well, Estelle, but I'm an artist not a businessman. People commission me for how I paint, not how I look. If your mother is happy for me to come as myself, then that's fine by me. I'll be there at three on the dot, but I won't be able to stay long as I have plans for the afternoon.'

Estelle pouted. 'No need to get all haughty, I was only trying to help.'

Take over more like. Which is one of the reasons he would never have a relationship with Estelle, even if she wasn't a client's daughter. He had no interest in women who wanted him to conform – he liked individuality.

Like Hattie.

An image of her clutching the tablecloth around her naked

body, the pretty stars-and-crescent moon tattoo clearly visible on the top of her right arm, flashed across his mind, followed by another one of her clad in black leathers, astride her motorbike. He'd never met anyone quite like Hattie. Then, he had an idea. If he could persuade Hattie to come with him, that would surely put Estelle off? But would Hattie agree to it?

'Perhaps I could bring my girlfriend, then I can stay a little longer,' he suggested.

He saw Estelle's eyes narrow. 'Girlfriend? You didn't mention this before.'

'We haven't been dating that long, although it's got serious very fast and I am going out with her on Sunday evening.'

Estelle's blood-red lips parted into a cunning smile. 'Of course, do bring her. I'd love to meet her.'

Marcus realised that rather than put Estelle off, the knowledge that he had a girlfriend was merely a challenge to her. And what if he couldn't persuade Hattie to come?

'I'll ask her, she might prefer to give it a miss.'

Estelle ran her tongue between her lips. 'Whatever she decides I'm sure we'll have lots of fun.'

Lady Thornwell returned then, brandishing his cheque, and Estelle walked off, swaying her hips seductively. She certainly wasn't going to be put off easily, Marcus thought. And how the hell was he going to broach the subject of coming to the party with him to Hattie?

It was about a quarter to eleven when Hattie finally heard a knock on the door.

'I'm sorry I'm so late, a couple of the diners really took their

110

time,' Marcus apologised. 'I was wondering whether to leave it until tomorrow but thought you might be waiting so I should at least explain.'

'No worries, I'm still up sorting out the kitchen. Come in.' She opened the door wide enough for him to step inside.

'Hello, Buddy,' Marcus said as he walked in. Immediately Buddy turned around and started squawking loudly. 'Bloody hell! Hello! Hello!' he shouted.

Marcus grinned. 'Well, you looked pleased to see me.'

Buddy was practically hopping up and down on the perch. He looked so animated as Marcus walked over to the cage. Hattie watched as Marcus thrust his hand in his pocket, took out a slice of apple and held it out to the parrot. Buddy took it very carefully with his beak, standing on one leg while he held the slice of apple with the other claw and started nibbling at it. She could hardly believe the change in the parrot. He really was very fond of Marcus.

'Well, you've cheered him up,' she said.

Marcus looked inside the cage. 'He's losing quite a few feathers, which is a sure sign he's stressed. I see you're managing to clean his cage without him getting out.'

'I got Lou to distract him, and Mali guarded the door while I cleaned the paper and changed the water. Not sure how I'm going to manage on my own, though; I'm scared he's going to escape and fly off again.'

'Once he gets used to you it'll be fine. He'll return to the cage if you leave the door open. He's just a bit confused about what's going on at the moment. Aren't you, fella?' Marcus said. Buddy squawked loudly and danced along on the branch.

Marcus dug a grape out of his pocket and held it out, close to the bars. Buddy walked down the bars head first, gripped the grape in his beak, climbed back up the bars again to the branch, where he stood on one leg, holding it with the other claw, and gently nibbled it.

Hattie felt a lump form in her throat. It was obvious that the parrot loved Marcus, and Marcus loved him. Was she being selfish keeping him?

He was her last link with Uncle Albert, she reminded herself, and she owed it to her uncle to keep his parrot in the cottage.

What about when the cottage was sold, though?

'What are you going to do with Buddy when you move?' It was almost as if Marcus had read her thoughts.

'Take him with me,' she replied, although she hadn't really thought that far ahead and wasn't even sure that it was a sensible thing to do.

'What and leave him in a city flat all day while you're out at work, then again in the evening while you go out with your mates?'

She didn't like the tone of his voice. How dare he make assumptions about her? He didn't even know her. She'd been stupid to think he'd changed, he obviously still disapproved of her, he'd only been pleasant because of Mali and Lou.

'Don't judge me, you don't know me.' She fixed him with a steely glare. 'I might not know much about looking after a parrot but I'll learn. For Uncle Albert's sake. I'm grateful for your help but please don't assume that I'd neglect Buddy if you weren't here. I'm not that kind of person.'

His eyes met hers, his expression unfathomable, then he

nodded. 'Point taken. I'm not saying that you're selfish and don't care about Buddy. I'm just trying to point out that this has been his home for years. His owner has gone, now I'm gone too, and soon you intend to whisk him away from his home. I'm not sure he'll survive all that upheaval.'

Hattie chewed her lip as she looked at the parrot. Was he right? *Other people move and take their pets with them*, she reminded herself. And she wouldn't be moving for a few months. Buddy would have got used to her by the time they found a buyer and the sale went through. She could see that Marcus's concern was genuine, but wondered if part of the reason he was so dismayed at her taking Buddy with her when she left was because he was fond of the parrot himself and would miss him. Which was a shame, but he couldn't care for Buddy with Mr Tibbs prowling around, could he?

She raised her chin determinedly. 'I'll spend more time talking to him, and if you could come around every now and again, let him out so he can have a fly around, then he'll be happier, and once I get more confident with him I can let him out myself. By the time I move, I'm sure he'll have got used to me and I'll have learnt to care for him.'

He nodded slowly. 'Look, it's late now, so I'll be off but we both have a big day tomorrow – Shanise said you're taking the photos of Ellie and Reece's wedding.' He paused, looking a bit awkward. She wondered if he was remembering the day he had snapped at her about photographing him.

'Look, sorry I was such a grouse about you taking a photo of my surfing,' he continued. There was a silence as if he was wondering what to say but then he blurted out, 'We haven't really got off on the best foot, have we? And I know that's mainly my fault for jumping to conclusions. In my defence, I thought the world of your uncle and have become very fond of Buddy. But that doesn't excuse my rudeness.' He held out his hand. 'Can we put it all behind us and be friends?'

Well, that was a surprise! He looked genuine, though, and she would like them to be on a friendlier footing. He was her only neighbour at the moment, and they'd both be working at the hotel tomorrow. She held out her hand. 'Of course.'

As their hands clasped she felt a frisson of awareness shoot through her and couldn't help noticing how his hand was strong but soft and rather than shaking hers, he was holding it; the feel of his fingers on her fingers; the soft smile on his lips; the wavy lock of hair that had escaped his low ponytail and was skimming his cheek, the silver earring clearly visible. She had to stop herself from reaching out with the hand he wasn't holding and pushing the lock of hair back, wanting to feel the texture of it between her fingers. It was as though they were both locked in that moment, gazing at each other, their hands touching, their bodies only centimetres apart, and she wondered if the same spark that was dancing through her body was dancing through his.

'How about I come around in the morning – about nine?' His voice brought her back to her senses and she quickly removed her hand, still not sure if it had been him holding onto her or her holding onto him. 'We can let Buddy out to have a bit of a fly around before we both have to go and prepare for the wedding. That will cheer him up.'

'That sounds great. Thanks.' Her voice sounded strange to her ears, high-pitched. False. She hoped he hadn't noticed.

'See you tomorrow, then.' Marcus put his head closer to the cage. 'Bye, fella.'

Buddy rolled his head to one side and peered at him 'Bugger off!'

Hattie burst out laughing and so did Marcus.

Chapter Seventeen

The silence hit Hattie as soon as she awoke the next morning. The last few days, she'd been woken by Lou's laughter, the TV or radio blaring, signs of life. Now Mali and Lou had gone home, she was on her own, which would have been fine in her flat in Bristol, but here, down in Uncle Albert's cottage, surrounded by memories of the happy times when they were all a family together, the silence was unsettling. 'Stop feeling sorry for yourself, you've got a busy day today,' she told herself. She had the wedding to photograph at two o'clock that afternoon, her first proper commission. She'd promised to be at Gwel Teg for twelve so she could take some photos of Ellie getting ready for the wedding. Then she remembered that Marcus would be around at nine o'clock, and it was gone eight now. She showered and pulled on a pair of shorts and T-shirt, then added a touch of light make-up and brushed her hair. She'd just got downstairs when there was a knock on the front door. She opened it to find Marcus standing there with a cup of coffee and a plate of toast.

'Morning,' he said as he stepped inside. 'Hope you don't

mind me bringing my breakfast with me, but I have to be at the hotel for eleven.'

'That's fine, I have to be there at twelve, so I can take some pre-wedding photos.' She led the way into the kitchen.

He munched a mouthful of toast, then replied. 'Makes sense. We'd better get cracking then.' He put the mug of coffee on the table, then walked over to the cage. 'Morning, Buddy!'

'Hello, hello!' Buddy squealed, jigging along the branch. 'Where you been?'

'You're a cheeky chappie, aren't you?' Marcus broke off a corner of his marmalade-covered toast and handed it to the parrot, who immediately scrambled down to grab it with his beak then went back up onto the perch to eat it.

'He loves toast and marmalade for breakfast,' Marcus said. 'I was thinking, we could open the cage and let him have a quick fly around while I eat my breakfast? Is that okay with you? He hasn't been out for a while now and must be desperate to stretch his wings.'

'What if we can't get him back in?' Hattie asked, worried.

'I'm sure we will. If not you could leave the cage open and the lounge door shut so he can't fly anywhere else. He'll probably be back in his cage when you come home.

So, she opened the cage as Marcus sat down to eat his breakfast. 'There you go, Buddy.' The parrot eyed her warily and stayed put. *Typical.* If she hadn't wanted him to come out, he'd have been out like a shot.

'I think I'll have some toast too,' she said, switching on the toaster.

She toasted two slices of bread and buttered them, added marmalade, then looked around as she heard a loud squawk.

117

Buddy was standing on the table beside Marcus, nibbling at a bit of toast from his plate. He looked so cute that she couldn't resist grabbing her camera and taking a photo.

Marcus looked over and grinned. 'I'll send it to you,' she promised, then remembered that she hadn't got his phone number. Heck, did that sound like she was fishing for it?

Marcus obviously mistook her sudden awkwardness as her wondering if she should sit down at the table. 'If you walk over slowly and don't make any sudden moves, you'll be okay to sit down,' he told her.

She walked over as slowly as she could and gently eased the chair out to sit down. Buddy swivelled his head around to stare at her, then swivelled it back and carried on pecking away at the toast.

'He really seems to be perking up,' Marcus said, his toast finished.

'I hope so. I do talk to him a lot, don't I, Buddy? And I always put the radio on when I go out. I thought some background noise might make him feel more secure.' She bit into her toast, feeling self-conscious now that Marcus had finished his. Toast was a noisy, messy thing to eat.

'Good idea,' Marcus told her, swigging back his coffee.

Buddy had turned to watch now as Hattie took another bite of her toast. Suddenly, he pattered over and snatched the last bit out of her hands, then scooted off to the other side of the table to eat it himself.

'Buddy! That's naughty!' Marcus scolded him, while Hattie burst into a peal of laughter. Marcus joined in too, his head thrown back, his eyes crinkling at the corners.

I wish he'd laugh more often, instead of being so grumpy and disapproving, Hattie thought.

'Bugger off!' Buddy replied, pecking at the toast.

'Good job I've got another piece.' Hattie picked it up off her plate, eyeing Buddy warily, although she was actually pleased that he'd come over to her, even if he had pinched some of her toast. 'Does he often snatch food like that?'

'Yes, given half a chance. He's a bit cheeky, and Albert indulged him. He was his only company – and that's not a dig,' he added, obviously noticing the look on Hattie's face. 'Make sure you scold him and shoo him away if he does, though. Buddy will rule the roost if you let him.'

'To be honest, I'm just so pleased to see him looking livelier and actually eating, that I haven't got the heart to scold him today.' Hattie finished her toast and picked up her mug of tea, thinking how surreal yet comfortable it was to be sitting at the table sharing breakfast with Marcus and Buddy.

Thankfully, Marcus persuaded Buddy back into the cage with another piece of toast.

'You really do have a bond with him, don't you?' she said as Marcus closed the cage door.

He glanced over his shoulder at her. 'I've known him years, remember. You'll get there in time.'

Would she though? She loved cuddly animals, dogs and cats that sat on your lap and let you stroke them; she didn't really know what to do with grumpy parrots who swore, sulked and pinched the food out of your hands. She was determined to keep persevering, though.

Marcus took his phone out of his pocket and dabbed at it

with his finger, 'Here's my number if you want to send that photo over.' He held the screen out so she could see the phone number on it. 'Best to keep a note of it anyway, in case you're ever worried about Buddy.'

'Thanks,' she keyed the number into her phone then selected the photo and sent it over to Marcus.

He immediately opened it and smiled. 'You've really caught Buddy's character well.' He put the phone back in his pocket. 'See you later at the hotel.'

And to Hattie's surprise, she found she was looking forward to it.

It took her a while to decide what to wear. 'You're the photographer not a guest,' she reminded herself, but even so, she wanted to look good – summery but smart. She wasn't one for dresses and finally settled on a pair of white-and-red, floral-print fitted trousers, a red sweetheart-necked top and red flat pumps. Then she picked up her camera bag, double-checked the equipment inside: camera, folding tripod, flash unit, spare batteries and compact flash professional cards, plus a piece of plastic sheeting for the bride and groom to sit on, if the grass was wet. It had been a while since she had photographed a wedding, and she felt a mixture of excitement and apprehension as she set off up the hill.

Mandy smiled and waved as she walked in. 'Go straight up, lovey. They're expecting you.'

Hattie took the lift up to the Silver Room where Ellie was getting ready. She could hear laughter wafting out of the room as she walked along the corridor, and the door was opened before she had chance to knock, by a pretty dark-haired woman dressed in a wispy peach-satin bridesmaid's dress that suited her smooth coffee-coloured skin perfectly.

'You must be Hattie, the photographer? I'm Abiya.' She opened the door to let her in. 'And I'm Kate.' Another woman with cropped fair hair and wearing an identical dress turned to smile. 'We're the bridesmaids.'

'Hello, Hattie.' Ellie looked at her through the dressing-table mirror where she was sitting applying lipstick. Her shoulder-length, chestnut-brown hair had been swept up into a loose chignon, with wavy tendrils hanging down each side of her face. She was already dressed in her wedding gown, an elegant off-the-shoulder white dress, from what Hattie could see of it. As Ellie leaned forward to apply another coat of lipstick, Hattie took hold of her camera.

'Hi. Hold that pose!' She clicked a couple of times, checked the shot, and smiled. 'That's a great start. Now, how about one of the two bridesmaids? Maybe one of you brushing the other one's hair?'

'I'll brush Abiya's hair, there's not much of mine to do anything with.' Kate grinned. She picked up the hairbrush and stood behind Abiya, smoothing it gently through her hair. Hattie clicked away. She took photos of the bouquets, of Ellie and the girls laughing together, and then one of Sue, standing in the doorway, looking so elegant in her powder-blue suit and matching hat.

'Are we ready to go?' she asked. 'The registrars are here, and all guests are seated, waiting for you.'

She held out her arm for Ellie to slip her arm through, and they set off. Ellie and her bridesmaids looked so gorgeous and sophisticated, Hattie took several photos of them, wanting the bride and groom to have plenty to choose from.

It was a busy afternoon. The wedding ceremony was followed by photographs outside. Hattie set the tripod up in the hotel grounds and took a close-up of Ellie and Reece with their hands entwined, showing off their wedding rings; the obligatory kiss; and the happy couple in the pagoda with the sun glimmering on the Atlantic Ocean below them – *very romantic* – as well as photos of Sue, Reece's parents and group shots of the guests. After the photos, there was a sit-down meal, and Hattie took some photos of the 'top table' and of the guests around the room.

Ellie and Reece came over to her when the meal was finished. 'Thank you so much for filling in at such short notice. Please come and join us at the reception tonight. And this time, leave your camera behind. You're invited as a guest.'

'That's really kind of you, thank you.' She was tempted to refuse, as she felt a little out of place, but she didn't want to hurt Ellie's feelings, and also thought it might be a good bit of networking.

'Any time after seven,' Ellie told her.

That gave her time to check through the photos and freshen up. 'I'll look forward to it. See you later,' she said.

She'd been hoping to see Marcus at some point in the afternoon, but hadn't even caught a glimpse of him. She guessed he'd been too busy in the kitchen, cooking the delicious three-course meal they had all been served. She knew that there was a table buffet tonight, so no doubt he was preparing that too.

She wondered if he'd be at the reception that evening. Sue had stressed that they were all like one big family at Gwel Teg, and they'd invited Hattie to the reception, so would that invitation extend to any of the staff? She hoped so. She was warming to Marcus a little; behind that grumpy, disapproving exterior, she'd caught a couple of glimpses of someone she really would like to get to know a lot better.

'Hello! Hello!' Buddy shouted as she walked through the door. She looked over, surprised and pleased to see the parrot hopping about on his perch. 'Well, you've cheered up,' she said with a smile. 'Hello to you too.'

She guessed it was Marcus's visit that morning that had cheered up the cheeky bird. It had cheered up her too, she thought, remembering how comfortable it had been to sit around the table with him, eating breakfast.

I hope he's at the reception.

She made herself a coffee and sandwich, then sat down at the table and checked through the photos on her camera. She was pleased with them, and knew that by the time she'd downloaded them onto her laptop and edited them, they would look even better.

Then she glanced at the clock and saw that it was gone six. She'd better get ready for the reception.

She looked through the clothes in her wardrobe, wondering what to wear. She wasn't a girly girl who wore clingy dresses or floaty skirts; she wore jeans, trousers and shorts, mainly. Something Adam had often complained about. She didn't like dressing up, but she did want to make an effort tonight, just in case Marcus was there. So far, he had only seen her in shorts and her biker leathers – not very feminine – *and naked, before you grabbed that tablecloth to wrap yourself in*, she reminded herself. An incident she'd prefer to forget!

She frowned as she looked through the clothes, then her eyes rested on a burgundy-satin jumpsuit she'd bought for a Christmas party. With its thin straps, v-neck and slinky wide legs, it was sexy but sophisticated. Even Adam had approved. She took it out of the wardrobe and held it up. Matched with her silver clutch bag and silver strappy sandals, it should certainly attract Marcus's attention.

She was so ridiculously excited about seeing him again, and in a situation where they could both relax and have a drink together. Maybe even a dance. The thought of Marcus's arms around her waist, of dancing close to him, sent a shiver down her spine. She brushed it away. She wasn't remotely interested in having a romantic relationship with him. They were neighbours, so it was only natural that she wanted them to get on.

Chapter Eighteen

Marcus scanned the crowded room, his eyes searching for the familiar short, white-blond shaggy bob, his ears listening for the sound of her voice with its endearing lilt. Was she here? He knew that Hattie had been invited to the evening reception, but wondered if she was too tired to attend after her day's work, or if she felt a bit awkward – after all, she didn't really know anyone here. He didn't intend to stay long, it had been a hectic day, with him and Shanise both run off their feet in the kitchen, and he had been tempted to go home and chill in front of the TV with an ice-cold can of beer, but Sue had suggested he bring his clothes with him and use one of the spare hotel rooms to shower and change, so that's what he'd done. He guessed that Hattie had gone home, though. *Would she bother to come back out again?*

Just as he thought she had decided not to attend, he heard a familiar laugh and turned his head. She was over in the corner, talking to a suave-looking dark-haired man. He could only see the back of her, but the way that classy jumpsuit clung to her bum made his pulse race. Then, as though she'd sensed him staring at her, she turned around and his pulse galloped when his eyes rested on the way the burgundy silk clung to her breasts and the deep V that led down to them. *Hot? She was flaming!*

She smiled at him and waved, and he wondered whether to join them but, feeling irrationally jealous that she was getting on so well with another man, he merely waved back and, using all the self-control he could muster, walked over to the bar to get a drink.

'Good to see you again, Marcus.'

He turned in surprise, not expecting to see anyone he knew there. He recognised the man's face as someone who had stayed at the hotel last summer and had complimented Marcus on the food, but struggled to remember his name. 'Hello again. Are you enjoying the wedding?'

'I certainly am, and as usual, the food was delicious. In fact, my wife –' he looked over his shoulder as though seeking his wife, then shrugged and turned back – 'We were wondering if you could do the catering for our silver wedding anniversary. We'd pay the travel expenses and put you up for the weekend, of course. We live in Exeter,' he added.

This wasn't the first time Marcus had been approached by one of the hotel guests to provide the food for an event for them, but whilst he enjoyed his job, he didn't want to spend his spare time cooking as well; he was an artist, not a chef, by heart. 'Thanks so much, it's an honour to be asked, but my spare time is pretty well tied up with my painting commissions,' he said.

The man nodded. 'I forgot you were an artist too. Shame. You could make a real career out of being a chef, I reckon. Have your own restaurant in no time.'

He didn't want his own restaurant; he wanted his own art

exhibition. *Dream on, Marcus*. His family certainly thought he was a dreamer, as he was sure did most of his friends, and this man obviously thought that Marcus would be better off spending his time cooking rather than painting, but at least he had a dream. He'd worked hard, built up his reputation over the years, and hopefully the painting he'd just finished for Lady Felicity Thomwell would bring more work his way.

'It's kind of you to say so, but that's not my ambition,' he said with a polite smile. He picked up his drink and turned around – and nearly bumped into Hattie who was on her way to the bar.

'Ooops, sorry!' he apologised as she took a quick step back. *God, that jumpsuit looks even more divine close up, and that cute stars-and-moon tattoo at the top of her arm looks really sexy.*

'No worries. The buffet looks fantastic, by the way. I've been tempted by the spring rolls and salad, and the carrot cake already.' She glanced over his shoulder at the guest who was now walking away from the bar with a couple of drinks in his hand. 'I think you could run a pretty good restaurant, too, but I don't blame you for preferring to be an artist. Mandy told me that you did that incredible painting of the ship in the storm on the wall in the reception. You're very talented.'

'Thank you.' He shrugged. 'Most people think I'm an idiot for preferring to try and make it as an artist. Not that I'm expecting to make a living with my art, I just prefer to spend my spare time doing that rather than cooking. Having a job gives me a regular wage coming in, and in my free time I want to paint and surf, not spend even more time in the kitchen.'

'I know what you mean, that's why I worked in an insurance office and did photography in my spare time. I didn't want to be self-employed, I wanted the security of an income, but now, well, I guess I'll give being self-employed a go while I'm down here doing up Fisherman's Rest.' She smiled at him. 'I'd better grab myself a drink while there's space at the bar. See you a bit later.'

He was tempted to offer to get her a drink, but Hattie struck him as an independent woman who bought her own drinks. And made her own decisions.

'And I'd better go and mingle.' He raised his glass. 'Have fun.'

Hattie was enjoying herself. Ellie and Reece had made her very welcome, as had their friends. Lucas, the best man and Reece's best friend, was a scream, charming and amusing. The brides-maids, Kate, a former flatmate of Ellie's, and Abiya, an old school friend, were good fun.

Abiya had told her that she had just got engaged. 'My parents want me to have a big Indian wedding, like my brother Deepa, but Milo and I want a simpler, quieter affair.' She grimaced. 'So, they are not very pleased with me at the moment.'

Hattie felt sorry for Abiya, caught between what she wanted and trying to please her parents. 'That's a shame, will they come round?' she asked.

Abiya nodded. 'Once my mother realises that no amount of pouting and emotional blackmail will change our minds.' She held her glass delicately, colourful bangles dangling from her wrists as she looked around. 'I think Ellie and Reece have the right idea, getting married in this gorgeous hotel. We want to do something like this. Have the wedding and reception all in the same place. It's so much easier.'

Hattie raised her glass 'A girl after my own heart.'

'What are you two gossiping about?' Ellie asked as she joined them, still wearing her wedding dress.

'Weddings.' Abiya flashed her a smile and nodded at her dress. 'You're not changing, then?'

'Definitely not. This is the one and only day I'll wear this dress so I'm making the most of it.' Ellie turned to Hattie. 'Thank you again for coming to our rescue by taking the photographs, Hattie. I can't wait to see them.'

'They'll be ready for when you come back from your honeymoon. Then you can choose which ones you want for your album.'

'That's perfect, thank you.'

Hattie chatted with them both for a while, then excused herself and went off to get some more of the buffet. Marcus was in front of her, his plate already piled up.

'Someone's hungry!' Hattie remarked.

'I'm starving! I haven't had time to eat all day, I've been too busy cooking. I haven't been home at all, I even got showered and changed here.' He picked up a spring roll and added that to his plate, before asking, 'How's Buddy?'

'He's getting used to me. He actually said "hello" when I got home earlier. I'm trying to teach him to say "Hello, Hattie" but he just turns his back on me!' She picked up a triangular salmon sandwich and put it on her plate. 'I think it cheered him up seeing you this morning. Pop round and see him tomorrow if you want.' Marcus must miss Buddy, she realised. 'I think he's missing Mali and Lou. The cottage was so lively with them there.'

'I bet you'll miss them too, they seem a fun pair.'

Hattie grinned. 'They are, and yes I will miss them, although

129

I have plenty to do, what with getting the cottage ready to put on the market and my photography work.' She saw his face cloud over and wished that she hadn't mentioned the cottage sale, it was obvious that Marcus still disapproved.

'And what will you do when it's sold?' he asked.

She shrugged her shoulders. 'Who knows? I might go back to Bristol, but my dad is in France, and my mum is in Portugal, I'm jobless and single. I could go anywhere.' She added a couple more salmon sandwiches, a vol-au-vent and some mixed salad to her plate and went to join Lucas who was waving at her to join his group.

They sat eating, chatting and drinking, then Lucas persuaded her to dance with him and they moved to the dance floor.

Lucas was good looking, and a great mover – far more energetic than her. She could see that he was a party person and liked to be the centre of attention, but he was fun too. She enjoyed his company, and when the music slowed down, happily slid into his arms for a smoochy dance.

'Do you ever come to London?' he whispered in her ear. 'I'd love to meet up with you again.'

She thought about it. It was tempting, she was sure she'd have a good time with Lucas, no strings attached, obviously, but the timing was wrong. She had too much to sort out to be travelling to London.

'Sorry, but I'm too busy at the moment. I'm in the middle of selling my cottage and setting up a new business,' she said.

'If you do, message me,' he told her. 'I'll send you a Facebook friend request.'

She nodded. 'Thanks.' She might just take him up on it.

After a couple more dances, one of the other women from

the crowd claimed Lucas, and Hattie was about to walk off the dance floor and give her feet a much-needed rest when she heard Marcus say, 'Fancy a dance?'

He'd unbuttoned the neck of his shirt now and rolled up his sleeves, his long hair free from its ponytail and curling on the top of his shoulders. He looked incredibly sexy, and even though she'd rationed the glasses of wine she'd had, she felt encased in a mellow glow. 'Sure,' she agreed.

He put his arms around her and drew her close as they moved to the music, and she nestled into him, savouring the warmth of his body, the tangy smell of his aftershave – the chemistry she had tried so hard to deny between them sizzling. Did he feel it too? she wondered, or was it just her? She looked up, wanting to see the expression on his face, and their eyes met, held. Hazel eyes that seemed flecked with gold under the disco lights. She stared into them, mesmerised. He did feel it, she was sure, and that knowledge made her breath catch in her throat. There was a question in his eyes now and she held her breath as his head lowered, then she threw caution to the wind and raised her lips to his.

Chapter Nineteen

Her head was throbbing. Hattie opened her eyes, blinked at the harsh sunlight, then quickly closed them again. She hadn't meant to drink so much wine, but it had been such a lovely day, the photographs had gone well, she'd had another couple of queries about commissions. And she'd danced with Marcus. She remembered that dance, his strong arms around her, holding her close, the tangy scent of his aftershave, his mouth brushing against her ear, trailing down her neck then kissing her slowly, deeply, making her heart race and her knees weaken underneath her.

Then another memory flashed across her mind, Marcus bending over the bed and kissing her. *Surely they hadn't . . . ?* She opened one eye tentatively and shot a glance at the space beside her. Empty. And thankfully there were no dents in the pillow where a sleeping head had lain. Marcus's head. She must have been dreaming. God, did she fancy him that much that she was actually dreaming about him now?

She rubbed her eyes and looked at the clock. Almost ten. She had totally zonked out. Good job it was Sunday. She yawned and sat up. Her throat was parched. She could do with a cup of coffee. She pushed the sheet back – it was too hot for a duvet – and set off downstairs, stopping off at the bathroom to go to the loo first.

'Bugger off!' Buddy squawked as she walked into the lounge. He was climbing up the bars of the cage, watching her.

'Nice to see you, too!' She walked over to the cage; it had been cleaned out and he'd got fresh food and water. She couldn't remember doing that. 'Morning, grumpy,' she said.

Buddy eyed her, cocking his head to one side. She really thought he was getting used to her. She'd do a piece of toast and marmalade and give him some, that would win him over. She walked into the kitchen, reached for the kettle, then paused as she saw a note propped against it. She squinted as she read the loopy blue writing:

You looked so peaceful I didn't want to wake you. Thanks for a fantastic night. And for agreeing to partner me for Lord Thornwell's birthday party this afternoon. See you later.

'Thanks for a fantastic night!' Oh God! It hadn't been a dream: she'd spent the night with Marcus. What the hell had she been thinking?

She needed a coffee – strong and black – then to get her head together. She couldn't believe that she'd actually slept with Marcus and couldn't remember any of it. Had she been that drunk? Had it been that uneventful?

And what was this birthday party she'd agreed to accompany him to? And for a Lord at that!

She put the kettle on and spooned coffee into a mug, her mind going back to yesterday evening as she poured in hot water, then added some cold to cool it down. She needed to get sober fast! She remembered dancing with Marcus at the wedding reception but nothing past then. She couldn't even remember getting home. She hoped that she hadn't shown herself up; she'd only just moved here.

She took the mug of coffee over to the table and sat down. She had to get her head straight. How could she face Marcus if she didn't remember what had happened between them? Then panic seized her. Had they taken precautions? What had she been thinking?

That's the trouble, you weren't thinking, you were drinking.

She groaned and put her head in her hands. This wasn't the first time she'd had a bit too much wine and done something she regretted. The trouble was, wine went to her head. One minute she was fine, and the next, that was it, total blackout. She had been determined to stick to two glasses but must have relaxed, and let her guard down because the photography session had gone well, so had an extra glass or two. Had Marcus encouraged her? Taken advantage of her? She shook her head, the memory of how it had felt to have his arms around her, of them kissing passionately, proving to her that whatever she had done, she had done willingly.

Well, now she'd have to man up and face him. Thank goodness she'd stayed on the mini pill after splitting up with Adam, because it helped regulate her heavy and irregular periods.

It would have been nice to actually remember the event though.

It couldn't have been that earth shattering if she couldn't recall a thing.

She took a huge gulp of her coffee, the bitter taste making her grimace. Well, it was no use sitting here moping, she needed to get a shower, then go and see Marcus, and find out exactly what they had done and what she had let herself in for today.

Just over an hour later, having eaten breakfast – cornflakes, as she had no bread for toast so couldn't do some for Buddy either – showered, and pulled on some denim shorts and a vest top, she went around to see Marcus. Taking a deep breath, she knocked on the door. *Just be casual*, she told herself, *tell him you can't remember the details of the birthday party, enquire about the dress code. Don't ask him outright what happened last night, be subtle.*

She knocked and waited. And waited. Then knocked again. No one opened the door. Where was Marcus? Had he gone back to bed to sleep off his hangover? She wracked her brains trying to remember if he was at work today but doubted it. Especially after working all day yesterday. Should she phone him or send him a text? She needed to find out if she'd agreed to go to some posh event where everyone wore dinner jackets and designer dresses. Well, she'd have to be the odd one out because she didn't possess a dress, never mind a designer one!

'Morning. Are you looking for me?'

She turned around at the sound of Marcus's voice. He opened the gate with his left hand, and had a carrier bag in his right hand, from which a sliced white loaf and some eggs peeked out.

'Want some breakfast?' he asked.

Her stomach rumbled. 'Thanks, but I've had some,' she replied, her eyes feasting on the eggs. She'd bet he had some bacon in there, too, and she would really love a bacon and egg sandwich. Her dish of cornflakes hadn't really soaked up the wine she'd drunk.

'What did you have, because all I could find in your cupboards was cornflakes?' He was almost at the front door now and must have noticed the expression on her face because he added, 'I was looking for bread to toast for Buddy. I cleaned his cage and gave him some fresh food this morning.'

'Mali and Lou ate me out of house and home and I didn't get round to doing a shop yesterday.'

'Well, come in and let me do you a decent breakfast. It's the least I can do.' He opened the door and stepped inside, leaving it open for her to follow.

The least he could do for what? For having sex with her? For persuading her to agree to accompany him to some posh dinner party later when she was too much under the influence of alcohol to refuse? She shook her head at both these thoughts, again remembering the way his eyes had looked into hers, how their bodies had moulded perfectly together when they'd danced, the heat up her spine when he had kissed her. She would definitely have consented to whatever they had done, although, yes, the alcohol would have clouded her judgement, weakened her ability to resist the effect Marcus had on her, especially when he already had a girlfriend. The effect he was having on her now.

She stepped inside. 'About this birthday party . . .'

'I hope you're not going to back out? I've told Lady Thomwell that I'm bringing a guest now.'

'The thing is . . . I can't remember anything about it and, well, I doubt if I've got anything suitable to wear to a posh party. I don't wear dresses. Don't even possess one.'

Marcus bent down and took a frying pan out of the cupboard. 'It's not that posh, it's a garden party. A pair of smart trousers will do.'

The only smart trousers she had were the smart black ones she wore for work. She bit her lip.

'No smart trousers either, eh? Well, I'm in the same boat. Estelle – that's Lady Thomwell's daughter – hired a dinner suit for me when she wanted me to accompany her to a do the other night. I've told her that I'm wearing my own clothes today, though. I've got a pair of cream chinos that look decent enough with a black shirt. I'm an artist, they can't expect me to dress up like a banker.'

That must be the posh woman she'd seen him with. Was he saying it was a platonic arrangement? Yet she'd seen her leaving Marcus's house the next morning.

'Two rashers or three?' he asked, pouring oil into a frying pan then cutting open the pack of bacon.

Her stomach rumbled. She couldn't resist saying, 'Two, please.'

He grinned. 'Do you mind putting the kettle on and making a couple of coffees?'

'Sure.' She filled the kettle and switched it on. Then asked the question that had been in her mind since she'd first seen him with the older woman in the sports car. 'Is Estelle the one you went out with the other evening? I thought you were . . . together.'

'It was a business event. And no, we aren't together, although

137

she would like us to be.' He placed the slices of bacon in the pan. 'Lady Thomwell commissioned me to do a painting for her husband's birthday – which is today at three by the way. The painting will be unveiled for the first time, so she invited me to be there. Estelle wants me to be there too. So, I asked if I could bring a guest.' He looked over his shoulder at her. 'To be honest, I asked her if I could bring my girlfriend.' He grimaced. 'Estelle's a bit full on, and won't take no for an answer, so I thought if I invented a girlfriend it might get the message across to her.'

Ah, now things were slipping into place. 'So, you want me to come along and pretend to be your girlfriend?'

He glanced at her. 'Sort of. I did explain all this last night.' He frowned. 'What do you remember about last night?'

Should she confess? She might as well, at least she'd know what went on then. 'Not a lot after our dance, to be honest. I was ... er ... surprised to see your note this morning. What time did you go?' That sounded vague enough, didn't it? Didn't let on she didn't know whether he'd gone last night or this morning.

Was that amusement she saw in his eyes? 'About one thirty. You were a bit ... tipsy ... so I thought I'd better see you home. I cleaned out Buddy and give him some food. Whilst I was doing that, you disappeared. I finally found you in the attic room fast asleep on the bed.

On the bed. Naked? But what about her dream of them kissing?

'I covered you over and you gave me a kiss goodnight, then I left you a note and went home,' he explained. 'Did you think I'd stayed the night and taken advantage of you when you were drunk?'

She folded her arms and looked straight at him. 'I wasn't *that*

138

drunk.' She'd let him decide whether she meant 'drunk enough to sleep with him' or 'drunk enough to forget it'.

He raised an eyebrow, then reverted his attention to turning over the bacon that was sizzling away in the pan. 'How many eggs?'

'One please.' She hunted in the cupboard for two plates, then opened the bread and placed two slices on each plate. 'Now, back to the dinner party. I really don't have anything suitable to wear. My wardrobe consists of work clothes, casual clothes and party clothes. Nothing suitable for a party on the lawn with a Lord and Lady. I think you should probably ask someone else to go with you.'

'There isn't time now and you promised.' He put the two slices of bacon on her bread then placed an egg on top. 'I've told you, it doesn't matter what you come in. We won't stay long. Wear whatever you want.'

'Biker leathers.'

He cut the bread in half and handed the plate to her. 'Sure, if you want to.'

It looked like she wasn't getting out of this. She took the sandwich and sat down at the table. 'Thanks.'

Marcus joined her with his own sandwich.

'A couple of hours and that's it, right?'

'I promise. And Hattie . . .'

She took a bite out of her sandwich and chewed it, waiting for him to finish his sentence.

'Can you sort of play up the "being my girlfriend" bit? Make it look really convincing.'

She rolled her eyes. 'Do I need to cling onto your arm and gaze lovingly into your eyes?'

'Nope, but a bit of affection now and again would be good.'

'Especially around Estelle?'

'Definitely around Estelle. The woman is a cougar.'

Hattie giggled, nearly spluttering out her sandwich. The afternoon might turn out to be fun after all.

Chapter Twenty

She'd handled that well, Marcus thought, after Hattie had gone. Not the slightest bit of coyness or embarrassment about whether they had spent the night together, yet he was pretty sure she couldn't remember if they had, she had been practically comatose when he'd left. The image of her sprawled naked on the bed flashed across his mind. After cleaning Buddy out, he'd gone up to check that she was okay, worried about her falling down those rickety, narrow attic stairs, and had been surprised to find the attic-room door wide open and Hattie lying on the bed. He'd tried not to let his gaze linger on the beautiful curves of her body, and had quickly covered her up, then gone back down and let himself out.

Back at home, he'd sat up for a while, thinking about how it had felt to dance with Hattie, their bodies touching, swaying to the music, her head resting on his shoulder. He'd been longing to kiss her all evening, and had hesitated, trying to assess what her response would be, before he finally had, his heart soaring like a released balloon when she had kissed him back. After a couple more drinks and dances, he had seized the moment and asked her to accompany him to the birthday party today and, to his surprise and relief, she had agreed. He had suspected that it was the influence of the wine that had made her agree so readily, and wondered if she would back out this morning, but no, she'd kept her promise.

He was looking forward to showing up with Hattie by his side. He had never met anyone like her, he thought. She was so uncomplicated, unabashed and beautiful. Another woman would have freaked out that he'd seen her naked on the bed – apart from Estelle, who would have tried to drag him into it with her – or read his note this morning and felt embarrassed wondering if they had slept together. Not Hattie. She was such a free spirit.

The more he got to know Hattie, the more he liked her and realised how wrong his earlier assumptions about her were. He was ashamed of how he had acted when they first met. She hadn't asked her uncle to leave her his cottage in his will, had she? And if her father wanted to sell his half and she couldn't afford to buy him out, what could she do? He should make the most of her living next door, she would be gone in a few months and then there would be a stream of holidaymakers coming and going at all hours of the day and night. Gone would be the peace and tranquillity he'd grown to love. Well, it had been good while it lasted.

He had to admit though that it wasn't losing the peace and tranquillity that bothered him so much as losing Hattie. He was getting fond of her, too fond. Maybe it hadn't been a good idea to invite her to Lord Thomwell's birthday party. Ever since Kaylee, he'd sworn not to have another holiday romance. He'd fallen for Kaylee hard when she'd come down to spend the summer with her grandparents. He'd always known she'd be going back to university but they'd agreed to keep the relationship going – then he'd taken the train up for a surprise visit one weekend and discovered that Kaylee had replaced him. He'd been devastated for quite a time. After that he'd vowed to stay clear of holidaymakers. Not that Hattie was a holidaymaker, but she was only passing through, there was no future for them and he was a bit too attracted to her. Then he thought of Estelle, and the risqué picture she'd sent him. He had to get her off his back, without hurting her feelings if he could, and this was the only way he could think of doing it. Besides, he was a big boy now, not a love-struck teenager. He could handle Hattie moving on.

Hattie uploaded the wedding photos to her laptop ready to edit them. The wedding had been lovely. Ellie and Reece had looked so happy, their faces wreathed in smiles. And Sue had been beaming with pride as she had walked along the red carpet with her daughter on her arm. Hattie smiled with relief as the photos appeared on her screen. They were good. Very good. She had even managed to capture the moment when Reece had turned to see Ellie walking towards him and their eyes had met. It had been a perfect wedding, and a perfect reception, and she was going to make sure she did them a perfect album of photographs to match.

Not the sort of wedding she'd want, though. The thought crept into her mind and she stopped to explore it. The only time she'd considered getting married was a couple of years ago when she had found out that she was pregnant. At first she'd been shocked – she and Adam had been so careful – then she

143

had started to feel pleased, imagining a little son or daughter, thinking that maybe she and Adam could get married, build their own little family. But Adam hadn't been pleased. He'd been cross, spouting off about not being ready to be a father yet, not wanting to give up his freedom. When Hattie had miscarried a couple of weeks later, Adam had hardly been able to conceal his relief, whereas she had been devastated. Seeing how upset she was, Adam had hugged her, tried to console her, told her it was for the best — and she'd known it was, because she and Adam weren't right together. Even if they had decided to take the plunge and get married, it wouldn't have worked out and then their child would have been the casualty of a divorce. To be honest, she didn't know many marriages that had lasted the course; look at her parents, and Mali and Ricki, and Ellie had told her that Reece's parents were divorced too.

Sometimes Hattie thought of the baby she'd lost. She knew that someday she wanted a child, but only when she had found the right partner. Marcus's face appeared in her mind and she pushed it away, she suspected he would be just as reluctant to settle down as Adam had been.

Marcus knocked on Hattie's door, wondering what she had decided to wear. Not that he minded — she looked amazing in anything. She opened the door and his eyes widened as he saw that she had taken him at his word and was wearing her motorbike leathers. She looked sensational, the trousers clung to her like a second skin and the top was sexily unzipped to reveal her cleavage.

'Will I do?' she asked.

He grinned. 'You definitely will.'

She grinned as she looked him up and down. 'You've spruced up well too.'

'Thanks.' He'd changed his mind about the cream chinos, deciding on a pair of black skinny jeans and a white collarless shirt, matched with black loafers. 'Right, let's do this.'

'Can we go on my bike seeing as I'm dressed for the part?' she asked. 'I've got a spare helmet. Or don't you like motorbikes?'

'Yes, I do, I had one myself for years.' But he'd always been the driver and didn't know if he fancied riding pillion, not being in control. There again, he did fancy wrapping his arms around Hattie's waist and cosying up to her. And it would be fun to pull up in front of the manor on Hattie's bike. That would make quite an entrance and he could just imagine Estelle's face. 'Sure, let's take the bike,' he said.

'You okay going pillion?'

'No problem.'

Everyone turned to look as they roared up the drive. Hattie gave her bike a final rev before coming to a halt. She'd enjoyed the ride here, with Marcus sitting on the back, his hands holding her waist. Adam had always refused to go on the back of the bike, she wasn't sure if it was because he hadn't felt safe or because he didn't like the idea of sitting behind a woman – not that he would have ever ridden a bike himself, he was definitely a car man, the sportier the better. Whereas Marcus hadn't seemed at all bothered about sitting behind and holding on to her. He was self-assured, confident of his own masculinity, and not so much of an opinionated chauvinist as he had first seemed.

They both dismounted just as a woman in a glamorous floral dress with a wide-brimmed hat almost floated over the lawn towards them. She looked about sixty, was very elegant and her clothes were definitely not off the peg.

'Marcus. We've been waiting for you.' Her eyes rested warmly on Marcus, then moved to Hattie, and her face broke into a welcoming smile. 'And who is this stunning woman?'

'Lady Thomwell, this is Hattie, my girlfriend.'

Hattie smiled as Marcus introduced her. 'Pleased to meet you, Lady Thomwell,' she said. 'Lovely place you have here,' she added, looking around admiringly.

Thomwell Manor looked like one of the stately homes she had sometimes visited with her mum on a Sunday. A very green, very well-looked-after lawn was at the front of the house, with a half-moon of steps leading up to the manor itself, and white lion sculptures each side of the door. There were a hundred or more people on the lawn, all dressed in their finery. There was a long table on one side of the garden, laden with sandwiches, cakes and drinks, and a few members of staff were standing behind it. More staff were walking around carrying silver trays with what looked like glasses of champagne on them, and handing them out to the guests. *Very impressive.* She wished she'd brought her camera with her; she could have got some great shots. She was tempted to use the camera on her mobile phone, but decided it was best not to.

'Rupert is due back very soon.' Lady Thomwell turned to Hattie and said conspiratorially, 'This whole thing is a surprise for his birthday. We're going to unveil the picture when he arrives. I must say that Marcus has done a wonderful job.' Hattie looked at the easel covered with a cloth in the middle of the lawn and guessed that was the painting. She couldn't wait to see it.

'That's very kind of you,' Marcus said, leaning forward to kiss Lady Thomwell, first one cheek and then the other.

'Do come and join us. Everyone is dying to meet you,' Lady Thomwell said.

Marcus smiled at Hattie and they both followed Lady Thomwell over the lawn.

'Marcus, there you are.' The blond-haired woman Hattie had seen driving the sports car the other night held up her hand and waved. She was wearing a white off-the-shoulder designer dress, that buttoned down the front and stopped just above the knees, to reveal long, slender legs. The white accentuated her golden tan, and the gold necklace, earrings and bracelet she was wearing sparkled in the sun.

'Estelle.' Marcus smiled at her, then reached out for Hattie's hand. 'Meet my girlfriend, Hattie.'

Estelle looked Hattie up and down languidly, her sharp eyes taking in the bike leathers, Hattie had now unzipped the jacket to reveal a black lacy vest. She gave Estelle a little finger wave. 'Hi there, Marcus has told me *all* about you,' she said sweetly.

'Not *everything* I hope, you rogue,' Estelle replied, pouting seductively at Marcus. 'Good to meet you, Hattie, you're not at all as I imagined.'

She made it sound like an insult but Hattie merely arched her eyebrows. 'Really? Now you're exactly how I thought you'd be.'

Estelle fixed her with a stony stare then slipped her hand through Marcus's arm. 'Now come along, Marcus, there are so

147

many people waiting to meet you. Let me introduce you to everyone.' She led him off, leaving Hattie standing by herself on the lawn with the choice of whether to traipse behind them or find someone else to talk to. Well, she could see why Marcus felt uncomfortable with Estelle, but he was big enough to stick up for himself. She wasn't running after them, she decided. If Marcus wanted her to pretend to be his girlfriend, he needed to start acting like her boyfriend.

'Hello, dear. Are you a friend of Estelle's?' an elderly man asked her.

She turned to him with a smile. 'No, a friend of Marcus, the artist.' Her gaze scanned the gardens admiringly. 'This is a beautiful place isn't it?'

'It is indeed. It's been in the Thomwell family for centuries. It was actually quite dilapidated when Rupert took over but he and Felicity have put a lot of money and hard work into it, and over the years have transformed the place.'

'Are you family?' Hattie asked him.

'Lifelong friends – ah, here's my son,' the man said as a tall, good-looking fair-haired man joined them. 'Jake, this is . . .' He paused as if realising that he didn't know Hattie's name.

'Hattie.' She held out her hand.

Jake smoothly lifted it to his lips and kissed it.

'Ah, the delightful photographer at Reece and Ellie's wedding yesterday. I attended the ceremony but had to leave early, I'm afraid. Business to see to.'

Fancies himself as a charmer, she thought.

'You're a photographer? And Marcus is a painter. How interesting. Do you both find the same subjects appealing, I wonder?' his father asked.

She had no idea what subjects Marcus found appealing. She'd only seen the painting of the ship in the storm.

'Sometimes, although I prefer to paint nature and Hattie loves photographing people, don't you?' She turned to see Marcus standing behind her. 'Sorry to interrupt but there's some people I want you to meet, Hattie,' he said.

So he'd managed to escape Estelle's clutches, then.

'I thought you were following us, but when I looked around, you'd gone,' he whispered.

'I don't follow,' Hattie told him with a smile.

For a moment their gaze locked, his hazel-with-a-hint-of-green eyes staring into hers, making her heart flutter. The chemistry between them was almost tangible; it was all she could do to stop herself from reaching out and touching his face.

'Then walk with me,' he said and held out his hand.

She took it, and they walked over the grass, hand in hand, just as a black limousine pulled up outside the manor.

Chapter Twenty-One

'It's Lord Thomwell. Now the ceremony can take place, and then after that we can make our excuses and go home,' Marcus said. 'If you want to, that is.'

'I'd prefer not to stay too long. This is not my kind of party, although it's a beautiful place,' Hattie told him.

'Marcus!' Lady Felicity was waving to him. Lord Rupert had joined her and there was now a crowd gathered in front of the covered easel. Hattie quickened her pace; she was eager to see Marcus's painting.

She took her phone out of her shoulder bag, preparing to take a photo as Lady Thomwell stood in front of the easel, ready to make a speech.

'I'm delighted to invite you all here today to celebrate my dear Rupert's sixty-fifth birthday,' she said. 'And to mark the occasion, I commissioned our local artist Marcus Wilson, to do a special painting. If you could come up and join me, Marcus.' She looked over at Marcus. Everyone else turned to face him too.

He shot Hattie a rueful smile and walked through the crowd – which had now burst out into applause – to the front.

Lady Thomwell then grandly swept the covering from the easel and Hattie gasped as the painting was revealed. Marcus had managed to recreate the style of an Old Master. The painting showed the Manor against a backdrop of a summer-blue sky, with Lady Thomwell and Estelle, dressed in crinoline dresses, with parasols, sitting elegantly on a blanket spread out on the grass, having a picnic. It was stunning. Marcus really was talented, she thought admiringly.

There was a round of applause, Lord Rupert gave a speech about how delighted he was, he and his wife exchanged kisses on the cheek, the waiters circulated with more silver trays of champagne and then everyone relaxed into a party atmosphere.

'So, how long have you and Marcus been together,' Estelle asked, sidling up to Hattie.

Hattie turned to her and smiled brightly. 'Oh, it's fairly recent.'

'I thought so, as he hasn't mentioned you all time he was here painting, and we got very close – as you can imagine.'

Estelle really did have a thing for Marcus, Hattie realised. She wondered if Marcus had been tempted to succumb to her charms, whether he would have taken up with her if she hadn't been the daughter of one of his clients. There was no doubt that Estelle was beautiful, elegant and self-possessed. Obviously wealthy, too. Although, she must be at least ten years older than Marcus.

'I'm not surprised, Marcus likes to keep his private life, private,' Hattie replied. 'He mentioned you, of course, and how he helped you out by going to a do with you.'

Estelle looked surprised but before she could reply Marcus joined them and interrupted.

'Excuse us, won't you, Estelle. Hattie and I have somewhere else to be.'

'You can't go yet, the party has only just started,' Estelle protested with a pout.

'Sorry, but I did say we couldn't stay long.' He slipped his arm around Hattie's waist. 'See you around.' And they both walked off to where her bike was parked.

'Where else do we have to go?' Hattie asked him.

'I'm going surfing, want to join me?' he asked. 'I've got a spare wetsuit that should fit you.'

She wondered if it had belonged to a former girlfriend but didn't ask. It wasn't important. 'Sure.' She straddled the bike and waited for him to get on behind her, but instead he pulled out his phone.

'Smile!'

Surprised, Hattie obligingly smiled. 'I thought I was the photographer,' she said when he'd taken the photo.

'I couldn't resist. You look great on that bike, with the Manor as a backdrop. I'll send it to you later.'

They went home to get changed into their wetsuits then headed for the beach. It was still warm, the sun was sparkling and glistening on the sea, white waves already building up and crashing onto the golden sand. Most of the families and holidaymakers had gone home for their evening meal so they easily found a secluded corner where they could surf in relative peace. Well, where Marcus could surf and Hattie could bodyboard – she'd learnt how to do that during her Cornwall holidays when she was a child. She'd love to be able to ride the waves like Marcus did though, she thought, as sitting down on the sand to catch her breath, she watched him in action. He really was good, good enough to do it professionally if he wanted to. Perhaps he did.

There was a lot she didn't know about Marcus, she realised. She hadn't known how good a painter he was until that afternoon, or realised his work was held in such high esteem. There were a lot of people at the party wanting to meet him, some of them wanting paintings done too.

She knew nothing about his background though, his family, his relationships. He obviously didn't have a current girlfriend but she had the feeling there hadn't been a shortage of them. He was good looking and, he definitely had an eye for the ladies, although he was in control of those emotions, judging by his refusal to bed Estelle, and how gentlemanly he had been with her the other night. Would she have had sex with him if he'd made a move? She rested her chin on her bent knees and considered it. There was no doubt that she found him attractive, so, yes, she thought, she might have gone for it if he'd made a move on Saturday but she was glad he hadn't. If she did decide to have sex with him, she'd definitely want to remember it the next day. Besides, she had the feeling that if she got involved with Marcus she would find him difficult to walk away from.

He was striding out of the sea towards her now, his wet hair dangling just above his shoulders. The tight wetsuit fitted him like a glove, stretching across his broad chest and muscular hips. As he got closer, she switched her gaze to a red-and-yellow hot air balloon floating in the sky, not wanting him to know she'd been looking at him. There was a banner advertising a local theme park on it.

'Have you ever been there?' he asked, looking up at the hot air balloon too.

'Yes, we always visited it when we were down on holiday, although I expect they have much scarier rides now. I used to go on the water ride with my parents; we've got a few photos of us all screaming as we got drenched with water.'

'Happy times.' He reached for his holdall, pulled out his towel and rubbed his hair dry.

'I thought so. Turns out Mum and Dad weren't so happy after all. At least Dad wasn't.' She hadn't meant to sound so bitter. It was all a long time ago, and thankfully both her parents were happy now.

'Still hurts, eh?'

She shook her head, not meeting his eyes. 'No, but I was mad at Dad for a long time. I felt like he'd abandoned us for a new life. We barely spoke for years. Until now, actually. I sometimes think that Uncle Albert left the cottage to both of us so that we'd have to talk to each other. He could have left it just to Dad.'

'And has it worked?' Marcus picked up his energy drink and took a long swig, then wiped his mouth with the back of his hand.

'I guess so, although our conversations are very short and always about the cottage. That's down to me, though,' she admitted.

'Still find it hard to forgive him?'

'I forgive him. I'm an adult now, I can see how relationships can fall apart, but I'm his child, his only daughter. He should have made an effort, even if I was a bolshie teenager.'

'You, bolshie?' His grin was teasing.

154

She grinned back. 'Anyway, enough about me. What about you? Have you always lived in Cornwall? Do your parents live here?'

'My dad died when I was a teenager. My mum and sister, Beth, live in Wales,' he told her. 'They've got a lot of land, they're into horses.'

'I'm sorry about your dad. Do you ever visit your mum and sister?' she asked.

'I take a drive up there about once a year. It's a bit of a trek and horses aren't my thing. We keep in touch through WhatsApp, though.'

'So the cottage isn't your family home?'

'It was my grandparents'. My mum grew up here. After my dad died, she remarried and went to live in Wales. I couldn't settle though, I felt more at home in Cornwall so I came back down to live with my grandparents. When they died, they left the cottage to my mum, sister and me. I bought them out. I've lived here since I was sixteen – eighteen years - and it suits me.'

'So you were left your cottage too ...'

He looked at her, knowing where the conversation was going. 'Yes, and I'm grateful, but it was already my home. I looked after my grandparents until they died, and bought my family out.'

'Whereas I neglected Uncle Albert and don't deserve Fisherman's Rest?'

He placed his hand over hers, hazel eyes sincere. 'I was being too judgey, I understand your circumstances better now.'

'But you still don't want me to sell?'

He rubbed her hand gently, his touch sparking desire within

155

her. 'I understand why you have to. Although, I'd prefer you not to sell the cottage to someone who will be using it as a holiday let.'

She bit her lip, her gaze drifting over to the sea. She'd prefer not to do that either. Actually, she was beginning to wish that she didn't have to sell Fisherman's Rest at all.

'Look, this is obviously a touchy subject, so why don't we declare it out of bounds? Come back to mine and I'll cook us a meal, open a bottle of wine and we can have a chilled-out evening.'

That sounded good. Really good. 'I'd love to,' she replied.

'Let's head off then, shall we?' He threw his towel and empty bottle in his holdall and stood up, then extended his arm to her.

She took his hand – his grip was strong but his skin was soft – and got to her feet, her own bag in her hand, and they set off up the hill, still hand in hand, an easy comfortableness between them. *I really am looking forward to this evening*, she thought. It would give them chance to talk in a relaxed setting. To get to know each other a little better.

As they reached the row of cottages, she saw a tall man with close-shaven brown hair and a small moustache sitting on the front garden wall of Fisherman's Rest. *What a cheek, why doesn't he find a bench?* She thought, annoyed. Then the man waved. She blinked and focused. There was something about him that seemed a bit familiar.

'Hattie!' The man waved again.

She felt Marcus stiffen beside her. 'It looks like you have a visitor?'

'I have no idea who he—' Then suddenly it dawned on her,

he was taller, older, had filled out a bit but yes it was definitely her stepbrother. 'Nick!'

'Didn't Owen tell you I was coming? I've been in England on business and have a few days to spare. When Owen said you had lots to do to the cottage so you could sell it, I offered to come down and help you.'

Chapter Twenty-Two

Nick switched his gaze to Marcus. 'I hope it's okay that I've come. Owen said he was going to clear it with you. I know we haven't seen each other for years, so if you prefer me not to stay with you I can get a B&B.'

Nick stay with her? That would be awkward. He'd been about fifteen last time she'd seen him and he hadn't exactly been friendly then. But then neither had she, had she? It was a long time ago though, and they were both adults now. He said he'd come to help and she could do with an extra pair of hands. Besides, it was half her father's cottage and Nick was his stepson so she should let him stay. She wished her father had warned her though. *Why hadn't he?*

'It's no problem to me.' She turned to Marcus who had released her hand and was now standing with his hands in his pockets.

'Marcus, this is Nick my stepbrother.' Then she turned back to Nick, 'This is my next-door neighbour, Marcus.'

Marcus nodded. 'Pleased to meet you.'

'I'm sorry, I had no idea that Nick was coming to help me. I'll have to come over another time,' Hattie said.

'Don't cancel your plans for me. Just let me in and I'll make myself at home,' Nick said.

Hattie hesitated. She'd been really looking forward to sharing a cosy evening with Marcus. She toyed with the idea of settling Nick in, then popping next door, but it seemed rude.

Marcus answered before Hattie could get her scrambled thoughts together. 'Don't worry, I'm sure you two will have a lot of catching up to do. We'll have the meal another evening.'

'If you're sure, that would probably be for the best,' Hattie said, trying to hide her disappointment. 'Do pop in and see Buddy whenever you want. Buddy is Uncle Albert's parrot,' she added, seeing Nick's surprised look. 'Marcus has been looking after him and they're very close.'

Nick nodded. 'Owen said you were looking after your uncle's parrot. That's great. I like parrots.'

'I'll leave you to it, then. Nice to meet you, Nick. See you soon, Hattie.'

She tried to hide her disappointment as Marcus opened his garden gate and walked down the path. She'd had high hopes for a lovely romantic evening and now it was all ruined. She sighed and turned to Nick. 'Come on then, let's get the kettle on.'

'I don't suppose you have a beer, do you?' he asked as she opened the front door.

'No beer, but I do have some fruit ciders in the fridge. Help yourself.'

'Bugger off!' Buddy shouted as soon as Nick walked in. He burst out laughing and went straight over to the cage. 'Hello, mate, you're a cheeky chappie, aren't you?'

Buddy cocked his head to one side as if he was listening.

159

Then he started squawking loudly, dancing along the branch and shouting, 'Bloody hell, who is it?'

Nick laughed. 'He's quite a character, isn't he?'

'He certainly is. It took him a while to get used to me, but he's settling down fine now, and I'm quite fond of him.'

'He's a yellow-naped Amazon, isn't he? My mate has the same breed. We used to flat share so I spent a lot of time with Molly, his parrot,' he said. 'Shall we let Buddy out for a bit? He looks a bit bored stuck in there.'

'I don't usually, not unless Marcus is here. He escaped once and I couldn't get him back in the cage.'

'I'll get him in no problem.' Nick glanced around. 'Are the windows shut?'

'Yes, I always shut them when I go out but ...'

Before she could stop him, Nick had opened the cage door. 'There you go, Buddy!'

Buddy immediately flew out, perched on the top of the fridge-freezer and started whistling.

Hattie bit her lip uneasily. She hoped Nick wasn't going to try and take over. 'You'd better be able to get him back in again or I'll be really annoyed,' she told him.

'I will. I promise.' Nick opened the fridge and took out a bottle of cider. 'Do you want one? I'll go shopping tomorrow and get some stuff in. I don't expect you to feed me, don't worry.'

'Well, that's a relief!' Hattie grinned, trying to lighten up. It was good of Nick to come all this way to help her sort out the cottage. It would be a lot easier with another pair of hands. 'Yes, I'll have one.'

Actually, Nick was good company. After Hattie had poured

160

him a cider and made a sandwich – the crust of which he gave to Buddy, who happily took it out of his hand and then flew to the top of the fridge-freezer to eat it – they sat chatting, sharing experiences of their childhood. Hattie was surprised to hear that Nick hadn't been happy about his mum remarrying either. In fact, he'd been just as resentful as she was and had set about making life very uncomfortable for her dad.

'Owen bore the brunt of my teenage years, I'm afraid,' he confessed. 'I really hated him moving in with Mum and made sure he knew it. I caused lots of arguments between them. They almost split up once. I feel awful about it now.'

And there Hattie had been, thinking her dad was having a lovely new carefree life over in France, whereas it now seemed it had been far from an easy ride. No wonder he'd barely had time to phone or come and visit.

'I was even worse when Lacey was born, felt like they wouldn't want to know me when they had "their own baby". I was a total berk. Didn't come to my senses until I left school and went to college. Finally, I grew up, realised that relationships are complicated and that Mum and Owen deserved a shot at happiness. And that your dad is a great fella. He's shown more interest in me and helped me more than my own dad.'

'I felt the same about Lacey too, at first,' Hattie admitted. She'd never stopped to think what life was like for Nick, but he was an innocent victim of this as much as she was. She wished she could go back and give that resentful teenage Hattie a shake. She could have spent her summer holidays in France every year and got to know her new family, that would have been awesome.

Mum wouldn't have liked it, though.

She'd have got used to it.

'Did Dad ever talk about me?' she asked.

Nick nodded. 'There was a photo of you on the dresser, beside the one of me and Lacey. He used to get excited every summer hoping you were coming over, then we could see he was hurt when you didn't. Not that I blame you.' A serious look suddenly came over his face. 'I was awful to you that first summer. I'm sorry. I guess I resented you – Owen had been so excited about you coming, Mum had been preparing your room and writing lists of the things we'd do for weeks. I felt like you were the star attraction and no one cared about me. Pathetic, I know.'

'And I felt like an outsider; you all seemed such a happy family unit. I didn't feel like I belonged. You had my dad, you saw him every day, whereas he seemed to have forgotten about me,' she confessed.

'Parents mess up their kids, don't they? You can't blame them, though, they're just trying to live their life and we're collateral damage. I guess I understand more now I'm older. God, I've had some relationship disasters. I'm just glad there's been no kids involved.' He looked over at her. 'Anyway, I'm sorry and I'd like to make it up to you. That's why I came here. When Owen told me all the stuff that had to be done to the cottage, I thought it wasn't fair to leave it all to you. I was in England and had a few days to spare so I thought I'd come and help out. And see if we could put the past behind us. We're family and I'd like to get to know my little sis better.'

He meant it, she could see that, and she felt a lump in her throat. She'd always wanted a brother or sister, perhaps it was time to embrace that she had both.

She held up her bottle of cider. 'I'll drink to that.'

He grinned and held out his, too. 'Here's to a better future relationship, sis.'

They clinked bottles. Suddenly she felt really glad that Nick was here, even if it did mean missing the evening with Marcus. Nick was family. And family was just what she needed right now.

Chapter Twenty-Three

'Breakfast will be ready in five minutes!' Nick shouted, banging on the attic door.

Hattie rubbed her eyes sleepily. 'Coming!'

It had been a surprisingly good evening. They'd chatted, drunk, eaten the fish and chips that Nick had insisted on going out to get, saying that Owen had raved on about the fish-and-chip shop in Port Medden so much that he simply had to try some, then chatted some more. Nick had told her all about his partner, Glenn, and how supportive Owen and Raina had been when he 'came out'. Hattie could tell that he was fond of her dad, and now had a good deal of respect for him.

At some point in the evening, Buddy had flown back into his cage and Nick had quickly fastened the door.

As Hattie reached for her dressing gown, she thought how pleased she was that Nick had turned up unexpectedly. If she had known he was coming, she would have been worried and tried to put him off, yet they had got on so well. He actually felt like a brother. She felt a bit sad about all the years they had both wasted resenting each other, but then maybe they'd had to go through that to be where they were now. And he wasn't going back until Saturday so she had his help for five whole days. They could get a lot done in that time.

She pulled the belt of her dressing gown tighter, then grabbed a pair of knickers and put them on too, not feeling comfortable totally naked underneath it when she had company.

Not that it had bothered her on Saturday night, when she'd evidently stripped off and laid on her bed, completely forgetting that Marcus was still there. Her thoughts drifted back to Marcus and the previous day on the beach, how they had been planning on spending the rest of the evening together until Nick turned up. Would they have ended up in bed?

Probably. And as much as she was sure she would have enjoyed it she was glad that Nick had interrupted their plans. Marcus was attractive – make that drop-dead gorgeous and incredibly sexy – but she didn't want to get involved with anyone right now; she needed to sell the cottage and sort her life out, no ties. And, she wasn't sure she could do casual with Marcus. She had the feeling that getting involved with him would only complicate things, and complications were something she could do without.

The aroma of bacon and eggs wafted up the stairs. This was the second time she'd had a cooked breakfast in as many days. She usually had cereal. She shouldn't feel that hungry after the fish-and-chip supper last night, but she did.

'Morning. Sit down. I was just about to dish up,' Nick said cheerily.

'This smells delicious. I can see I'm going to be piling on the kilos while you're here if I'm not careful,' she said, pulling out a chair and sitting down at the table.

'Rubbish, there's nothing to you!' he scoffed as he heaped

165

bacon and eggs on a plate and placed it on the table in front of her.

He put a plate of bread in the middle of the table and two glasses of orange juice, then came back with another loaded plate and sat down opposite her. 'Anyway, I don't do a fry-up every day, it's bad for my figure too,' he patted his stomach. 'But we're going to need to keep our strength up for the big tidy up today.'

They planned on going shopping for what they needed then doing a general declutter today, then spend the next couple of days cleaning up and painting. She was also hoping to get a new bathroom suite fitted before Friday as she wanted Nick to spend the last day relaxing. 'I'm not having you coming over and not seeing anything of Port Medden,' she'd said firmly. She could spend the next week tidying and decluttering upstairs ready for Jonathan to take the photos the following Monday. Nick told her that Owen and his mum had struggled all last year as they'd hardly had any guests at the B&B, which was normally booked up weeks in advance. She felt guilty when she learned how her dad and stepmother had struggled financially – she should have realised herself how all the Covid-19 restrictions the previous year would have affected them – and understood now why her father was desperate for a quick sale. It would be good for her too, she was starting to get a bit settled down here, and far too fond of Marcus. She needed to sell the cottage and sort out her life. She was glad Nick had come over to help her – by the weekend, the worst of the work would be done.

She'd just finished her breakfast when her dad phoned. He was apologetic about not letting her know Nick would be coming, saying that Nick had only told him yesterday and he'd meant to message but they'd had a bit of a crisis at the B&B – a burst water pipe. Hattie reassured him that it was fine and that she and Nick were starting on the clear-out today. 'I've arranged with Jonathan for the photos to be taken next Monday and to put the cottage on the market then. Jonathan is confident of a quick sale,' she told him.

'Thanks so much, Hattie. I really appreciate this.' There was a pause. 'Have you thought about what I suggested about you coming to stay with us for a bit when the cottage is sold? It would be good to spend some time together.'

'It's really kind of you, Dad, and I will think about it,' she said. And she meant it. Over the last couple of weeks she'd felt herself getting closer to her dad, and the talk with Nick last night had got rid of any lingering resentment. It was time to build bridges.

They chatted a little longer, the most they had talked in years, and Hattie promised to keep him updated with the progress by sending photographs. And to keep a note of what she was spending so she could be reimbursed when the cottage was sold.

'Now how about we ring around and see if we can get a plumber to fit a bathroom suite for us this week first? We can order one and they can pick it up for us. Then we can go out and get some paint and get started on the big tidy up,' Nick suggested afterwards.

'Sure. We can go into Truro. We should be able to get everything we need there,' she told him.

She googled plumbers on her phone, and after a couple of calls found one who could pick up and deliver a bathroom suite on Thursday for them, and would get rid of the old one too, thank goodness. They looked on the website link he sent them and chose a basic white one, a new shower head for the shower over the bath and a glass screen to replace the discoloured curtain. It was all done in less than an hour.

'Now let's go shopping,' she said, closing the laptop.

'Your car or mine?' Nick asked.

'I don't have a car, only a motorbike,' she replied.

Nick looked surprised. 'A bit of a wild one, aren't you? Okay, my car it is then. And luckily it's an estate so we'll get a lot in the boot.'

Marcus came back from his early morning surf to find Hattie and her stepbrother about to get into the car. Hattie waved to him casually and Marcus waved back. Last night he'd been planning a cosy evening for the two of them, maybe even hoping they'd spend the night together, but all that was gone now thanks to Nick turning up. Hattie had said that she was staying for the whole summer but it seemed her dad had other ideas. He was obviously desperate for the money from the sale of the cottage.

It was a shame. He'd enjoyed Hattie's company yesterday and she'd certainly got him out of a bit of a tight spot with Estelle. He shrugged, there was no sense bothering about something he couldn't change.

He fixed himself poached eggs and toast then went up into the attic to paint. He stayed there, engrossed in his art, for a few hours. Then he became aware of someone talking outside; it sounded like Hattie. He got up and walked over to the back window to look out. There was a pile of furniture and boxes in the back yard next door. They'd obviously started clearing out the cottage. He wondered how much of the stuff they would get rid of.

Then he saw Nick come out carrying a painting. It was the one he had painted for Albert a couple of years ago, of some fishermen tending their boats by the harbour. Albert had been really touched and had hung it up over the fireplace, saying that he wanted to be able to see it and remember his fishing days. Marcus had spent many an evening with Albert, both of them sipping a tot of whisky as the old man sat in his rocking chair, talking – in between smoking his pipe – about his life as a fisherman. Albert had some good tales to spin – whether they were all true or not, Marcus was never sure, but he could be entertaining company. Other times he could be quite brusque and, every now and again, would shut himself away saying he didn't want company. Marcus never took offence, his own grandad was like that sometimes, and would take himself off to his shed for some quiet time. Marcus and his nan knew to leave him be for a while. So he used to leave Albert for a day or two then pop around on some pretext of wanting his opinion about something or bringing a treat for Buddy, or – as Albert got older – some food from the hotel that would have gone to waste if Marcus hadn't taken it home.

He frowned as he looked at the painting. Were they throwing it out? If so, should he ask for it? He knew that it was silly to feel peeved about it, he guessed a painting like that wouldn't fit into the modern flat Hattie would be moving into, and she didn't know he'd painted it, did she? She probably hadn't spotted his signature in the bottom-left corner. He shouldn't be so quick to jump to conclusions, though, they could be moving it out so that they could paint the room.

He'd go down and ask, maybe offer to lend a hand.

'What shall we do with all this? It's junk mainly, but maybe a charity shop would be interested in it?' Nick said as he came out carrying another box of stuff.

'There's one in the town, we can take everything there,' Hattie called from inside.

So they are chucking it all out. Well, they weren't taking his painting to a charity shop, no way! He'd ask for it back and hang it on the wall himself, it would be nice to have something to remember Albert by. He'd been like a substitute grandfather to him.

Chapter Twenty-Four

Hattie came out then, carrying a tall lamp that had seen better days.

'Hi. You been painting?' she called over the wall to Marcus.

'Obviously,' he said curtly – why else would he be wearing his old paint-spattered clothes? – then saw her frown and wished he hadn't sounded so off. He swallowed. 'You've started clearing the house out, then?'

'Yes, Nick's only here until the weekend so we need to get done as much as we can before he goes.' She thrust a floppy strand of hair back off her face. 'There's such a lot to do.'

'Well, don't throw that painting out – I'll take it.' There he was again, sounding all huffy and abrupt.

She looked at him in surprise. 'Oh ...'

'If it's not a problem?'

She shook her head. 'No, of course not.'

Nick looked over at her. 'I thought you—'

'No, it's fine, let Marcus have it. He painted it, didn't you?'

So, she knew that and was still going to dump it? 'I did.' He walked over to the wall. 'I'll take it now, if that's okay?'

Nick shot Hattie a glance.

'Of course.' She picked it up and passed it over the wall. 'It's a good painting.'

Not good enough to keep, evidently. 'Thanks.' He took it off her and carried it into the house.

Well, the closeness of yesterday was well and truly gone. To think he'd been planning on cooking her a meal, spending the evening – and maybe the night – with her. But now her long-lost stepbrother had showed up, all she could think of was selling Fisherman's Rest.

They need the money from the cottage. And it isn't just her decision, he reminded himself.

Even so, she could have kept some of Albert's stuff, and the painting had looked good over the fireplace, given the cottage's character. He expected that they wanted it to look bland though, and that the painting and Uncle Albert's things would all look out of place in the modern home Hattie would be buying for herself.

He studied the painting. It needed a clean, the frame was filthy and the painting itself was smoke-stained – Albert had been far too fond of that pipe of his, to the detriment of his health, but whenever Marcus, or the doctor, had suggested he cut down, he'd always said, 'When your time's come, it's come. Until then, I'm going to make the most of the few pleasures I have.'

Marcus welled up as he thought about the old man. He put the painting down by the side of the sofa. He'd clean it later. Right now, he needed to grab something to eat then go back up to the attic to continue painting. Yesterday's garden party had led to talk of another couple of commissions and before they got finalised he wanted to finish the painting he was working on.

Half an hour later, a mug of coffee in his hand, he climbed the narrow steps to the attic. The painting was of a woman dressed in black leather astride a motorbike, her white-blond hair blowing in the wind. *Bike Rider* he'd called it but he might as well have called it *Hattie*, because that's who the woman was. He'd copied it from the photo he'd taken of Hattie that day at Thomwell Manor, obliterating the background. It was as if Hattie was looking out of the painting at him. She was laughing, her eyes sparkling. She was *alive*.

This was one painting he had no intention of selling.

'Why didn't you tell him that you were keeping that painting?'

Hattie shrugged. 'He painted it. And he spent far more time with Uncle Albert than I did, so I think he deserves it more.'

'The thing is, I think he got the impression that you were dumping it. And as he painted it, that probably bugged him.' Nick leant back against the sink and folded his arms. 'Are you two an item or what? You seemed pretty close on Sunday night but now you seem a bit edgy around each other.'

'No, we're not. He needed someone to partner him to a garden party so I agreed to do it.' She told him about the painting he'd been commissioned to do for Lord Thomwell's birthday. 'He's a really talented artist.'

'I can see that by the fishing boats painting he did for your uncle.' He cocked his head to one side. 'So, you're not interested in him, then?'

'A romance with my next-door neighbour is the last thing I

need right now,' she told him. 'Now, how about helping me with these boxes instead of speculating on my non-existent love life?'

He grinned and did a mock salute. 'Your wish is my command.'

Hattie smiled. Nick hadn't even been here twenty-four hours but already they had slipped into an easy familiarity. It was nice to have an older stepbrother, she decided, especially right now when she was trying to get the cottage sorted to put on the market.

By the end of the day, the back yard was so full they could barely move, but the lounge was completely empty bar a couple of chairs and the heavy wall unit. They scrubbed the doors and walls first intending to get up the next morning and start painting.

'I hope it will all be safe out in the back yard,' she said. 'There's no forecast of rain so it should be dry enough, and surely no one will want to pinch old stuff like that?'

'I wouldn't think so.'

'Now, how about we pop out for a walk along the harbour and a drink?' Nick suggested. 'I think we deserve it after all our hard work.'

'Sounds good to me,' she agreed. She'd found it quite sad sorting through Uncle Albert's things, and although she didn't admit it to Nick, she was disappointed that Marcus had asked for the painting back; she'd wanted to keep it as a reminder of her uncle, and of Marcus. How could she deny Marcus it, though, when he had painted it? And been like a son to Uncle Albert? She could see how all this must look to him – no one had been to see Uncle Albert for years and now here she and

Nick were going through the cottage quicker than you could say 'inheritance'. They must look like a right pair of vultures.

She hated this feeling guilty all the while. And she was far too bothered what Marcus thought of her. He really was getting under her skin. The sooner the cottage was sold and she was away from him the better.

Chapter Twenty-Five

Straight after breakfast the next morning, Hattie and Nick both donned the overalls they'd bought yesterday, and got ready to start painting the lounge.

Buddy was watching them beadily from his cage. *He must be wondering what's going on*, Hattie thought. All these people coming and going – her, Mali and Lou, and now Nick. And all this upheaval. Then another thought struck her.

'Do you think Buddy will be okay with the paint fumes?' she asked worriedly.

'I hadn't thought of that. We could put him in the back garden while we paint,' Nick suggested.

Hattie shook her head. 'I don't trust Marcus's cat, Mr Tibbs. He sneaked in yesterday when we had the back door open to carry the stuff out, and I had to shoo him off. He stalks Buddy if he gets the chance. Marcus said Mr Tibbs even jumped on the cage once when he was looking after Buddy, that's why he brought him back to Fisherman's Rest and came in regularly to feed and check on him instead.'

Maybe she should put Buddy up in the attic – at least he

would be out of the way of any paint fumes there, or of Mr Tibbs if he sneaked again, and it was a lovely bright room.

She mentioned it to Nick. 'Marcus has a small travel cage. I'll ask him if I can borrow it to carry Buddy up to the attic in. We'll struggle trying to carry that big cage up the two flights of narrow stairs and it could unsettle Buddy.'

'That sounds like a good idea, if you can transfer him without him flying off.'

'Marcus can, he's used to it. He's probably back from surfing now. I'll pop around and ask, I'll only be a few minutes.'

She went around next door and knocked loudly, knowing that Marcus was often up in the attic painting. She actually felt a bit awkward seeing him after how close they had been at the weekend, and then the business with the painting yesterday.

'Coming!'

Marcus opened the door, his hair dishevelled, T-shirt paint-stained as though he wiped his brushes on it, and in cut-off denims and bare feet.

'Sorry for disturbing you …'

'It's fine. It looks like you're busy too.' His eyes lingered on the overalls she was wearing.

'Actually, we're just about to start painting and thought we should move Buddy up to my room because of the paint fumes.' She paused. 'I was wondering if I could borrow your travel cage and if you could help me get him into it?'

Marcus ran his hand through his hair. 'The fumes could be bad for him, yes. Look, why don't you leave him with me until you've finished? He might be better off here.'

Hattie shook her head. 'It's kind of you to offer but Mr Tibbs sneaked in yesterday and I had to shoo him away from the cage.

And I really would like to keep him with me. I don't want to unsettle him any more than we have to.'

Marcus nodded. 'Point taken. Well, give me a few minutes and I'll bring the cage around.'

'Thanks so much.'

Marcus shut the door and went back inside, leaving Hattie to turn and walk away wondering why he hadn't asked her in and how they'd got so formal all of a sudden when at the weekend they'd been laughing and dancing together.

True to his word, Marcus came around ten minutes later, now with trainers on his feet and carrying the travel cage and a banana.

'All right, mate?' Nick looked up from the dust sheet he and Hattie were spreading over the unit that had been too heavy to carry out.

'Just come to move Buddy.' Marcus looked over at Hattie. 'Can you give me a hand?'

'Sure.' She eyed the banana. 'I'm guessing that's to tempt him into the smaller cage?'

'It is.'

'Hello! Hello!' Buddy squealed excitedly as soon as he saw Marcus. 'Where you been?'

'Hello, Buddy.' Marcus went over to the cage and Buddy whistled loudly, then climbed down the bars as Marcus put his face to the cage.

'Well, he sure loves you. That's the chirpiest I've seen him,' Nick said.

'He's got to know me over the years. I used to pop round most nights after work. Albert was in the habit of sitting up late and liked me to join him for a chat and a drop of whisky,' Marcus said. As before, Marcus used the banana to tempt Buddy into the smaller cage. Then he quickly pushed the cage door shut.

'Want me to carry him up to the attic for you?' he asked.

'It might be best, then I can open the doors for you, I don't want to make him jittery,' Hattie said, leading the way out into the hall.

'I'll get cracking with the painting then, while you two move the bird and settle him in.' Nick grabbed one of the big tins of paint and a roller.

Marcus carried Buddy, talking reassuringly as he walked up the two flights of stairs.

Thank goodness she'd made her bed that morning and not left any underwear lying around, Hattie thought as she opened the attic door. 'Shall we put him on that chest of drawers by the window? It's nice and light there,' she suggested.

'Good idea.' Marcus walked over and gently put the cage down. 'There we are, boy. You're staying up here for a while,' he said.

Buddy was sitting on the perch, head to one side, staring at him. Marcus took the other half of banana out of his pocket, opened the cage door slightly and dropped it in. 'Have another treat,' he said.

Buddy hopped down, grabbed it, and carried it up to the perch where he balanced on one leg, held the piece of banana with his other claw and nibbled it.

They both watched him in an awkward silence and Hattie wondered if, like her, Marcus was remembering the last time he had been in her bedroom. When he had helped her home drunk from the wedding reception and she had stripped off and got into bed, too drunk to care that he was there. Was it really only a few days ago? How had they gone from that to being so self-conscious around each other.

'He seems happy enough here,' she said to break the silence.

'He'll be fine,' Marcus said as they both walked out of the room.

Hattie carefully closed the door behind her.

'Nick seems okay, how are you both getting on?'

'Good. Better than I thought we would. He's given me a different insight into my dad. I think I might have been a bit harsh on him.'

'Well, I'm sure your dad understands. Divorce is never easy, especially for the children who feel they've been left behind by one of the parents.'

'Yes, that's how I felt. I never thought about how it was for Nick, having his father replaced. I'm going over to France for a visit when the cottage is sold.' They were down the stairs now and, as they walked into the kitchen, Hattie saw that Nick had made a start on painting the lounge ceiling and was singing along to a music station on the radio.

'You stopping for a bevvy, mate? There's some cans in the fridge if you want one,' he called to Marcus.

'Thanks but I need to get back.' Marcus thrust his hands in his pockets. 'I've got Thursday evening off, though, why don't you two come around for a meal? It's probably going to be difficult for you both to cook while you're decorating and stuff.'

His offer took Hattie by surprise. 'That sounds great, doesn't it, Nick?'

'A chef cooking for us? Nice! Count me in,' Nick agreed. Then he paused, paintbrush poised, and glanced at Hattie. 'Unless you'd prefer a cosy evening for the two of you?'

180

'Of course not,' Hattie said quickly, even though she would have liked that. A lot. 'You must come too.'

'That's settled then. See you about seven?' Marcus said.

'We'll be there. Thanks,' Hattie told him. 'I'll see you out.'

'It's fine. I know the way. You've got enough to do here. See you tomorrow.'

'Are you sure you wouldn't have preferred a meal for two?' Nick asked as they heard the front door close behind Marcus. 'I'm happy to have a pub meal on my own. I don't want to play gooseberry.'

'Don't be silly, I told you we're just friends.'

'Yep. You told me that, but your face when you see him tells me different. And I can tell he feels the same about you. Still, I'm not about to turn down a free meal.' He dipped his roller in the tray he was holding. 'How's this looking?'

'Good. I'll start on the walls.' Hattie picked up a paint tray and poured some of the white emulsion into it, then grabbed a roller and started on the long lounge wall.

They worked side by side, singing along to the radio, all morning. By the time they stopped for a late lunch, the lounge was almost done.

'It really makes a difference, doesn't it?' Hattie said as Nick put the kettle on and she made them cheese and ham sandwiches.

'Yep, I reckon this place will be snapped up.' Nick put two mugs down on the table. 'I'm sorry I can only stay until Saturday, but hopefully it will all be done by then.'

'It's fine. I'm really glad of your help. I'll go to the market on Saturday and pick up some colourful curtains and cushions. I'll send you some photos of the finished look. I'll be sending some to Dad too.'

After lunch, they painted the kitchen then moved the furniture back inside.

Then they had a shower and went out for a pub meal.

'Thanks for coming down to help me. The cottage looks much better already,' Hattie said as they tucked into their sausages and mash.

'You're welcome. I'm pleased that I could help,' Nick said, swallowing a spoonful of mash.

Hattie speared a sausage and took a big bite out of it. 'So am I,' she said.

Chapter Twenty-Six

By the time the plumber arrived with the bathroom suite early on Thursday morning the living room and kitchen were looking clean and tidy, the hall, upstairs landing, and the bathroom walls had been painted and Nick and Hattie were cleaning down the doors upstairs. It took most of the day for the plumber to take out the old suite and fit the new one – Nick helped a bit. Hattie tidied up Uncle Albert's bedroom, shoving things into the cupboard and wardrobe until she had time to sort them out. All that mattered at the moment was that it looked clean and tidy for the photographs, and for viewings.

Although it was only a basic white suite, with the new shower and a clear screen it really looked good.

'This looks so much better. I'll get a new blind and light shade too and a colourful bathmat.' She was already imagining the colour scheme, coral and white she thought, with a heated towel rail with a fluffy towel hanging on it, a cheerful coral bathmat, a cream roller-blind . . . Then she remined herself that Jonathan had told her to keep the colours neutral.

'Good idea.' Nick surveyed the room thoughtfully. 'It could

do with retiling and new windows ideally, but the new buyers will probably sort that out.'

'There's such a lot of potential here, isn't there?' Hattie said. 'A bit of money and TLC and it could make a lovely home.'

'You're right. Not my cup of tea, though, I prefer something more modern. And with central heating. I bet it's freezing in the winter. I'm amazed the old guy didn't freeze to death.'

Hattie hadn't thought of that. She'd guessed Uncle Albert hadn't wanted the upheaval of having radiators fitted. Or hadn't got the money, she realised. According to Albert's will, apart from the cottage, there had only been a couple of hundred pounds in his bank account that he'd left to the RNLI. Maybe he'd been living hand to mouth, huddled around a gas fire in the lounge, and only the gas heater in his bedroom upstairs. How did he manage when he had a shower? she wondered. The thought made her feel sad and once again she felt a twinge of guilt that she had lost touch with him.

'I expect you could get radiators put in. Has Marcus modernised his place much?' Nick's voice cut through her thoughts.

'What?'

'Does he have central heating? Has he replaced the windows?'

Hattie cast her mind back to the couple of times she'd been in Marcus's cottage. 'He's replaced the kitchen cupboards and put doors in the archway but I've no idea about central heating or the windows. I've not noticed. I've only been in the lounge and kitchen,' she added.

'Well, it'll be up to the buyers to make any other changes. They might want to put a couple of radiators in to make it more comfortable for holidaymakers who stay out of season.' Nick stretched. 'Well there's just time for us both to try out the new shower before we head next door. I'll go and put the kettle on if you want to go first?' He checked his watch. 'What time did he say to be there?'

'Seven,' Hattie replied. 'I haven't heard from him since yesterday, though, so I wonder if I should text and check that it's still on.' She still couldn't believe that he'd invited them both.

Nick looked surprised. 'Why would he cancel?' He shrugged. 'But yeah, go ahead if you feel you should. We can always go out for a pub meal if he has changed his mind.'

Hattie wondered whether to text or phone Marcus, then decided to phone – she'd be able to pick up on his mood better if she could hear his voice.

'Hi, Hattie, is it all going okay?' Marcus's voice sounded warm and friendly, she noticed with relief.

'Hi, yes. We've had a new bathroom suite fitted and painted the bathroom walls. It's all looking good.'

'That's great. You're not calling to say that you're too busy to come for dinner, are you?'

'No, I was double-checking the time you wanted us there – unless you're busy and want to cancel?'

'Definitely not. I've already started the prep. Any time after seven is good. We can have a drink before the meal. And I have plenty of wine so there's no need to bring anything.'

'I don't want to come empty-handed . . .'

'Just bring yourselves, it's all in hand. You can return the favour another time, if you feel guilty.'

Was he inviting himself around to hers for a meal? 'I'll hold you to that,' she said.

★　　★　　★

185

Marcus had been thinking about what to cook for Nick and Hattie ever since he'd dished out the invitation to them, and had finally decided on grilled salmon with dauphinoise potatoes and roasted vegetables, followed by warm brownies and ice cream. Simple, but tasty. He didn't want to be ages in the kitchen cooking, leaving Hattie and Nick to entertain themselves.

He hadn't actually planned on inviting them around for a meal, the words had just come out of his mouth before he'd even realised he was going to say them, spurred on by a desire to see Hattie again. They'd had such a wonderful weekend – he'd felt that they'd grown closer, reached an understanding – then Nick had arrived and suddenly it was back to being distant again. That was probably his fault for getting all huffy over the painting. He'd seen her eyes cloud over as though she'd sensed that she'd done something wrong but wasn't sure what it was. She probably wouldn't have spoken to him again if she hadn't needed the travel cage for Buddy – and his help getting the parrot into it. Which would have been a shame, as he liked Hattie. Really liked her.

Well, don't get too hung up on her, she's only here for the summer, he reminded himself as he turned the oven on to warm up then set about peeling and slicing the potatoes. When that was done, he placed them in a bowl with grated garlic and seasoning, poured cream over them and mixed it all well before transferring into a large gratin dish. The dauphinoise needed to go in first, as they took the longest to cook. He pressed the potatoes down firmly with the back of a spoon and put the dish in the now-warm oven. He wished that it was a meal for two, and that he was spending the evening with just Hattie as they planned for the other night, but now he thought that probably wouldn't be a wise thing to do. Hattie would be moving away soon so it might be best for them not to get too close. Maybe it was a good job Nick would be there. Besides, he seemed like a decent guy and Marcus was looking forward to a pleasant evening. It had been ages since he'd had company around for dinner. It wasn't something he did often, unless he was dating someone but even then he often preferred to eat out. His home was his sanctuary. And it had been a while since he'd dated anyone long enough to invite them around for a meal.

He took a white linen tablecloth out of the bottom cupboard and put it on the table, his mind going back to the red, checked, plastic tablecloth Albert had always used, the one Hattie had wrapped herself up with. As a chef, Marcus knew the importance of presentation – not just of the food but of the table too. His nan had always had a supply of tablecloths and serviettes, using different ones to suit the occasion, and most of them were still as good as new. Marcus preferred white linen, it always looked good and you could use any colour serviettes with it. Today he was using red. And sparkling crystal glasses – his grandmother's. He took her box of silver cutlery out of the cupboard too, without stopping to ask himself why he was going to so much trouble for his next-door neighbour and her stepbrother.

The table was laid, and everything almost cooked, when Hattie and Nick knocked on the door. Marcus took a deep breath to still the ridiculous butterflies that were somersaulting in his stomach and went to let them in.

Chapter Twenty-Seven

'That was a delicious meal,' Hattie said, rubbing her stomach as she pushed aside her now-empty plate.

'It certainly was,' Nick agreed. 'That salmon was cooked to perfection.' He put his thumb and finger together and kissed them to show his appreciation. '*Parfait*.'

'Thank you.' Marcus stood up and reached out for the dirty plates but Hattie was already piling them up. After he'd cooked them a heavenly meal like that, she wasn't going to sit there and leave Marcus to clear up.

'Anyone want dessert?'

Nick's eyes lit up. 'Yes please!' He certainly loved his food, Hattie thought in amusement.

'What is it?' she asked, her tummy felt so full she was sure she couldn't squeeze in another morsel.

'Warm chocolate brownie with cream or ice cream. Or you can have cheese and biscuits.'

How could she resist chocolate brownie with cream? She'd find room for it somehow. 'Chocolate brownie, please,' she called as she carried the plates over to the sink.

'And for me. Need a hand?' Nick offered.

'You could open another bottle of wine,' Marcus suggested and Nick immediately got up to get one out of the fridge. They'd brought two around with them, despite Marcus telling them not to.

Marcus looked good in his stone-coloured cropped trousers and black T-shirt, Hattie thought. He'd tied his hair up into a man bun which showed off his chiselled cheekbones and amazing eyes. She got the impression he'd made an effort. Was it for her? She had made an effort too, putting on a pair of floaty patterned trousers and a lacy vest top and even some mascara, powder and a darker shade of lipstick, as well as a dab of concealer to hide the shadows under her eyes. She was tired, and knew that Nick was too; they'd both worked really hard the last few days, but she was delighted with the results. And glad that Nick had come over to help her. She liked Nick, he was easy company, laid back and amusing. He treated her fondly, like a little sister, and she knew that it had done her good to have him there.

Marcus took the brownies out of the oven and placed them on the cooling rack. There were already three empty dishes waiting on the worktop, so Hattie got the cream out of the fridge while Nick opened the wine.

'I see you've modernised your cottage but managed to keep the character of the place too,' Nick said as they sat down with their desserts. 'I like the light oak cupboards; they open the kitchen up a bit. I noticed a couple of radiators so am guessing that you've got central heating too?'

'Yes, I had it put in a couple of years ago. My grandparents lived here all their married life, and their parents before them, so the cottage needed tidying and modernising, like Albert's cottage does, but I didn't want to lose the character.' He took a sip of his wine. 'How are you getting on with things next door?'

'It's mainly a "tidy up what you see" job, but the new bathroom suite has made a big difference, as has painting the walls and decluttering, although Hattie still has loads to do. I feel guilty leaving her to it really.'

'There's no need. You've been an amazing help,' Hattie assured him.

'Is there much left to do?' Marcus asked.

'Wardrobes, cupboards to declutter, and the shed. Uncle Albert was a bit off a hoarder, every cupboard I open is brimming with stuff.' Hattie reached for the jug and poured a little more cream onto her brownie.

'I'd help tomorrow but she's refused to let me do anything else.' Nick broke off a chunk of the brownie with his spoon and put it in his mouth. 'Mmmm,' he mumbled appreciatively.

'I've insisted that Nick has tomorrow off and comes for a tour of Port Medden. He goes back Saturday morning and I feel guilty that he's spent the whole time he's been here doing up Fisherman's Rest,' Hattie explained.

'I don't mind, that's why I came over,' Nick said, his mouthful of dessert now finished he started to scoop up another spoonful.

'Even so . . .'

'Let me know if you need a hand. I can help any afternoon. It's no trouble, so don't feel awkward about asking,' Marcus offered.

'Thanks,' said Hattie. Then she added impulsively, 'Why don't you pop around tomorrow and see what we've done? We're out in the daytime, but maybe after your shift at the hotel? If it isn't too late?'

'Thanks, I will. I'm actually doing the afternoon shift again tomorrow as Shanise can't make it – family stuff,' Marcus told her. 'I'll be finished for seven thirty.'

'Even better, come around about eight, then. We'll be back by then and it will still be light enough for you to see it all clearly.'

When they'd finished the dessert, Nick washed up, Hattie dried it all, and Marcus put everything away. Then they took another bottle of wine and their half-full glasses into the lounge.

Hattie's eyes rested on the painting over the fireplace; it was the one from Uncle Albert's cottage. The one Marcus had painted and thought she was going to throw away, only it looked much brighter now. Marcus had obviously cleaned it.

'She wasn't going to dump it, you know,' Nick slurred, following Hattie's gaze.

'What?' Marcus looked at them both, puzzled.

'That painting.' Nick gestured towards it with his glass, almost spilling some wine as he did so. 'She took it down so we could paint the walls. She was going to keep it to remind her of her uncle. And probably because you'd painted it, too.'

Damn! Trust Nick to loosen his tongue now he'd had a drink. Hattie felt terrible as she saw Marcus's eyes widen. 'Why didn't you tell me that, Hattie?' he exclaimed.

'Cos she thought you really wanted it, and as you were the one who painted it—'

'Nick!' Hattie chastised him, mortified. 'I told you not to say anything.' She turned her gaze to Marcus, hoping that her cheeks weren't as red as they felt. 'Please ignore him, he's had too much wine. Of course you should have the painting back.'

191

'You really weren't going to dump it?' Marcus asked, his eyes holding hers.

She shook her head. 'Definitely not! But I honestly don't mind you having it.'

Marcus walked over to the fireplace and took the painting down. 'Then please take it back and excuse me for jumping to conclusions. Again.' He walked over and placed it down by the side of the chair she was sitting on.

She couldn't make out whether he was pleased or not. 'Are you sure? You have a gap there now . . .'

'Which will soon be filled by a painting that I'm currently working on.'

'Then, thank you.' She flashed him a big smile.

Nick swallowed another mouthful of his wine. 'So, all your paintings aren't commissions or for sale then? You keep some yourself?'

'Most of them are, yes. But this one that I'm working on is just for me.'

'Thank you for a lovely meal,' Hattie said as she and Nick got up to leave after what had been a very pleasant evening. She hadn't enjoyed herself so much for ages, Marcus had been relaxed, laughing and chatting away, and Nick was entertaining company, especially with a few glasses of wine inside him. She was quite reluctant to go, but it was gone midnight now.

'Don't forget to pop in tomorrow evening,' Hattie turned to remind Marcus as she and Nick walked up the path. 'We'll bring Buddy down into his big cage then too, and you can take the travel one back home with you.'

'Sounds good to me,' Marcus said. 'Enjoy your day out tomorrow.'

They both waved and linked arms for the short walk next door. 'Can't have you falling over, you seem a bit unsteady on your feet,' Nick said.

'Cheek! You're the one who's tipsy. I'm holding you up!'

'You're both tipsy! And so am I!' Marcus said with a grin, watching them totter up the path.

'He definitely fancies you,' Nick said as soon as they were back in Fisherman's Rest.

'No, he doesn't.' Hattie shook her head firmly. 'I told you we're just friends.'

'Yeah, but you both want to be more. Don't deny it.'

'I think you need a coffee.' Hattie walked over to put the kettle on, her heart skipping inside her chest. *Was Nick right, did Marcus fancy her?*

Chapter Twenty-Eight

'It all looks amazing. It's like a different cottage. I never dreamed we could transform it so much in just a few days. Thanks so much for your help,' Hattie said as she and Nick sat in the kitchen having a late breakfast the next morning. Even though they'd done the cottage on the cheap, it was enough to give it a fresh new look. She passed Nick a mug of tea. 'I think I might put a coat of paint on the kitchen cupboards too. It would be great to put in some new ones, like Marcus has, but at least painting them will brighten the kitchen.'

'You could get a new sink too, that would make a big difference.' Nick blew on his tea to cool it down. 'I wish I could stay longer; I know that there's still a lot more to do. Clearing out the wardrobes and cupboards is going to be a massive job, goodness knows what's in them.'

'I can do the rest of the sorting out bit by bit, and Marcus will help me. He might even want to keep some of Uncle Albert's things,' Hattie told him. 'Even if we sell the cottage quickly it will take at least six weeks for the sale to go through. That's plenty of time for me to clear out the rest of the things.

I've told Dad that if I come across anything I'm not sure of, I'll take a photo and send it to him. I don't want to be throwing out any family heirlooms!' She wiped her hands on her shorts. 'Right, now, I'll clear these mugs and then we'll have that tour of Port Medden that I promised you.'

'Sounds good to me. I'll just give Glenn a call. I'll be down in about ten minutes.'

'Take your time.' Hattie quickly washed the plates then went into the back yard. They'd cleared everything from it now, and had dropped anything that was broken at the local tip and then given the rest to a couple of charity shops. She wanted to get a few flowering tubs to make the yard look really pretty. She could put some pots out the front and paint the bench too. It would make the cottage look more inviting, cared for. She had to see Ellie and Reece tomorrow, but she had the rest of the afternoon and Sunday free, plenty of time to do what she had in mind. Jonathan was coming on Monday with a photographer.

She heard the back door open next door and looked over the wall to see Marcus coming out. 'How's it going?' he asked.

'Good. We've tidied up and are off to have a walk around Port Medden now. Are you still popping around later to check out our hard work and have a goodbye drink with Nick?'

'I'll be there straight after work,' Marcus promised. 'It's going to feel a bit weird being on your own when Nick has gone, isn't it?'

'It will but I've got plenty to keep me occupied. And Buddy is good company now he's got used to me. Mind you, I'll be glad to move him back downstairs, he wakes me up at stupid o'clock shouting "bugger off" to the seagulls!'

Marcus chuckled. 'Yes, you can really hear them in the attic room, can't you? Do they disturb you?'

'They did at first, but I've got used to them now, but Buddy screeching at the top of his voice always jolts me out of my sleep and once he's awake he's non-stop chatter!' She was getting very fond of the parrot, though, and was pleased that he was finally settling down with her.

'Okay, I'm ready to go – ah, hello, Marcus. How's your head this morning? We got through a bit of wine, didn't we?' said Nick, appearing in the back yard.

'Nothing a strong black coffee couldn't sort out.' Marcus didn't point out that it was Nick who had drunk most of the wine. He checked his watch. 'Sorry, I've got a meeting with someone who wants to commission a painting so I need to get going. I'll see you both tonight. Got to dash.' He raised his hand in a wave and then was off.

'I presume we're having a walking tour? I'm not sure all that wine is out of my system yet,' Nick said.

'Yep, all the best places are within walking distance.' Hattie sat down on one of the rusting chairs. 'I'm so grateful for your help, Nick. This would have all taken me ages.'

He grinned at her. 'We make a good team.'

Hattie grinned back. 'We do. But it's not something I'd like to do too often.'

'Me and Glenn bought a run-down cottage and have been doing that up as and when we can alongside our jobs. It's taking longer than we'd like, though.' Nick sat down on the other chair beside Hattie. 'We've toyed with the idea of going part-time so we can do the house up quicker, sell it on and buy another one, but were a bit worried about making the commitment. Now,

I'm thinking it might be a good idea. I can't believe what we've done in a few days.'

'Neither can I. When I came down as a child, I remember the cottage as bright and cheerful. There were pots of flowers in the back yard, and around the front door, I remember their smell – and the smell of cooking from the kitchen. It was lovely. I had a shock when I saw how scruffy and neglected it had got, but I guess as he got older Uncle Albert let things go a bit. Marcus said that he was lonely. It's so sad.'

'I know. It sounds like Marcus kept an eye on him, though, and the woman next door, so he said last night. You couldn't help if you didn't know, could you?' Nick pointed out. He got to his feet. 'Right, let's start this sightseeing tour then. And can we stop off for a pub lunch maybe?'

'Sounds good.' Hattie grabbed her bag, locked up the cottage and then they set off down the hill to the harbour.

The day passed quickly and very pleasantly, starting with a walk around the harbour front, the local art gallery – where they were both chuffed to see two of Marcus's paintings on display – and a paddle in the sea. They stopped off at the Old Sea Dog for a pub lunch washed down with a fruit cider. Then they had a wander around the shops, where Nick bought a few souvenirs to take home and Hattie spotted some yellow cushions which she simply had to buy.

'It might have been an idea to take the car,' Nick said as they walked back to the cottage, their hands full of bagged-up cushions.

'They will look great on the sofa, they'll really add colour to the room,' Hattie told him.

She was right. The vibrant yellow cushions transformed the

old brown sofa and brought a splash of much-needed colour to the living room. 'Now, I can pick out the yellow in flowers, or rugs, or lampshades. It'll look really bright and cheerful,' she said, feeling really pleased with how much they had transformed Fisherman's Rest.

Hattie's phone started to ring. She glanced at the screen and saw it was her dad, video-calling her. 'It's Dad,' she mouthed, swiping the screen to answer. There was a crackle and then Owen's face appeared.

'Hello, love. Is this a good time? I just wanted to check how you and Nick were getting on with tidying up the cottage.'

'We've done more than tidy it, we've transformed it. Let me show you.'

Taking the phone from room to room, she showed him what they'd done.

'That looks brilliant. I think I could do with you two over here helping with the hotel renovations.' Owen was clearly impressed.

'Maybe me and Glenn can talk to you about that ... but I'll have to discuss it with him first,' Nick said, peering over Hattie's shoulder.

'You're going to take a chance on setting up on your own then?' Owen clearly knew what Nick was talking about and Hattie felt a bit sad that Nick had a closer relationship with her dad than she did. She pushed the resentment away. The past was done with – at least she and her dad were building a stronger relationship now.

'We're still talking about the details but yes, I think we're going to give it a go,' Nick told him.

'That's great. And seriously, thank you both for all your hard work there. I really think this will make a huge difference to how quickly the cottage sells as well as to the price. And I really need a quick sale.'

'It's going on the market Monday, Dad,' Hattie told him.

'That's such a relief,' Owen told her.

Then Raina joined in and they all sat chatting for a while. Owen gave them a bit of a tour of the hotel, and even Lacey gave them a wave and a cheery 'bonjour'. For the first time in years, Hattie felt like she had her dad back. It was a lovely feeling.

'You've done a good job on this,' Marcus said approvingly as Hattie and Nick showed him around after they'd transferred a very perky Buddy back into his large cage in the corner of the lounge. 'I'm not usually a fan of white walls but it's opened up the rooms, and those yellow cushions really brighten it up.'

'Gorgeous, aren't they? I fell in love with them as soon as I saw them,' Hattie told him.

'You should have seen the struggle we had carrying them home!' Nick quipped. 'We decided to walk, rather than take the car, in case I was still over the limit, and then we ended up loaded up like packhorses.'

Marcus grinned. He could imagine. 'The new bathroom suite makes a difference too. That's one of the things I changed as soon as I moved into Curlew Cottage.' He nodded. 'I reckon this will get snapped up.'

Why did that make him feel sad? He had always known that Hattie was only here temporarily.

'I'm going to have to accept the first reasonable offer; I'm sorry if it's someone who wants to rent it out as a holiday let but my dad can't afford to wait.' He could see that Hattie was genuine.

'It's okay, you do what you've got to do. I'll cope.'

He opened his rucksack and took out a dish covered in tin foil. 'I don't know if you two are hungry but there's some leftover casserole here from the hotel. It'll only go to waste.' The same words he used to say to Albert.

'That sounds perfect. Does it need warming up?' Nick asked.

'It should still be hot, it's in an insulated dish,' Marcus replied.

'I'll get the plates,' Hattie said, going over to the wall cupboard where the plates were kept.

'I'll open a bottle of wine.' Nick went to the fridge.

Marcus grinned as he watched them. Nick and Hattie had certainly jelled this week and he was pleased for Hattie. When she'd told him about her parents break-up and her father moving to France, he had got the impression that she'd been a lonely, resentful child but now, thanks to Albert leaving this cottage to Hattie and her father, that all seemed to have changed.

It was a noisy, fun meal, with them all exchanging anecdotes and memories. They demolished the casserole and swigged glasses of wine. Albert would have loved this, Marcus thought, remembering how he used to sit with the old man, sharing leftovers from the hotel and sipping a glass of whisky. But Albert had gone. And soon Hattie would be gone too.

He watched her talking to Nick, her face alive, her eyes sparkling, and thought how much he was going to miss her.

'Well, I need to be getting to bed, I've got a ferry to catch tomorrow and if I drink any more wine I won't be fit to drive.'

Nick held out his hand to Marcus. 'It's been good to meet you, mate, and if you ever decide to take a trip over to France do look us up. Better still, pop over with this one. She's coming for a visit once the cottage is sold.' He grinned at Hattie. 'Maybe we'll even persuade her to stay there.' He bent down and kissed her on the cheek. 'Night, sis.'

'Night.'

'Night,' Marcus replied automatically, his head reeling at Nick's words. Was Hattie seriously thinking of living in France?

Chapter Twenty-Nine

Nick left early the next morning and Hattie went straight to the Saturday market to look for curtains and a new blind. She found some pretty white curtains with tiny yellow roses on them that would go well with the yellow cushions, and some light blue blinds for the bathroom. She bought some new duvet covers too, knowing they would brighten up the bedrooms. As she stuffed her purchases into the saddlebags and top box on her motorbike, though, she thought about getting a car. It would certainly come in handy for shopping, and if she wanted to expand her photography business she could do with getting some props and would need a car to carry them around. A motorbike had been great when she lived in Bristol, she could get in and out of the traffic so much quicker, and it was easy to find a parking space, but she didn't fancy moving back into the city. She was enjoying the slower life in Port Medden. Maybe she could move to Exeter instead?

She pulled up outside the back gate of Fisherman's Rest just as Marcus came out of his yard. He looked at her packed bike in amusement. 'You've been shopping, I see.'

'Yes and I got a little carried away.'

'Well, next time let me know and I'll give you a lift in the van. It'd be safer than carting all that on your bike.'

'It's quite safe. The saddlebags and top box are fixed on tight, and I'm not over the weight,' she retorted, then checked herself. Marcus was only offering to help. 'But thanks for the offer. Actually, I did want to pick up some big tubs for the back yard tomorrow and they'd be difficult to carry on the bike. Don't worry if you're busy,' she added quickly.

'I'm not and yes I'd be happy to take you. I might even get some for my back yard,' he told her. 'You're making my cottage feel a bit shabby with all your refurbishments.' He walked over to the gate and unbolted it for her so she could wheel the bike in. 'Want help unpacking that?'

She shook her head. 'No, I'm good thanks. I'm just taking it inside and then I'm off to see Ellie and Reece; they're back today and want to discuss some things with me.'

'I'm working tonight – want to share a nightcap when I come home or is that too late for you?' he asked.

'I'd love to; it's going to be quiet without Nick.' She hadn't been on her own much in the two weeks she'd been here, she realised. First Mali and Lou had come to stay, then Nick. Now she would be on her own until the end of next month when Mali and Lou broke up from school for the summer and were planning on coming down again. Mali had offered to cancel this as the cottage would be on the market with people viewing it, but Hattie had assured her it wouldn't be a problem to have them there.

'I'd love that. See you later, then. About ten thirty?' She knew that the last meal served at the hotel was nine thirty, then Marcus always tidied up the kitchen.

'See you!' he set off down the hill.

It was comfortable, this friendship with Marcus, Hattie thought as she watched him walk down the hill, hands in his pockets. He was a nice guy. Thank goodness they'd got past that awful hiccup at the beginning. Her thoughts went back to how they had been planning on going back to Marcus's cottage after the garden party. If Nick hadn't turned up, they might be more than friends now, they might be lovers. Her pulse quickened at the thought of Marcus's hands caressing her body, his mouth on hers . . . She shook the thought away. It was a good job Nick had turned up; she didn't need the complications of a love affair, not when she had to find herself a new home. But right now, she had half an hour to unpack this stuff and get to Gwel Teg.

She unlocked the back door and took everything into the kitchen, said a quick 'hello' to Buddy then grabbed herself a yoghurt out of the fridge to tide her over. She thought about getting changed but didn't want to keep Ellie and Reece waiting. It wouldn't look professional.

Hattie finished the yoghurt, and, after a quick check of her make-up, set off.

Mandy looked up from the computer screen at the reception desk as Hattie walked in. 'Afternoon, lovey. Go straight through to the private quarters. Ellie and Reece are in the garden.'

'Thanks.' Hattie indicated her shorts and top. 'Do I look all right? I've been shopping and didn't have time to change.'

'You look gorgeous,' Mandy assured her.

Hattie threw her a grateful smile and walked through into the garden. Ellie and Reece were sitting at the green ornamental metal table drinking lemonade. They both stood up as she came out and Hattie was relieved to see that they were both wearing vests and shorts too.

'Did you have a nice honeymoon?' she asked.

'It was wonderful.' Ellie gave her a hug, and Reece kissed her on the cheek. 'Would you like a glass of lemonade?' he asked.

'I'd love one, thank you.'

They chatted for a while about the honeymoon, and how Hattie was settling in, and then turned the conversation to the wedding photographs. 'They are all gorgeous, it was hard to make a selection,' Ellie told her. 'And there are a couple I really like but I don't like my expression on them. I wonder if you can do anything about that?'

'Yes, I can swap the faces. Can you show me which ones you want replaced, and the ones you want them replaced with?'

When all that was sorted out, they chose the album they wanted and then Sue came out too with a plate of sandwiches and cakes. Sue wanted a few photographs as well so Hattie made a note of her choices.

'There's something else I wanted to ask you, Hattie,' Sue said. 'We're updating the hotel website and adding a "Meet our Staff" page. I wondered if you would be interested in taking the photos of the staff for us?'

Hattie was delighted. Her photography work was certainly taking off since she'd come down to Port Medden. She was beginning to think she might make a success of it, after all.

'I'd love to,' she said. 'What timeline did you have in mind?'

Then she realised Marcus was a member of staff there – she would have to take a photograph of him. The thought of his sensual mix of tawny and hazel eyes staring into the camera lens made her heart flip.

He's just a friend, she reminded herself. *And that's the way it's staying.*

The hotel had been busy this evening and Marcus had been rushed off his feet. A couple of guests had come into the dining room at twenty-five past nine, wanting a three-course meal. 'I know it's past last orders, but can you do it, please?' Sue had asked, so Marcus had agreed. It had meant he was late cleaning up, though, and it was almost eleven before he was knocking on Hattie's door, bottle of cava in his hand. He'd texted her to say he'd be late, of course, saying it was fine if she wanted to cancel, but Hattie had replied swiftly to say he should drop by, she wasn't going to bed quite yet.

'Back again,' Buddy squawked as soon as Marcus stepped into the lounge. 'Back again.'

Marcus laughed. 'Well, that's a new one! He's really chirped up, hasn't he?' He went over to the cage to talk to the parrot. 'Hello, Buddy, how are you?'

'Fine and dandy! Fine and dandy!' He danced along the perch.

'I haven't heard him say that for ages! Albert taught it him,' Marcus said. 'He looks so happy and settled here now.'

'He never shuts up,' Hattie said with a grin. 'He's really cheeky.'

'It's good to see him looking so much better.'

He sounded so wistful that Hattie glanced at him. 'Are you missing him? You can come and see him anytime.'

'I am a bit,' Marcus confessed. He held up the bottle of cava. 'I've brought this so we can celebrate.'

'Celebrate what?' she asked.

'You being the official hotel photographer. Word travels fast,' he said with a grin.

'Who told you?' she asked. Then she guessed. 'Mandy?'

'Yep, she's taking the credit, of course, telling everyone she spotted your talent right away.' He put the bottle down on the table. 'It will certainly give your photography business a boost. Reece and Ellie have connections.'

'I know. I'm chuffed.' She took two glasses out of the cupboard and took the cava over to the sink to open it, just in case it sprayed everywhere. 'Thanks for this,' she said, as the cork popped out.

'You're welcome.' He held out his glass. 'To Hattie!'

Hattie clinked it with her glass. 'To us!' As soon as the words were out of her mouth, she realised how they sounded. 'Because you've got some new commissions for your paintings,' she added quickly.

He grinned. 'It looks like things are looking up for both of us.'

They chatted easily for a while, and had another glass of cava each, then Marcus got up to leave. 'See you in the morning,' he said. 'Will nine thirty be okay? The garden centre doesn't open until ten on a Sunday and I'd like to go for a surf first.'

'Do you go in the sea every day?' she asked.

'If I can, yes. Winter and summer. It keeps me fit. I love being out there, riding the waves, just me and the ocean. It's a wonderful feeling.'

No wonder he was so fit. Memories of his taut, toned body flashed into her mind.

'I'll take your word for it. It's a bit early for me. I'm shattered.

It's been hard work doing up the cottage this week. Nick and I have had loads of late nights.'

'I'm sure you have. Well, I won't keep you up any longer. Pop around any time after nine thirty tomorrow. I'll be back and showered by then.'

She nodded, her eyes almost closing of their own accord. She'd have to set the alarm. At this rate she'd be still asleep at midday!

Chapter Thirty

It was actually almost ten when Hattie knocked on his door the next morning. 'Sorry, I overslept,' she said.

She still looked tired, Marcus thought, noticing the dark shadows under her eyes. She was really working hard to sort out the cottage, determined to get the best price for her dad.

'It's not a problem if you prefer to go another day,' he told her as she followed him inside.

'No, I need to go today. Jonathan is coming to take the photos tomorrow.'

'Then let's go!' Marcus grabbed his bunch of keys off the table.

The garden centre was busy, even that early in the morning. 'I'm glad we didn't come any later, there's loads of customers with big pots of plants in their trolleys. I don't want the best to have been taken,' Hattie said.

'Are there any particular plants you're looking for?' Marcus asked.

'I want the garden to look vibrant and summery. I thought hanging baskets by the back and front door, and two pots outside the front door, and smaller ones dotted around the back yard. Maybe in some unusual pots – like that.' She pointed to a big boot-shaped pot overflowing with assorted petunias. 'And that gorgeous cascade corner planter. I can just imagine that full of primroses and fuchsias and we could have a pot of lavender, and some begonias . . .'

She wandered amongst the plants, considering what to buy thoughtfully then putting several pots into the trolley as she pushed it along.

She really was taking doing up the cottage seriously, you'd think she was doing it for herself to live in, not for strangers, Marcus thought. She was struggling a bit with the trolley, though, it seemed quite unwieldly.

'How about I push the trolley and then you can be free to wander around looking at the plants,' he offered, wanting to help but not wanting it to sound like he was taking over because she couldn't manage.

'Thanks.' She passed it to him and dashed off to look at some garden statues. Surely she wasn't going to buy one of those? thought Marcus, looking at the display.

She studied them all for a while and then came back with a small mermaid statue. 'This can go in the front garden,' she said as she carefully placed it in the trolley.

The trolley was now brimming with a variety of plants and pots. 'Do you think you might have enough now?' he asked. 'I know you want the cottage to give a good first impression but if the new owners are buying it for a holiday rental they probably won't want a lot of plants to look after.'

'If they don't want them, I'll take them with me,' she said.

'I've decided that I want a house next time, not a flat. It's lovely to have a garden and a bit more space.'

'Have you always lived in a flat?' he asked.

'Since my parents split up, yes. There was only me and Mum, and she was working, so a flat was easier, and cheaper. Then when I moved out I went for a flat too.' She looked around. 'All I need now is a tin of white paint for the bench. I should be able to get that here, shouldn't I?'

'I should think so, but it will probably be in another section.'

They found the paint and paid up, loaded it all in the van then went back inside for a coffee at the little café.

'You know, since Nick and I have done up the cottage, I've really seen the possibilities for it,' Hattie said as she stirred sugar into her coffee. 'It could be so pretty. I remember when we used to come down for the summer and Uncle Albert used to do a fry-up every morning, the smell of bacon used to waft up to our attic room and I couldn't wait to come down for break-fast. And I used to help him water all his pots and baskets. He kept it so lovely. I guess it all got too much as he got older.'

Marcus saw tears fill her eyes and she quickly lowered her gaze to stare into her coffee cup.

He'd judged her wrong, he realised. She had cared about her uncle and now staying here in this cottage was bringing back painful memories for her, of happier times when he was alive and when her parents were still together. She hadn't selfishly forgotten about him; she'd been a child, battling with her parents' divorce and trying to hold her life together. Albert had never reached out to anyone, had always been stubbornly self-sufficient, how was anyone to know that he was struggling? He hadn't even wanted his family to know.

'This must be difficult for you . . .'

She raised her eyes to meet his. 'It is a bit. I want to do right by Uncle Albert and I feel awful that we're selling the cottage, but Dad needs the money to save his home and business, and I need to get myself a home too.' She bit her lip. 'I don't know how Uncle Albert would feel about his cottage being a holiday let but there's nothing I can do about it. Much as I'd like to live here and make it a home again, I can't. I need to sell.'

She hadn't meant to say that out loud. It was something that had been stirring in her for the last few days, as she and Nick had gone through Uncle Albert's things and tidied up the cottage. It had made her see the cottage through different eyes. When she had first come down to stay, Fisherman's Rest had been a haven, a refuge until she could sort out the mess her life had become, but over the last couple of weeks it had become a home. She could feel herself putting down roots in Port Medden, growing closer to Marcus, and now she'd been offered more work for Gwel Teg too. It was as if the little Cornish town was opening up its arms and welcoming her, and she longed to snuggle into them and enjoy the safety and comfort, but she knew that she couldn't.

'Is that how you really feel? That you want to live at Fisherman's Rest?' Marcus asked softly.

Hattie chewed her lip. 'I'm being silly; it's all the memories and nostalgia, I think. And it's such a lovely place."

'Is there no way you could buy your dad out?'

212

She frowned. 'I don't see how. My redundancy money, when I get it, won't even cover a fifth of his share, and I need some money to live on. It's going to take some time to build up my photography business enough for me to earn a regular wage.' She was wondering if she should get a part-time job too – she didn't think she could cope with the insecurity of being self-employed. At least, not while she's just starting out.

God, listen to her, she sounded pathetic. He must think she was a right whinger. Uncle Albert had rescued her and her dad; she shouldn't be resenting having to sell the cottage. She should be grateful he had left it to her, and given her the chance to restart her life.

'Listen to me moaning! Honestly, I'll soon get the money together to put a deposit down on a lovely little house. I'll be absolutely fine.'

She finished the last of her coffee. 'Shall we go? I can't wait to get all these plants in place.'

Marcus stopped to help her, insisting that he had nothing else planned that day, and they spent the afternoon putting the pots in place and painting the bench. There was enough paint to do the table and two chairs in the back garden too.

'It looks fantastic. Thanks so much for your help,' Hattie said, gazing around at the back yard which was now an abundance of colourful plants in pots. She had moved her motorbike in front of the shed, to make more room for the pots.

'How about we go for a stroll along the harbour now, then grab something to eat?' Marcus suggested. 'I don't know about you, but I'm starving.'

She was too. 'Sounds great but I need a quick shower and change, shall we meet in half an hour?'

'I'll give you a knock.'

It was lovely how Marcus and she had become such good friends after such a rocky start, Hattie thought, as he went out of the gate then into his own back yard.

The trouble was, not only did she not want to sell the cottage, she didn't want to be friends with Marcus either. She wanted to be lovers.

Well there was no point in doing that. It would make it even harder to move away.

Chapter Thirty-One

Jonathan arrived with the photographer dead on time on Monday morning. 'Well, you've done a great job on this in the time you've had,' he said, clearly impressed. 'I love the splash of colour against the white walls and all those pots in the garden have really brightened the place up. I can't believe that you've done all this in such a short time.'

'My stepbrother came over from France to help me,' Hattie told him. 'And Marcus next door helped me with the garden yesterday. Do you really think it's made a big difference? I still have the wardrobes and cupboards to empty,' she added.

'There's time for that, potential buyers won't expect the cottage to be empty and ready to move into. But yes, this has all definitely added to the price and increased the marketability. I think we could up the price by at least another ten thousand. Let Terry take some photos, then I'll go back to the office and email you the details through. We could have it for sale on our website for tomorrow.' I've already emailed some of the clients on our list who had stated an interest in property like this and we've got three wanting viewings.'

It's all happening so fast. Too fast.

'Let me know what days and times are okay for viewings. Or you could give me a spare key and I can let potential buyers around if you aren't in? Obviously, we won't walk in unannounced. I'd let you know the days and times beforehand.'

She'd prefer Jonathan to show people around, she decided. It would make it more detached and professional. 'That sounds good. I'm in and out at the moment doing various photography jobs,' she told him, handing him the spare front-door key. 'I'll try to leave the place tidy at all times.'

'Don't worry about that, people can see beyond a few dirty plates and an unmade bed,' Jonathan told her. He took a label from his briefcase, wrote *Fisherman's Rest* on it and put it on the key fob. 'Have you thought about what you're going to do when the cottage is sold? If you want to stay local, I could look out for a place for you if you let me know your budget? We deal in rentals too.'

Did she want to stay around here? 'I'm not sure what I'm going to do yet, but thanks. I'll give it some thought and get back to you. Now, I'm sorry but I've got to dash as I've got a photography job in just under an hour.'

Jonathan nodded and held out his hand. 'Pleasure to do business with you.'

She shook his hand. 'Likewise.'

As soon as Jonathan had gone, she grabbed a sandwich, then set off for Gwel Teg, where she was due to take the first few staff photos. Those of Sue, Mandy, Harry the handyman and Shanise, a couple of the waitresses and the two cleaners. Marcus was working this evening, so she was coming back to photograph him, the bar staff and the rest of the waiting staff.

216

It was an enjoyable afternoon. Hattie had suggested that the staff should be photographed as naturally as possible, doing their jobs, and Sue had agreed. So, Mandy – wearing an extra-bright red lipstick – was photographed at her desk, Harry was holding a drill, about to put a shelf up, Shanise was dishing up a meal, etc. There was a sense of fun about it, and the photos were natural but effective. 'You've really got a talent for this, Hattie. You seem to capture the natural character and warmth of people.'

'Thank you. That means a lot,' Hattie told her. And it did. It made her feel more confident about being able to make some sort of living out of her photography. She'd checked her bank balance this morning and it had frightened her how much her savings had gone down and her credit card balance gone up; she'd used that to pay for the bathroom suite and some of the other things she'd bought for the cottage. 'My redundancy money will be in soon and then I can pay that off,' she reminded herself.

It brought home to her though how much she needed to sell Fisherman's Rest. There was no point in her being sentimental, she needed the money.

She was walking down the hill back home when her phone rang. It was Jonathan. 'We've got a viewing for Wednesday and two for Friday,' he told her. She could hear the enthusiasm in his voice. 'I can handle them for you if you're out.'

That was quick. Jonathan had been sure there would be a lot of interest in the cottage and it seemed he was right. Well, she was going to have to keep the place tidy, that was for sure. And she was going to have to decide where she wanted to live.

'Want me to look out for places to rent for you?' Mali asked when she called her once she'd made herself a cup of coffee back in the cottage. 'Do you fancy a flat or a house this time?'

'A house. I want a garden where I can put plant pots and a table and chairs. Look what me and Marcus did yesterday.' She changed the screen view so Mali could see the yard. 'Isn't it gorgeous?'

'Beautiful.' There was a pause on the other end of the phone. She could almost hear Mali's brain cogs working. 'You don't want to move, do you?' she asked.

'No,' she admitted, 'I feel so at home here. And I've got more photography work at the hotel, and a couple of other jobs too. I guess it's like taking a long holiday, you don't want to go back home, but once you're back then you're fine, and slip back into your old life again.'

She didn't want to go back to her old life, though. And to be honest, Mali and Lou were about the only people she missed. She'd got on well with the other members of the insurance firm that she'd worked for, but it hadn't been her dream job, and the people she'd met here in Port Medden had made her feel so welcome. Mandy, Sue, the couple at the café. Marcus.

She could stay here. She could rent somewhere. She shook her head. No, that wouldn't work.

She could go to France, like her dad had suggested.

For the first time in her life, she felt rootless, as if she had no anchor, and that both scared and excited her.

'Turn towards the camera now and keep stirring the pot,' Hattie instructed.

Marcus complied, half-turned towards her, his right hand

stirring the beef goulash. Hattie was frowning in concentration, her white-blond hair tucked behind her ears, as she took a few shots from different angles.

She was a good photographer, he knew that; he'd seen some of her shots. He thought back to the day he'd told her off for taking a photo of him surfing. She must have thought he was really up himself.

'There, that should be enough.'

'How many photos do you need?' he teased, although he knew that she'd taken a few so she had plenty to choose from.

'Only one, as you know. And you look really cute with that hat and apron on.'

Marcus wrinkled his nose, knowing she was teasing him back. He always tied his hair up when he was cooking, and donned a chef's hat and apron, it was part of the hygiene standards the hotel insisted on. 'I guess I'm not going to be the sexiest one on the website.'

'It's about looking professional but natural, not sexy,' she told him. Then she winked. 'But you're not too bad.'

'Thanks.' He stirred the pot again, dipped a spoon in to taste it and added a bit more salt before turning back to Hattie. 'Are you almost finished now?'

'Just the evening bar staff to do and that's it.' She ran her fingers through her hair to release it from behind her ears. 'Jonathan phoned. He's got three viewings already.'

Marcus raised an eyebrow. 'That was quick. How do you feel about it?'

She shrugged. 'Well, it's not to say any of them will make an offer. I mean, homes can be on the market for ages. But I guess I'd better start emptying out those wardrobes and cupboards.'

219

'Want me to come around and help tomorrow?' he offered.

'What about your painting? Don't you have a new commission?'

'I start it next week, so I can help you out for a couple of days before then. I'm guessing we might need my van to shift some of the stuff.'

'That would be great, thanks. I've got to pop out in the morning, a couple want me to take photographs of their baby, but I'll be back midday.'

'See you after lunch then.'

She nodded, gave him a little wave and went out to carry on with her photographs.

Marcus turned back to his cooking. The hotel was pretty full and the restaurant packed tonight, so he was too busy to think about Hattie's news, but when he walked past her cottage later that evening and saw the light on in the lounge, he thought how quickly he'd got used to her living next door. He was going to miss her.

Chapter Thirty-Two

'I remember this. I didn't realise he still had it.' Marcus picked up a navy flat cap from the pile of clothes, hats, shoes and boxes that they had just pulled out of the wardrobe in Uncle Albert's room.

Hattie glanced over. 'I remember him wearing a cap too. I'm not sure if it was this one.'

'I wouldn't be surprised. It was looking quite tatty when I first met him. He used to practically live in it, but then one day he started wearing a brown cap instead. I guessed the navy one had got too tatty and he'd dumped it.' His gaze skimmed the assortment of stuff on the floor. 'Looking at all this, he didn't dump much!'

'Lots of old folk are like that. In their time, you made do and mended, my gran was always saying that.' Hattie bit her lip and busied herself picking up the clothes and pushing them into one of the black bags they'd brought up with them so that Marcus wouldn't see the tears that had sprung to her eyes. She'd been close to her maternal grandparents and it had hit her hard when they'd died.

She felt an arm wrap around her shoulder. 'Still miss her, eh?'

So he had noticed. She nodded numbly. 'At least she had grandpa, and when he died, me and Mum used to visit her. I hate to think of poor Uncle Albert being on his own.' Damn, why was she getting all sentimental? It was looking at all this stuff, the remnants of her uncle's life, imagining him all sad and lonely. No one to care about him, no one to talk to. And he'd been so jolly and kind when they'd stayed with him every summer. She couldn't bear to think of him huddled in that rocking chair by the fire, a blanket over his lap to keep him warm, and only Buddy for company.

He had Marcus too.

Marcus's arm tightened around her shoulder. 'He liked his own company, and me and Winnie used to pop in.'

'I guess.' She nestled her head into his shoulder, taking comfort from his embrace. 'We should have kept in touch, though. Made sure he was okay.' Her dad should have, anyway, Uncle Albert had been his brother. But then he'd barely had time for her, his daughter, never mind his much-older brother who lived down the bottom end of England!

She heard Marcus catch his breath. 'Look, I'm sorry. I was too hard on you about that, I know I was. I had no right. Albert never complained about not seeing his family. I don't want you to feel bad about it. This must be a really emotional time for you.'

She lifted her head to reassure him that it was all right, but he was looking down at her, his eyes darkening as they met hers, and she couldn't speak, the words were caught in her throat as she drowned in his gaze, her heart thudding so loudly in her chest she was sure he could hear it. Then he was pulling her

222

closer to him, and he was lowering his head, and she was raising hers to meet his lips, and they were kissing but it was like a kiss she had never experienced before. A kiss that made her pulse race and sparks of desire explode through her body. A kiss that was getting deeper and deeper as Marcus caressed the back of her head with the hand that wasn't holding her shoulder, and she reached her right hand up to lightly stroke his cheek.

'Hattie, do you want me to stop . . .' he murmured, his voice thick with longing.

She knew that he was asking her if she wanted to back out now before they went any further and for a moment she thought about it, the foolhardiness of getting involved with someone like Marcus when she would be leaving soon, but it was too late, she could no more pull away than she could stop breathing. She wanted this. She wanted it more than she had ever wanted anything, and she could tell that Marcus did too. She shook her head. 'Please don't.'

Afterwards, as they lay on the bed they had both moved to – without either of them saying a word – Marcus thought back over what had just happened. Their hands had started to remove each other's clothes, then explore each other's bodies, before making passionate love. He gazed down at Hattie in his arms, her face flushed, her eyes sparkling, her gorgeous body – that had until a few minutes ago been lying on top of his – was now curled up by his side. She was beautiful and sexy . . . and they really shouldn't have done that. He'd promised himself he wouldn't give in to his desire for her, that he would keep their relationship on a friendly basis. Some willpower he had.

'Well, that was unexpected but wonderful,' she murmured, kissing him on the lips. 'Now, is this where you tell me it was a big mistake and we go back to being friends?'

He turned towards her. The question had been teasing but her expression was earnest. The way she was looking at him gave him the impression she felt the same way as him. He kissed the tip of her nose. 'Definitely not a mistake for me. How about a summer romance with no strings attached?' he said lightly.

Her lips widened into a smile and she reached out and wrapped her arms around his neck. 'Perfect,' she said, pulling him closer.

Chapter Thirty-Three

They finally managed to prise themselves away from each other to have a quick shower, get dressed again and finish sorting out the stuff they'd pulled out of the wardrobe and was still sprawled all over the floor. If she hadn't got viewers coming the next day, Hattie would have been tempted to leave it there, but now she had to make sure that the cottage was relatively tidy.

'Right, that's it all done,' Marcus said when the bedroom floor was finally clear and everything was bagged up. 'Now, how about we dispose of these and go for a swim. It's a gorgeous afternoon.'

He was right, it was, and she really wanted to spend some time with him while they had the chance. 'Deal,' she said.

'I'll put this in the van, then and grab my swimming shorts.' Marcus leaned over and kissed her on the lips.

She wound her arm around his neck and pulled him closer, deepening the kiss.

'Carry on like that and we may have to give swimming a miss,' he whispered in her ear when they finally stopped for breath.

She eased herself out of his embrace and tapped him on the nose with her finger. 'No chance. I haven't had a swim in the sea since I've been here and this is the perfect afternoon for it. You'll have to wait until later.'

His eyes twinkled as he grabbed two of the bags. 'I'll hold you to that.'

Hattie picked up the remaining two bags and followed Marcus down the stairs with them, almost bubbling inside with happiness. Okay, so she hadn't planned on getting involved with him, but what the hell. He was gorgeous and they were good together. Why not have a bit of fun? They both knew the score, a summer romance, no strings attached.

An hour later, they were both walking, hand in hand, across the soft, warm sand of the quiet beach Marcus had taken her to. She loved the feel of his hand in hers, of walking beside him side by side, of the way he squeezed her hand now and again and, when she turned to look at him, the way he smiled as if right here, right now, with her, was just where he wanted to be. It was just where she wanted to be too. Walking over this gorgeous beach, her flip-flops dangling from one hand, her feet sinking into the golden sand, the sun shining down on them both. She felt happy, free and . . . cared for.

There was barely a ripple on the turquoise sea, which was quite far out now, and the beach was almost deserted. Most of the holidaymakers would have gone home now the half-term break was over, Hattie realised. She knew that the main influx of visitors would come in July and August, as she and her parents had done. Some of the locals hated this summer invasion, even though they needed the money the holidaymakers spent. She could understand that feeling in a way, it was so peaceful and tranquil now, whereas when they had visited in August the streets had been so crowded her mother had always insisted she held Hattie's hand, convinced she would be swallowed up in the crowd and never seen again, and the beach had been so packed it had been difficult to find a space to sit.

'Here okay?' Marcus's voice cut through her thoughts and she blinked, then realised they had stopped a short distance from the water's edge. 'It's dry here and the tide won't be coming in for a few hours yet.'

She nodded. 'Sure. We don't want to have to walk a mile out to the sea.' She put her flip-flops down on the sand and pulled off her vest, then wriggled out of her shorts. 'Race you in!'

'Hey, give me chance!'

She sprinted off as he started to pull off his top, eager to swim in the ocean as she used to do when she was younger, her father always swimming alongside her to make sure she didn't get into trouble, her mother, not a strong swimmer, watching anxiously on the beach until they both finally came out and joined her on the sand. Her parents had both loved her, even if they had stopped loving each other, she reminded herself as her foot touched the water, its coldness making her hesitate for a moment. She'd forgotten that there was always a chill to the Atlantic Ocean – even in August she'd had to brace herself before she ran in.

'Too cold for you?' Marcus teased as he raced past her and dived in, his powerful arms crashing through the water as he did the crawl.

'Nope!' she shouted and dived in too, catching her breath as her body hit the cold water, but as soon as she started swimming – the breaststroke for her – she warmed up.

Marcus was ahead but she didn't care. She was enjoying the feel of the water around her, the sun on her back, the glorious-ness of her surroundings. She'd promised herself that she would come swimming every day, yet she'd been here over two weeks and hadn't been for a swim once. Well, now she had settled in and done the worst of the tidying up, she might get chance to come more often.

Marcus was swimming back to her now. When he reached her, she turned and they both swam back towards the shore, stopping when their feet could touch the sand, and without either of them saying anything, turned to each other and melted into an embrace. As Hattie stood there, wrapped in Marcus's arms, the sea lapping around her thighs, she thought that she had never felt happier.

'Shall I pop around tonight after work or are you busy?' Marcus asked as they sat on the soft sand, Hattie sitting between Marcus's outstretched legs, her head resting back against his bare chest, his arms wrapped loosely over her shoulders. He kept his tone deliberately casual, wanting to see her but not wanting to sound too clingy, as if he was pressuring her. They both had things to do, they couldn't spend every minute together.

She tilted her head back and looked up at him. 'Now, that sounds like a lovely idea.'

He lowered his head and kissed her. 'Shall I bring supper?'

She edged forward and half-turned towards hm. 'Please. It's such a bonus to be dating a chef.'

He wrapped his arms around her and eased her closer. 'Are

you saying that you're only going out with me because of my cooking skills?'

'Hmm, I can think of another skill I quite like . . .'

'Only quite?'

She kissed him deeply, then pulled away, her eyes full of mischief, and stood up. 'Stop fishing for compliments, we need to get going. You've got work in a couple of hours and I have a house to tidy for tomorrow.'

For the potential buyers.

He scrambled to his feet, pushing away the thought of how much he would miss her. It could take months to sell a house, he reminded himself. Their romance would have run its course by then.

Wouldn't it?

They chatted easily on the short journey home. As he pulled up to park the camper behind the cottages, he saw Winnie standing by her car, boot open, taking out a box. Several other boxes and bags were piled in the boot. She was back.

'Afternoon, Winnie. Is your sister better?' he asked as he opened the door to get out. Hattie was already scrambling out of the other side.

'She is, thank you. I'm afraid I did a bit of shopping whilst I was there too. Very enjoyable but I'm wondering whether it was sensible. I've no idea where I'll put it all.'

'Let me help you take it inside.' Marcus walked over to the boot, and Hattie followed him.

'That's very kind.' Winnie's sharp eyes flitted across to Hattie. 'And who's your young lady?'

'I'm Hattie, your next-door neighbour,' she said.

'Oh goodness, you're Owen's daughter! You have the same eyes. So pleased to meet you, dear. Albert talked about you a lot.'

Marcus saw Hattie's eyes cloud over and knew she was feeling guilty again.

'Albert left his cottage to Hattie and her dad, so she's come down to sort things out,' he quickly filled in for her.

'Well, it's lovely to meet you, Hattie. And very kind of both of you to help me with my shopping. I appreciate it.'

They all grabbed a box each and carried it over to the gate. Winnie passed the keys she was holding in her hands to Marcus. 'Open it up for me, will you, dear? If I put this box down I'll never pick it back up again.'

Marcus bent one knee and balanced the box he was carrying on it, then unlocked the gate, pushed it open and stood back to let first Winnie, then Hattie, through.

'Just put everything down by the back door, I can take it all in,' Winnie said, putting the box she was carrying down then holding her hand out for the keys. Marcus passed them to her, winking at Hattie as Winnie opened the door, then followed her inside.

'Sorry, but I'm not letting you carry all this in. I'll bring the boxes into the kitchen and leave them there. I'll put them here, make it easier for you to unpack them,' he said, placing his box onto the kitchen table.

'Stubborn as always,' Winnie said with a smile.

Hattie placed her box by Marcus's and then they all went back out to get the next batch. A couple more journeys and the boot was unloaded.

'Thank you both. Will you stop for a cup of tea?' Winnie was already reaching for the kettle.

'I'm afraid that I have to go. I'm due in work soon,' Marcus told her.

'I will, thank you,' Hattie said to his surprise. He wondered if she wanted to take the opportunity to meet her next-door neighbour or if she didn't want to refuse.

'See you later, then,' Marcus said, kissing Hattie on the cheek.

'I'll have a bottle of wine chilling.'

'Sounds great. Bye, Winnie!' He waved and left, leaving the two women to chat.

After a quick freshen up and change, he dashed down the hill to work. He prided himself on never being late but he was cutting it fine today.

'Have a good day at the beach, did you?' Mandy asked, a knowing smile playing on her lips as he dashed into the reception.

'What?'

'You were spotted. With Hattie. Looking very close.' She was delighting in teasing him. 'I knew it as soon as I saw her. I knew you two belonged together. I had this feeling.'

Mandy and her feelings, Marcus thought in exasperation. 'We're just having a bit of a summer romance, Mandy. Nothing serious. Hattie put the cottage up for sale yesterday and has two viewings already. She'll be gone in a couple of months.'

Even as he said the words, he felt his stomach sink.

Mandy folded her arms across her chest and looked at him. 'She hasn't left yet, lad, and my feelings are never wrong.'

Well, this time they are, Marcus thought, as he went through into the kitchen to take over from Shanise. Hattie had no intention of staying in Port Medden. And yes, he had a feeling he was going to really miss her but he would just have to deal with it. He'd known the score, and he certainly wasn't going to be heartbroken like he had been with Kaylee.

Chapter Thirty-Four

'Good morning, gorgeous.'

Hattie stirred and opened her eyes as Marcus kissed her on the forehead, then the nose, before finally resting his lips on hers. She wrapped her arms around his neck and enjoyed the passionate kiss, thinking that even though this was the first morning she had woken up in bed with him, it seemed so natural. Just as natural as it had felt to suggest he stayed the night when they were both snuggled up on the sofa after eating the chicken hotpot Marcus had brought with him, and drinking the bottle of Pinot Grigio she'd had cooling in the fridge. Not that they'd got much sleep, hence why she was feeling so tired and groggy.

Not that she was complaining.

'Want a cuppa or shall we . . . ?' Marcus left the question dangling but his hands left no doubt as to what he was suggesting, and she felt the stirring of desire rise in her again.

'We definitely should,' she said, all thoughts of grabbing more sleep going out of her mind as she turned to him.

It was much later when they finally got out of bed. 'Fancy coming surfing with me?' Marcus asked.

Actually, she did, but should she? Jonathan was bringing the first viewers along today. Mind you, did she want to be here while they traipsed through Uncle Albert's cottage and discussed whether to buy it or not?

'Sorry, I forgot, you've got a viewing, haven't you?' said Marcus. 'What time are they coming?'

'Ten thirty and it's . . .' She glanced at the clock. 'Heck, it's nearly nine now. I need to shower and tidy round. I think I'd better give surfing a miss.'

'No problem. I'll go home and shower too. Good luck with the viewing, I'll see you later. Yes?'

She nodded, wishing he didn't have to dash, but then she had plenty to do herself and Marcus usually went surfing earlier so was probably eager to go.

He kissed her again, then left.

She got out of bed, smoothed down the sheet, pulled the bedcover over and plumped up the pillows before getting into the shower. By the time she'd had her shower and was dressed, she'd decided that she did want to be here when the viewers – a Mr and Mrs Howes, Jonathan had said – came. Apparently, they were looking for a holiday home for themselves rather than to let out, so she was hopeful they would think Fisherman's Rest was right for them. Besides, it would be good to get some feedback after all the work she and Nick had done.

She tried to remember some of the tricks she'd read about how to make a home appealing when you wanted to sell it: 'put colourful flowers in a vase' – it was too late for that now; 'brew proper coffee' – but she always had instant; 'have fresh bread baking' . . . hmm all those were no-goers. 'Make everywhere look clean and tidy' – she could do that. She dashed around spraying everywhere with 'Summer Breeze' air freshener, plumping up curtains, straightening towels, and clearing the work surfaces, wanting to make sure the cottage looked at its best.

When there was finally a knock on the door – bang on time – she was a bag of nerves. She was so desperate for them to like the cottage, now she had spent so much time on it and put in so much hard work. Fixing a welcoming smile on her face, she went to the door, her hopes sinking as she caught the words 'the garden's so small'. Not a good first impression, she thought as she opened the door. Jonathan and a couple in their mid-forties, she'd have guessed, stood on the step in front of her.

'Morning, Hattie. This is Mr and Mrs Howes,' Jonathan said.

'Do come in.' Hattie stepped aside to give them room to step into the hall. The woman raised an eyebrow as her sharp eyes rested on the worn carpet then flitted over to the scratched lounge door. Damn she'd meant to get a new carpet but hadn't got round to it. 'It needs a little updating,' Hattie quickly said.

'Shall I take over, Hattie?' Jonathan asked, obviously not trusting her to big up the selling points of the cottage.

'Please.' She nodded.

Jonathan opened the door into the lounge. 'As you can see, there are still many of the original features,' he said enthusiastically.

The Howes exchanged 'not very impressed' glances.

'When was that gas fire last serviced?' Mr Howes asked.

'Er . . . I don't know, sorry. It was my uncle's cottage,' Hattie replied.

'So, it's basically one long room with an archway,' Mrs Howes remarked as her eyes swept the room then rested on Buddy, who had been asleep up until they'd arrived.

'Bugger off!' he squawked and Mrs Howes gasped and turned furiously to Hattie.

'Sorry, my uncle was a fisherman …' Hattie said awkwardly, wondering if she should have moved Buddy up into the attic. Marcus had left the smaller cage with her in case she needed it.

As they walked around the cottage, uttering comments like, 'it needs a lot of work' when they were in the kitchen, 'it's a bit small' when they went into the bathroom, with its newly painted walls, shiny new bathroom suite and light blue blinds, and 'isn't there an en suite?' as they looked around the main bedroom, Hattie felt cross on Uncle Albert's behalf.

'My uncle was a fisherman and lived here for over fifty years,' she said as Jonathan led them out into the back yard. 'I think part of its charm is that it's so traditional.'

'Of course. We were looking for somewhere more modern, though,' Mr Howes said a little more kindly.

'And with more of a garden,' said Mrs Howes, looking around disparagingly at Hattie's colourful pots.

Hattie wondered if their comments were aimed at making her reduce the price, she'd heard that some viewers did that, and surely they couldn't be totally oblivious to the character of the cottage. Well, they weren't the sort of people she wanted to see living here. She wanted to sell the cottage to someone who appreciated it, who loved it as much as Uncle Albert had. As much as she was starting to. So when they had finally left, and Jonathan returned a few minutes later to tell her they weren't making an offer, she felt like cheering.

'We have another two viewers on Friday, and one of them, a Mr Paterson, wants to buy a holiday let so I've got high hopes that he will make an offer. I'm sure this is exactly what he's looking for,' Jonathan told her. 'And there are several other people on my list too. The cottage will be sold in no time, I'm sure of it.'

She nodded. 'See you on Friday, then. And could you please do those viewings? I have to go out.'

She had an appointment to take some 'new baby' photographs, and then a multi-generation one, for a couple who lived in Truro. She was really looking forward to doing that and was glad that it clashed with the time of the viewing. She didn't think she could take anyone else walking around the cottage sneering at everything.

She texted Marcus: **The viewers don't like the cottage** ☹

A text came pinging right back: **So we've got longer together then. Want to come around for a coffee? I'm back from the beach now. Xx**

She grinned as she read it. **Be there in 5!** she texted back.

'Morning, dear, how did the viewing go?' Winnie asked as Hattie locked the front door behind her. Surprised, she turned to face her next-door neighbour, who was tending to her flowering baskets, then realised that of course she would know Jonathan and guess that the two people with him were potential buyers. 'They didn't like it, they wanted somewhere more modern,' she said.

'Well, I'm sorry to hear that, dear. I know you must be anxious to sell and get back to your normal life.' She sounded genuine.

'I am, but how do you feel about me selling the cottage?' Hattie asked her. At the moment, the three of them got along fine; new neighbours could spoil the happy balance of the block of three cottages and she felt a bit bad about that.

Winnie put her watering can down and walked over to the wall. 'Change happens, that's life. We were quite pally, Albert, Marcus and me, we kept ourselves to ourselves but we were there for each other and I like that.' Hattie nodded and Winnie continued, 'But Albert has gone and you must do what's best for you, dear. My daughter lives in Australia. When I go, this will be hers and I'm quite sure she will either sell the cottage or let it out to holidaymakers. This is my life, not hers. Just like Fisherman's Rest was Albert's home, not yours. Unless you want it to be.'

Winnie looked at her with such warmth that Hattie wanted to hug her; the guilt she'd felt at what effect selling the cottage would have on her neighbours faded away a little. 'Thank you. I was a bit worried that you might be upset.'

'Don't you worry yourself about me, and let me know if you need any help with anything. I know Albert was a hoarder.'

Hattie grinned. 'He certainly was. I will, thank you.'

Winnie nodded and returned back to tending to her plants. She was glad she'd spoken to her, Hattie thought, as she opened her gate and went next door. She felt a lot better about selling the cottage now. Although, if today's couple were anything to go by, it wasn't going to sell as quickly as Jonathan had thought.

Chapter Thirty-Five

'Now, if you could all stand around Lily, in a half-circle and smile down at her,' Hattie said. She'd already taken several photos of the three-month-old baby on her own – she was adorable and had cooed away happily – so it was time for some more group photos. She'd taken one of Lily in her parents' arms, surrounded by both grandparents, great grandparents and great-great grandmother but now she wanted just the women in the family. She placed a shawl on the table and Lily in her Moses basket upon it and asked the women to gather around. The baby was lying peacefully, she really was an angel.

The women got into place, all turning their gaze upon the baby in front of them. Hattie focused her camera, glad that she had brought the travel tripod with her to hold it in the perfect position. The flash unit was already in place. 'I don't want you to smile for this shot, just look at Lily,' she said. 'Ready?' She took a few shots, then stood up.

'Now, can you all please look at me and smile for this one?'

The women looked at the camera, their faces wreathed in smiles. 'Ready? Smile!' Again, she took several shots. This was the first time she'd been commissioned to take some multi-generational photos and she wanted them to be perfect. There were five generations of women. The oldest, the great-great grandmother, was eighty-nine, she had told Hattie proudly. It would be an iconic photo.

'Thanks so much, Hattie. This means a lot to us,' Julia, Lily's mother, said as Hattie folded up the tripod, then put it and her camera in the camera bag. 'If you leave me a couple of your cards, I'll pass them around. I'm sure some of the other mothers at the mother and baby club will be interested in having photographs taken too.'

'I need to have some cards printed out, but I've got a couple of flyers here. Will they do?' She took out a few flyers and handed them to her. She knew that she needed to have some business cards done eventually but these would be fine for now. She'd have to think about getting a website up and running too.

'Perfect.' Julia took the flyers and put them on the side. 'I can't wait to see the photos. When will they be ready?'

'I'll email you over a selection to choose from on Monday,' Hattie told her. 'Then they'll be ready by the end of the week.'

I love doing this, she thought, as she said her goodbyes and went out to where her bike was parked by the garage. She'd always enjoyed taking photographs but now she seemed to get real pleasure out of it. *It's as if I'm finally being me*, she thought. Was that because she was doing the work she wanted to do, or because she was here, in Port Medden? The little town certainly had a charm to it.

She checked her watch. Jonathan would be showing another potential buyer around the cottage now. There were two viewings today, fifteen minutes apart, so she'd told him to make a cup of coffee if he wanted while he was waiting for the second one. She wondered if any of them would like the cottage enough to make an offer. And if they did, what would she do then?

Marcus dipped his brush into the black paint on the palette and applied a few more strokes to the painting. Then he stood back to study it. It wasn't often a subject consumed him like this one, he was filled with a desire to finish it but also a dread, as if once the painting was finished, Hattie would be gone – going out of his life as quickly as she had come into it.

And it was almost finished. A bit more work on the face, he hadn't quite got that 'loving life' expression right. Would he be able to capture that on canvas? Hattie would, with her camera. She was so talented; she really had the knack of taking 'people photographs'. He thought of the photographs she'd taken of the hotel staff, where she seemed to have captured everyone's personality. She would make a go of her photography business, he was sure.

He heard voices outside and went to the window. Hattie had said that Jonathan was showing two lots of viewers around this afternoon, this couple must be one set. They were out in the back yard, talking to Jonathan. They looked interested. Would they make an offer?

His stomach twisted a little at the thought of Hattie leaving. He turned back to the painting, his eyes resting on the white-blond hair, the wide blue eyes, that gorgeous curvy figure clad in black leather, legs apart astride her bike. The zip of the jacket was half down to expose her sun-kissed neck and a hint of

241

cleavage – he shut his eyes as he remembered caressing her soft skin, scooping those beautiful firm breasts in his hands, kissing those red lips, his hand running through that silky white-blond hair, pressing her closer to his chest. *Hattie*. She looked sexy, exciting, full of life.

He was falling for her, he realised. He'd been falling for her since they first met, and soon she would be gone. All he would have left of her would be this painting.

Jonathan and the couple had walked back inside now. Marcus moved away from the window and back over to his painting. He'd finish it later or tomorrow. He needed to get out, go for a walk, get his head straight. He hadn't meant to get involved with Hattie, but he had. Now, he didn't know what to do about it. Where did they go from here? He was at work tonight, should he suggest calling in again afterwards? If he did, would she think that he was after sex again? If he didn't, would she feel ignored? Relationships were complicated, that's why he tried to avoid them. His days were busy, he didn't want or need a woman in his life to complicate things.

She'll be gone soon, he reminded himself, *she's only a temporary distraction*. But that didn't make him feel any better.

He made his way to the quiet beach at the end of town, as he always did when he felt restless. Hands in pocket, he stood gazing out at the sea: grey-blue today, and a bit choppy. He looked up at the sky. They were due for some rain later.

He walked back along the seafront by the harbour. It was mid-June now and already there were a few holidaymakers down, but in another month, when the schools closed, and they were all arriving would Hattie be leaving, he wondered, ready to move on?

He turned the corner to the cottages and saw Hattie heading towards him on her motorbike. She waved and he waved back, then she turned to go round to the back of the cottages and he headed that way too. He arrived in time to see her pull up by his van, turn off the engine, and remove her helmet. Her eyes were sparkling, that 'full-of-life' expression on her face that he was trying so hard to capture. He focused on her face, trying to imprint it on his mind, wanting to take his phone out and capture it but not sure he would ever be able to.

'Hi, how did it go?' he asked, walking over to her.

'Good. The baby is gorgeous and I got some fantastic shots. You been for a walk?' She was dismounting now.

'Yeah, it looks like we're going to be having some rain.' They were walking over to the gates now. Should he ask her in? 'How did the viewing go?'

'No feedback yet. Jonathan said that he thinks one of the couples might be interested, but he's not sure. He's got another couple of viewings for next week.' She paused at her gate. 'Time for a cuppa and a catch up with Buddy?'

'Sure. Did he behave himself today, do you know?'

'Apart from a couple of "Bloody Hells" but apparently both viewers were amused and thought he was cute.'

Buddy whistled as Hattie walked in. 'Back again,' he squawked, hopping about happily on the branch.

Hattie grinned. 'Hello, cheeky chappie.' She looked at Marcus in delight. 'He's really getting used to me, isn't he?' she asked.

We both are.

'He is. Shall we let him out for a fly around while we're having a cuppa?'

243

'Good idea. You open the cage while I put the kettle on.'

As soon as the cage was open, Buddy flew straight to the top of the kitchen cupboards and peered down at them. 'Hello, hello!' he squawked.

'Hello!' Hattie set the mugs of coffee down on the table, then picked up a banana. 'I'm going to see if he will take some off me.'

She sat down and slowly unpeeled the banana, then took a big bite out of the top. 'Want some?' she asked, holding it out to Buddy.

The parrot cocked his head to one side as if considering this, then flew over to the table and pattered over to Hattie, squawking excitedly. He stopped in front of her, jerked his head forward and took a bite out of the banana. Her face lit up. 'Look! I think he actually likes me now.'

'I'm sure he does,' Marcus agreed as their eyes met and locked. The air became charged with tension, excitement, and anticipation as their gaze deepened. Her eyes were bigger now, the blue deeper, flecked with tiny sparks of silver.

'Hattie,' he murmured as they both leaned forwards, as if unconsciously drawn to each other like metal to a magnet.

They both jumped as Hattie's phone rang. She drew back and reached for the phone on the table beside her, checking the screen first to see who was calling. 'It's Jonathan.'

Marcus held his breath as she answered the call. Her expression changed to one of shock, and she glanced at Marcus then away again.

'Okay, Jonathan, thank you. I'll talk to Dad and get back to you.'

Marcus waited, his heart thudding.

'We've had an offer on the cottage,' Hattie said.

Chapter Thirty-Six

Hattie was stunned. Although Jonathan had told her that he didn't think it would take long to sell the cottage, she hadn't expected to get an offer that quickly! It had only been on the market a few days. It was three thousand pounds less than the asking price but she was sure her dad would accept it. It was still a lot of money and seven thousand higher than Jonathan had first quoted, thanks to her – and Nick's – hard work Although, of course the money she'd spent on the cottage had to be deducted from that.

'Are you going to accept it?' Marcus asked.

'I don't know. I need to discuss it with Dad. I'm pretty sure that he will want to, though.'

'Right. Well, I'll finish this and leave you to it. I've got to go to work in a bit.' Marcus finished his coffee and took the mug over to the sink. 'Want me to help you get Buddy back in the cage or are you okay with it?'

'He'll go in himself in a little while, I'm sure, but thanks for the offer,' she told him, her mind in a whirl. They had a buyer. She could hardly believe it.

'I'll get off, then. I can see that you're in a hurry to phone your dad and tell him the news.'

Hattie threw him a distracted smile. 'Thanks. I'll message you later. Let you know what we decide.'

As Marcus headed out of the door, she was already dialling her dad on WhatsApp for a video call. After a couple of rings, he answered, the phone buffering as his image appeared on the screen. 'Hi, Hattie. Everything okay?'

'We've had an offer on the cottage, Dad. Three thousand below asking price but Jonathan said that it's a cash sale, which means it will go through in about six weeks. What do you think?'

'Oh, Hattie, love, that's brilliant. That's saved my bacon. I was beginning to think that I'd have to take out another loan. We're hand to mouth over here.'

As Hattie listened to the relief in her dad's voice, she felt her heart sink. She knew that he'd be pleased with the offer, that he desperately needed the money, yet somehow she'd been hoping he would refuse the sale.

'Are you okay with accepting the offer? It's only three grand less and worth it for a quick sale, surely?' her dad said.

'Yes, you're right. It's fine by me,' she assured him.

'What are you going to do when the cottage is sold? Have you thought any more about coming to stay with us, give you chance to think about your next step?' he asked.

She had no idea what she was going to do. And tempting as it was to take up her dad's offer, she knew it wouldn't work out. It was one thing going to visit him once she had sorted out a home for herself but another to go and stop with him indefinitely. Yes, they were back on a friendlier footing now and she would like to spend some time in France with her dad and his family, and to see Nick again, but this wasn't the right time.

'Thanks so much, Dad, but maybe I can come over later in the year? Christmas, perhaps? Right now, I really need to get myself a home and start building up my photography business. Maybe even get a part-time job.'

'Of course, whenever suits you.' There was a pause. 'Look I know we agreed to pay you back out of the sale for what you spend doing up the cottage. But I want you to have more than that. I'm instructing my solicitor to give you an extra ten thousand pounds of the money. And please don't argue over this. It's thanks to your hard work and time that's the cottage has sold so quickly.'

It was a nice thought, and she appreciated it, but she didn't want to take his money, he needed it. 'It's fine, Dad. I've lived here rent free and I've enjoyed sorting things out.'

She pushed away the thought that she didn't want to leave the cottage. Or leave Marcus. She had always known it wasn't forever. It had only ever been for the summer. They would still have a couple of months together, while the sale was going through.

They chatted a bit about the formalities, with her dad promising to come over to sign the papers when the buyers were ready to exchange.

'What about all the furniture? All Uncle Albert's things?' she asked.

Her dad sighed. 'I'm afraid that it's all going to have to be dumped. I know it's sad but I've got no room for anything here. If there's anything you want, take it, but apart from that get some house-clearance people in. We'll take whatever it costs you out of the sale of the cottage.'

'There's papers and photos too,' she told him.

'Put them to one side. I'll come over the weekend before the sale goes through and look through them. Anything important, I'll take back with me . . .'

His image started to flicker.

'Sorry, love, I'm losing the connection. It's because I'm outside. Message me if you need me and I'll phone you back later.'

'Okay. Bye, Dad.'

Well, that was it, Fisherman's Rest was sold. She had about six weeks to find herself a new home.

She phoned Jonathan to let him know they were accepting the offer; it went to answerphone so she left a message. Then she texted Mali to let her know the news and tell her that she and Lou needed to come down for their holiday as soon as school had finished for the summer as she wasn't sure how quickly the sale would go through.

Mali phoned straight back. 'I've got a free period,' she explained. 'It's wonderful news, isn't it? I can't believe you've got a sale so quickly.'

'Neither can I. Now I've got to decide where I want to live and get myself a new home.'

'Why don't you move in with me and Lou while you sort yourself out?' Mali suggested. 'You don't want to make a rushed decision, take your time.'

'Thanks. I think I'm in shock. I don't know what I want to do.'

As she ended the call with Mali she realised that she felt lost, adrift. She'd started to feel at home down here, building up her photography business. And then there was Marcus. She was falling for him, she acknowledged.

Then she realised that she hadn't messaged him to let him

know that they'd accepted the offer. She took out her phone and typed a message quickly. Perhaps they could meet later and talk about it.

Marcus read Hattie's text again.

I've spoken to Dad and we've decided to accept the offer.
I told Jonathan and he said the sale will only take about
6 weeks. Hattie x

So that was it. The cottage was sold and in six weeks' time Hattie would be gone. Out of his life forever. There was no mention of see you later. Or I'll miss you. She had barely said goodbye to him earlier, too busy dialling to tell her dad that the cottage was sold, which had said volumes to him. And now rather than phone him and talk it over she had sent him a text ending with one single, solitary kiss.

Well, that's his fault, wasn't it? He'd suggested a 'no strings' summer romance. He'd always known that Hattie wasn't here to stay. They hadn't made each other any promises. She wasn't to know that he had fallen for her.

So, where did they go from here? Continue with their romance until the house was sold and Hattie finally rode off into the sunset on her motorbike?

He shook his head. He couldn't do that. They should never have made love but he knew he wouldn't be repeating it, not now he knew the effect Hattie had on him. He wasn't going there again. Hattie was leaving and he wasn't going to get his heart broken a second time.

Except the feelings he'd had for Kaylee were nothing compared to the fire Hattie lit up in him. He had to protect himself and keep away from her as much as possible. It was the only way he would cope with her moving away.

He thought carefully about how to respond to her message, then finally typed out a reply:

I'm pleased for you. You must have a lot to do with the sale going through so quickly. Let me know if I can help. Marcus x

He read it over, it was light and friendly, like her text. He wanted to put 'please don't go. I'll miss you. I love you'. But he didn't. Obviously, his feelings for her were deeper than hers for him, otherwise she would be upset about going, trying to find a way to stay. He knew that she had no choice but to sell the cottage but she could rent a place in Port Medden. If she loved him as he loved her she would talk to him, discuss options with him.

I love her!

The words had popped into his mind without him thinking about them, but he knew they were true. *I love Hattie.*

And she obviously didn't love him. Well, he would cope with it, and there was no way Hattie would find out how he felt. He didn't want sympathy, apologies or guilt. He read his message again and pressed send.

So that was it, no 'see you later' or 'shall I pop around to chat?', no 'I'll miss you' or 'I didn't expect it to be that quick'. Just 'let me know if I can help'.

Hattie's heart ached as she reread Marcus's text. She had been so stupid to get so close to him. She'd known from the start that she was just another holiday romance They had both agreed 'no strings attached'. Only she'd gone and fallen for him, hadn't she?

Well, he hasn't fallen for you.

That's why he hadn't asked to come round to talk to her, or offered to pop in after work tonight. She was moving on, the summer romance was over.

They had been so close and now it was like there was a chasm between them.

You had sex, once, that's all.

It had felt more than 'just sex'. Afterwards, he had held her in his arms, stroked the back of her hair as she had lain listening to his heart thudding in his chest. And he had kissed her before he left, a proper kiss, gazing into her eyes as if she was the only woman in the world who mattered to him.

She hadn't imagined it all, surely

He's probably like that with all the women, she told herself. She'd thought he was a womaniser when she'd first met him. That's how it is with surfers and artists; they're like magnets for a lot of women, aren't they? She was just another in a string of women falling for Marcus. Like Estelle. He flirted with everyone. Even Mali.

And she had gone and fallen for his charm. Stupid her. Well, if he wanted to forget what had happened between them then that was fine by her. She would pack up the cottage and make herself a bright new Marcus-free life.

Chapter Thirty-Seven

Marcus was surprised to get a call from Lady Thomwell the next morning.

'Afternoon, Marcus,' she said when he answered. 'I wondered if I could have a word?'

Surely she didn't want him to do another painting. 'Sure. What about?'

'A friend of mine is holding an art exhibition in London for up-and-coming artists, and I'd like you to exhibit one – or more – of your paintings. There's a substantial cash prize for the most distinguished piece of work, and smaller amounts for second and third place.'

'How substantial?' Marcus asked.

'Five thousand pounds,' she replied. 'Are you interested?

He thought about it, his mind running through the paintings he'd done. There was nothing very recent, most of his work just lately had been commissioned. There was the painting of the sunset over the sea he'd done last autumn . . .

'I'll have to check if I've got anything suitable. Most of my recent work has been sold,' he said. 'I'm guessing there isn't time for me to paint anything new?'

'The exhibition is in just under three weeks. Does that give you enough time?' Lady Felicity asked. 'I'm going to London for the exhibition and staying with a friend for the week. So I can take the painting down for you and bring it back. Do think seriously about entering, you're very talented and this will be good exposure for you.'

'I'll see what I can do,' he said. 'Thank you for telling me about it.'

After the phone call was finished he went up to the attic to look at the collection of paintings he had there. The sunset one was good, but not his best. He really wanted to do something new. Something different, something so vibrant that it would almost seem alive.

Then an idea struck him. Buddy. With his bright-green plumage, yellow nape and red-and-yellow tail feathers, the parrot would make an ideal subject for a painting that would really stand out. He wanted to bring out his cheeky personality too. Then he remembered the photo Hattie had taken of Buddy pinching a piece of toast from his plate. She'd sent the photo to him. He took his phone out of his pocket and selected the photo gallery. There it was. Buddy perched on the table, head bent towards the plate, a piece of toast in his beak. He zoomed in on the parrot, cutting out the background detail. That would make a great painting. And give him something to remember Buddy by when Hattie had gone. If he made a start straight away, he should be able to finish it in time. He sent a text to Lady Thornwell confirming that he would enter the competition.

If he worked flat out he could do it, and it would take his mind off Hattie leaving.

The next couple of weeks passed quickly for Hattie. Too quickly. The survey had been done on the cottage, Hattie had cleared out most of the clutter, and time was ticking by. Mali had found a couple of houses to rent within ten minutes from her and Lou so Hattie was going up to see them this weekend. Although Mali had told her that she was welcome to Lou's bedroom as long as she needed it, as Lou could move in with her, Hattie thought it was best for her to have her own home, so wanted to rent for six months. Then she could take her time looking around for a house, make sure she got the right one.

Hattie had hardly seen Marcus. He seemed to be avoiding her as much as she was avoiding him. She knew he was working on a new painting, and that the hotel was so busy now that he occasionally did an extra shift, but their closeness had gone. There had been a distance between them since she'd accepted the offer on the cottage. She guessed it was because now Marcus knew she was going he didn't see any point in continuing to see her. Maybe he had already moved onto someone new. A summer romance, they'd both agreed, but now it wasn't even a friendship. And she missed him.

She grabbed her bag and went out the back where her bike was parked, then stopped for a minute to take in the colourful pots, the white table and chairs. She loved this place. And she loved Marcus. Her heart wrenched at the thought of leaving them both.

Oh, stop being maudlin, she told herself. You'll be fine once you've gone. When you have a brand-new home, new opportunities.

She opened the gate and pushed the bike out, then bolted it behind her. As she got astride the bike, she saw Marcus pull up in his camper van. She paused, waiting for him to get out, thinking it would be rude to just ride off without saying hello.

He nodded at her. 'How's it going?'

'Okay. The survey is done, everything's underway. I'm going up to Bristol tomorrow for the weekend to look at a couple of houses to rent.'

'So, you're moving back up near Mali then?'

'Yep.'

He thrust his hands in his pockets, his eyes not quite meeting hers. 'Well, I'm glad it's all worked out for you. Really, I am.' He shuffled his feet. 'We ought to get together, have a drink or something before you leave.'

'I'd like that.' The words sounded croaky even to her ears. 'I was going to call around actually. I wondered if you would mind checking on Buddy when I'm gone? I'll be back Sunday evening, so it's only two nights but I'll worry about him.'

'Of course.' He sighed. 'Look, I don't want things to be awkward between us, especially as we're still neighbours for the time being. Can we forget that we ... er—'

'Had sex,' she finished for him.

Something flashed over his face but it was gone before she could catch it.

'Can we forget it happened and just carry on as friends? Meet for a drink, make the most of the couple of weeks we have left?' he said.

'I'd like that,' she agreed, her heart thumping. She'd missed him.

'How about tonight, before you go? I've got a Thursday evening off for once. Then you can give me the keys so I can check on Buddy too?'

'That'll be great. We could go to the Old Sea Dog? Shall I give you a knock about eight?'

'Perfect. See you later.'

Marcus watched Hattie ride off, her words repeating in his mind. 'Had sex,' she had said bluntly, which is obviously all it had been to her. She hadn't experienced the heart-thumping he had, his touch on her skin hadn't been as electrifying as hers had been on his, their kisses hadn't melted her heart like they had his. He had done it again, something he had sworn never to do; he had fallen for a summer visitor. Only this time, the love he felt was far deeper and stronger than it had been for Kaylee. This time he felt like his heart was being ripped out and he would never recover.

Why had he suggested that they be friends again, and still see each other, when it hurt so much, and when all he wanted to do was shut himself away?

Because it hurt even more not seeing her. And that would be how it was permanently soon enough. Hattie would ride off on that motorbike of hers and be gone out of his life forever. So, he wanted to make the most of the time they had left together, seize every moment, even if it meant he had to hide his feelings, never kiss or touch her. He wanted to burn every memory he could into his mind so that he could replay them over and over again when she had gone, taking the sunshine in his life with her.

He pushed open his gate and walked inside. Hattie had well and truly captured his heart and there was nothing he could do about it.

That evening, as they sat in the Old Sea Dog having a drink and both looking a bit awkward, he told Hattie about Lady Thornwell's phone call in an attempt at light conversation. 'I've been painting Buddy but I'm struggling to get across his cheeky character so it'll be good to spend some time with him this weekend. I was thinking of asking you if I could pop around and see him anyway.'

'How marvellous! I can't wait to see it.' She was almost clapping in delight. 'You can pop around any time, bring your paints and stuff with you and work in the kitchen if you want. Or take Buddy around to yours in the travel cage and paint him in your attic.'

'That would probably be the best idea as the light is so good there. I was wondering if you'd mind me taking him this weekend? I'll keep him well away from Mr Tibbs. Lady Thornwell is coming to collect the painting on Monday.'

'Of course.' She was smiling now. 'I'll be leaving about four tomorrow, to try and avoid the Friday traffic. So come around any time before then.'

The awkwardness was gone now and they both chatted away easily, then walked home together arm in arm.

'Want to come in for a coffee?' Hattie asked when they reached the row of three cottages.

He'd have loved to, thought Marcus, but he didn't trust himself not to kiss her and then that might lead to them ending up

257

in bed again. It might be just sex to Hattie, but it meant more than that to him.

'I'd better not, I've got an early start in the morning. I'll collect Buddy tomorrow about five thirty.' He leant forward and kissed her on the cheek 'Night, Hattie.'

Chapter Thirty-Eight

'Hattie!' Lou ran to the door in delight as Mali let Hattie in. 'Hello, Looby-Lou, how are you?' Hattie knelt down and gave the girl a hug.

'I'm good. Especially now you're coming to live near us. You've got my bed this weekend,' she added. 'I'm sleeping with Mummy.'

Hattie smiled. 'Thank you, Lou, that's very kind of you.'

'You can take some of my fluffy toys in bed with you, if you want. All except Bumble, he's coming in Mummy's bed with me.' She grabbed Hattie's hand. 'Do you want to see the bedroom.'

'Let's show Hattie later, Lou. I bet she could do with a drink and something to eat, she's had a long journey,' Mali said gently.

Lou looked so disappointed that Hattie said, 'It's okay, we can go and check out the room then I can have a drink.'

'Coffee, lemonade or wine?' Mali asked.

'Coffee please, but wine later would be lovely,' Hattie told her.

Lou proudly showed her the single bed with the light-blue

and yellow stars duvet cover and matching curtains beside it, as well as the row of cuddly toys that sat along the bottom of the bed. 'You can choose any one you like.'

'It's a lovely room, Lou. Thank you for letting me stay in it,' Hattie told her.

'That's okay, I like snuggling in with Mummy sometimes. Not all the time, though, cos she snores and pinches all the duvet.'

'Cheeky madam,' Mali shouted from the kitchen, where she'd obviously heard every word.

Hattie felt her spirits lift. A weekend with Mali and Lou was exactly what she needed right now.

Later, when Lou was finally worn out and fast asleep in bed, Mali poured them both a glass of wine and sat down on the sofa beside Hattie. She kicked off her shoes and tucked her legs underneath her. 'Now, tell me all the goss. How are things with you and Marcus?'

'Friendly. We don't see much of each other, really. We're both busy.'

Mali picked up her glass of wine and took a sip. 'That's surprised me. I thought he fancied you and you are definitely into him.'

'I am not!'

Mali studied her over the rim of her wine glass. 'So, that's it, friends? Not even a kiss?'

Hattie chewed her lip while she tried to think about how to phrase her answer.

Mali narrowed her eyes and stared at her. 'Hattie . . .'

'Well, okay we did . . . er . . . get a bit close, but it was only the once and it meant nothing.' *Liar.*

Mali put her wine down on the coffee table and turned to face Hattie. 'How close?'

So Hattie confessed.

'And it was that bad neither of you wanted a repeat performance?'

'It wasn't bad, it was good.' *Make that earth-shatteringly good.* 'Then I got the call to say we had a buyer for the house and Marcus backed right off. I guess he thinks it's a waste of time getting involved with each other as I'll be leaving soon.'

'And what do you think?'

Hattie hesitated, then decided to be truthful. Mali was her best friend. 'I think I've fallen for him, but I know that there's no future in it so it's best if we keep a distance from each other. I'll be gone in a few weeks.'

'Are you sure that he doesn't feel the same way?' Mali asked.

'Positive. He suggested that we forget all about that one incident and just be friends until I go. So, we went out for a drink last night, chatted, then he walked me home and kissed me on the cheek.' She picked up her glass of wine. 'And earlier tonight he came around to collect Buddy because he's looking after him while I'm away, and didn't even bother giving me a peck on the cheek, just got Buddy into the travel cage, said he hoped I enjoyed my weekend and that one of the houses was suitable, then went.' She'd been so disappointed, that when he'd left, she'd almost burst into tears and had had to give herself a stern talking to.

'Bummer! Well, you'll soon forget about him when you're back in the swing of things here. We've got three fab houses to see, one is only around the corner, which I think would be perfect, but obvs you have to choose what's best for you.'

Hattie took a long sip of her wine, and as she felt the liquid slide down her throat, she felt herself relax. Mali was right, she would be fine once she was in her own little house in Bristol.

They spent the evening chatting away. Mali wanted to know all about Nick and was surprised when Hattie told her about her dad's offer to go and stay with them once the house was sold.

'So, you and your dad are getting on now, then?'

Hattie shrugged. 'Sort of. I realise that I was a bit hard on him; he was struggling to adapt to his new life and I made it difficult for him to see me. I will go and stay with him, Nick is great and I'd like to get to know my stepfamily more, but not until I'm settled.'

'You never know, you might like France and want to live there. Although, me and Lou would miss you like mad.'

'No, I don't fancy living abroad. Mum's been really supportive too, she's been on a Caribbean cruise the past few weeks but messages me when she can and has offered for me to stay with her and Howard as long as I want. I'm beginning to realise how lucky I am to have two parents living abroad. Lots of free holidays.'

'Sounds good to me.' Mali held out her wine glass. 'Here's to new beginnings.'

'New beginnings,' Hattie repeated as they clinked glasses. She was feeling so much better. Being with Mali always cheered her up. Her friend was right. This was a new beginning for her and she should seize it with both hands.

The weekend didn't turn out as she'd planned, though. She'd been looking forward to going back to Bristol again, staying with Mali and Lou, checking out the houses Mali had found her to rent. But it had seemed so strange. She felt as if she had come back to somewhere she used to live and didn't belong to anymore. It felt too loud, too busy. The houses were modern and warm but she couldn't imagine living in them. She kept comparing them to quaint, cheerful Fisherman's Rest with its gorgeous sea view. As she walked around the streets with Mali and Lou, she kept thinking about the picturesque houses and cobbled streets of Port Medden.

Mali had seen something was wrong. 'Your heart isn't in this, is it?' she'd asked yesterday when they had looked around the last house on her list.

Hattie had shaken her head. 'I'm sorry, Mali, but I don't feel like I belong here anymore. It's weird. I know I've only been in Port Medden a few weeks but I feel at home there, and I love Uncle Albert's little cottage.'

Mali looked thoughtful. 'If you really don't want to move from Port Medden, why don't you rent a place down there when the house is sold, as we suggested before? You could save the money from the house sale and when your photography business is up and running, or you get a job, you could put it down as a deposit and buy somewhere to live.'

'I love the cottage, though. I don't know if I want to live anywhere else. I wish I could afford to buy Dad out, but I've got no chance of doing that.'

'Is it Marcus or the cottage you're in love with? If Marcus moved out from next door, would you still want to live there?' Mali asked her.

Hattie thought about it. She did love Marcus, yes, but she loved the cottage and little town too. 'I think I would, yes.' She looked at Mali pensively. 'I can't explain, but I feel so at home there.'

'Oh, Hattie, I'm so sorry.' Mali gave her a big hug. 'Look, I'd love you to stay here with me and Lou but I think that maybe you should get right away when the house is sold. Go and stay with your dad or mum for a month or so, get your head together.'

Hattie thought she had a point, so promised to think about it. Mali persuaded her to stay one more night. 'You're tired, don't travel down now,' she said. 'Let's have a drink and a catch up.'

Hattie thought that sounded a great idea.

Chapter Thirty-Nine

It was Sunday evening before Marcus finally finished the painting of Buddy. Marcus put down his brush and stepped back, his eyes resting on the painting in front of him, the parrot's head bent towards the plate, a chunk of toast in his beak, which it was obvious he'd snatched from the piece of toast on the plate, his eye seeming to stare out of the picture back at him. It was cheeky, fun, and colourful. Was it good enough? It was all he had time for. The exhibition was on Tuesday and Lady Thomwell wanted to pick up the painting tomorrow to take down to London. He didn't expect to win – there would be artists far more talented than him entering – but he wanted to enter because Lady Thomwell had asked him personally and the prize money wasn't to be sneezed at. He wouldn't sell the painting, though, he had decided. It would be good to have a memory of Buddy when Hattie had left, taking the parrot with her. To have a memory of them *both*, he thought, looking over at the painting of Hattie in the corner.

Just then, his phone rang. Thinking it was Hattie, to let him know what time she'd be home, he answered it without checking. It was Lady Thomwell.

'Is your painting finished, Marcus?' she asked.

'Yes, just,' he replied.

'Then I'll come and get it. I'm in the area and want to set out early in the morning.'

'The paint is still a bit wet,' he told her. 'I'd rather bring it over tomorrow morning.'

'No, don't do that. I'm leaving early so I'll collect it on the way to London. Are you sure you don't want to come with me? My friend has a spare room you can use. You could make some useful contacts at the exhibition.'

She couldn't seem to understand that it wasn't his scene. He liked painting. He didn't like putting his paintings on display and listening to people make comments about them – good or bad. It made him feel awkward.

'I can't spare the time, I'm afraid, but thank you for taking the painting for me. I'll see you in the morning.'

Hattie texted a little while later to say that she was staying over at Mali's again tonight and would be back tomorrow morning. He felt strangely disappointed. Knowing that she wasn't next door had made him feel out of sorts all weekend. He wondered if she had chosen the house she wanted. Two or three more weeks and she would be gone. The knowledge that he would never see her again was eating into him. *You'll get over it*, he told himself.

He was tired. He'd worked flat out all weekend to finish the painting. He grabbed a shower, something to eat and collapsed into bed. He was woken the next morning by his phone ringing.

Hattie?

He grabbed it, only to discover that it was Lady Thomwell again.

'Where are you, Marcus? I've been banging on your door for five minutes.'

Shit! He glanced at the clock. It was nine. He'd been totally zonked. 'I'll be right there,' he said. Ending the call, he grabbed his shorts and pulled them on, then headed for the door, running his hands through his messy hair as he pounded barefoot down the stairs. He opened the door and was greeted by a surprised stare from Lady Thomwell and a cheeky wink from Estelle. He hadn't known she was going too.

'Did we get you up, dear?' Lady Thomwell stepped in without waiting to be asked and Estelle followed, her eyes drifting over his naked torso and back up to his face.

Marcus groaned. Why hadn't he pulled on a T-shirt?

'I'll just get the painting, it's up in the attic.' He turned to walk down the hall to the stairs and realised that the two women were following him.

'We'll come with you. I'm dying to see where you work,' Estelle said.

'And there might be another couple of paintings we could take. You aren't confined to one entry, you know,' Lady Thomwell added.

There was nothing for it but to let them in to his studio.

'Bugger off!' Buddy greeted them as they all walked into the attic.

'Goodness, you keep a parrot up here!' Lady Thomwell exclaimed. 'And you've painted him! That's wonderful. Look at this, Estelle.'

But Estelle had spotted the painting of Hattie and was walking over to that.

'Estelle?' Lady Thomwell turned. 'What are you doing? Oh goodness, that is striking!'

Marcus supressed a groan as she walked over to his painting of Hattie too. Why hadn't he covered it up?

'This is your girlfriend, isn't it? The one you brought to Rupert's birthday party?' said Lady Thomwell. 'She looked stunning in those leathers.'

Marcus nodded. 'The parrot belongs to her. I'm looking after it while she's away for the weekend.'

Lady Thomwell was walking around the painting, studying it from every angle. 'You must enter this in the exhibition too. It's stunning. So much character. Isn't he talented, Estelle?'

'Beautifully painted, darling, and how sweet that you've painted your girlfriend,' Estelle said. 'I prefer the parrot painting, though. He's such a gorgeous bird.'

'I think I prefer this one. It's got a look of wildness about it,' Lady Thomwell said, nodding her head as she walked around the painting of Hattie. 'You can almost hear the bike starting up ready to go, and feel the young woman's adrenalin coursing through her. She looks like someone who enjoys life and lives it to the full.'

Exactly like Hattie, Marcus thought. And right now, she was planning her next adventure.

He could feel Estelle's eyes on him, feel her brain ticking. 'Such a shame she's moving away. You'll miss her, won't you? I guess you painted her portrait as a reminder. That's so sweet,' she said languidly.

Her words took him by surprise. How the hell did she know

268

that Hattie was moving away? He quickly pulled himself together. 'Yes, she's selling the cottage but she's not moving that far. We can see each other at weekends.'

'She's going to Bristol, isn't she? My friend Hilary said. Hattie took some photos of Charlotte riding her horse, they were very good, so Hilary tried to book her for Charlotte's birthday party photos in September but Hattie said that she was moving away to Bristol soon,' Estelle explained, obviously noticing Marcus's surprised expression.

'Well, it's not set in stone yet but, yes, she's thinking of going back to Bristol. She's been over there this weekend looking at property,' he said. 'She'll be back any time now.'

'How nice.' Estelle smiled sweetly at him.

'We really must be going. I'd like to take both these paintings, if I may, Marcus. They are wonderful. I'd be very surprised if one of them didn't win a prize.'

Marcus hesitated. 'I'm not . . .'

But Lady Thomwell was adamant. 'Don't worry, I'll look after them. You'll have them back safe and sound next week.'

What could he say? 'Let me wrap them both up and carry them down for you.'

'We've had to park around the corner, Branson is waiting in the Rolls,' Lady Thomwell said.

The chauffeur got out when he saw them approaching and opened the boot which was full of suitcases and baggage. 'Just place them on the suitcases, dear, they will be perfectly fine,' Lady Thomwell said. 'I promise I will take good care of them. You are a very talented young man and I am quite certain one of these will win a prize.'

He hoped so, he could do with the money. And he did trust

Lady Thomwell to look after his paintings, he knew that she had great respect for art. He lay the pictures flat on top of the suitcases and closed the boot. 'Thank you for entering these for me.'

'It's a pleasure, dear.' Lady Thomwell kissed him on the cheek, then got into the back of the Rolls. 'Come on, Estelle. We must go.'

'Hang on, I need a pee,' Estelle said, turning to Marcus. 'I couldn't quickly nip to your loo, could I?'

He wanted to refuse her, but it would be rude so he nodded, hoping he had left the bathroom tidy, and they both walked back to Curlew Cottage. As soon as Marcus opened the door, Estelle shouted, 'Thank so much,' and dashed past him. He waited on the doorstep and she returned a few minutes later.

'Right, I'll be off,' she said, wrapping her arms around his neck and giving him a big kiss on the lips – just as Hattie rode past on her motorbike.

Chapter Forty

Hattie rode around to the back of the cottages, stunned. She pulled up outside the back gate of Fisherman's Rest, and tried to pull herself together, the shock of seeing Marcus and Estelle kissing in the doorway of his cottage coursing through her. Marcus and Estelle! He had begged Hattie to go to the party with him so he could avoid Estelle's advances, and now he had invited her to his house as soon as Hattie's back was turned, and there he was standing on the doorstep kissing her goodbye. And that wasn't a friendly kiss. That was a 'just got out of bed' kiss. And if the kiss didn't prove he had just got out of bed, his tousled hair and half-naked body certainly did. How could he?

She parked her bike up in the back yard and let herself in, expecting to hear Buddy squawk 'Where you been?' as soon as she stepped foot into the lounge, then realised Marcus had him. Damn, that meant he'd be bringing him back soon and right now Marcus was the last person she wanted to see. She felt such a fool, there she'd been, thinking of him all weekend, missing him, wishing she wasn't leaving, whereas he hadn't given her a moment's thought, he was too busy bedding Estelle.

You don't own him. You both agreed to be 'friends only', remember. And now he isn't working for the Thomwells, Estelle isn't the daughter of a client any longer, so perhaps he's decided to date her. And he had every right to. He was single. He could date who he wanted.

She had to forget about him. She had her own future to work out. And she wasn't going to waste a moment of it thinking about Marcus, that was for sure!

What was she going to do, though? She felt lost. Adrift.

She looked up as she heard a knock on the front door. That was probably Marcus bringing Buddy back. Well, she was going to keep cool and not let on that it had bothered her seeing him kiss Estelle. Not that it had; she was over it.

'Hi, Hattie. Glad to see you back.' He was holding the travel cage with Buddy inside it, and looked a bit awkward. 'Look, sorry about that with Estelle . . .'

'You don't have to explain, you're perfectly entitled to kiss your girlfriend.'

'She isn't my girlfriend.' He sounded frustrated.

'Oh, of course she isn't, you don't have girlfriends, do you? You just have friends that you sleep with now and again . . .' she retorted.

Marcus recoiled as if she had slapped him across the face. 'Lady Thomwell came to pick up my painting for the exhibition. I managed to get it finished in time and Estelle—'

She cut him short. She knew what she'd seen and didn't want to hear his lies. 'I don't want to know. You don't have to explain to me. I'm just a friend. And I won't be here much longer. When this cottage is sold, I'm going to France, so you can see who you want. Fill your boots.' She held out her hand. 'I'll take Buddy. Thank you for looking after him.'

'Hattie, you've got it all wrong,' Marcus protested.

'It really isn't important. If I could just have Buddy.'

'At least let me transfer Buddy into the big cage for you.' Marcus walked past her and carried the cage into the lounge. Hattie watched sulkily as he opened the cage doors and Buddy hopped into the big one. Then he put the travel cage down and turned to Hattie. 'If you'd just let me explain ...'

'I don't want to hear it. Please go.'

His eyes held hers and she saw the spark of anger in them, the tight set of his jaw. Tough, she didn't want to hear his excuses. He could do what he liked with his life.

'If that's what you want,' he said.

'It is.'

She showed him out and shut the door behind him. Then she went back into the lounge, curled up on the sofa and cried.

Finally, her tears spent, she got up, wiped her eyes, and put the kettle on for a coffee. After Adam, she'd promised herself that she would never let a man break her heart again, and now look at her. Marcus wasn't worth it any more than Adam had been. She was going to pull herself together and get on with her life.

She'd just sat down with her cup of coffee, when her phone rang. It was her mum; Hattie guessed she must be back from the cruise now.

'Hello, darling. How are you? I've been dying to call you but the reception on the ship has been terrible,' Caroline said. 'Have you managed to sort out somewhere to live? You know that you're welcome here.'

'I know, Mum. Thanks. Dad said that too.'

'Really? Are you both on better terms, then?'

'I guess we've had to have more contact because of selling the cottage. And Nick came over to help me.' She filled her

273

mother in on what had been happening the last few weeks while she had been sailing around the Caribbean.

'I'm pleased that you're both getting on.' There was a pause, then she continued, 'I'm sorry if you felt that you had to take my side when we divorced and that's why you didn't see more of your dad. That wasn't fair of me. I was just so hurt.'

That was a first, her mother apologising! 'It's okay, Mum. I was angry with him too.'

'Well, it was all a long time ago, and I'm happy with Howard, so time to let it all go. I'd be delighted if you wanted to come and spend some time with us while you sort yourself out, but I won't mind in the least if you decide to visit your father instead. I promise you. I want you to do what's best for you. I want you to be happy.'

Hattie swallowed the lump in her throat. 'Thanks, Mum. Now, tell me all about your holiday.'

They chatted away for a while, exchanging news.

'Call me soon, let me know how you're getting on, and what you've decided to do,' her mother said as she ended the call.

'I will,' Hattie promised.

That was her priority, deciding what to do. And, as her mother said, she had to do what was best for her. This was her life.

'Hello, Hattie!' Buddy suddenly squawked. 'Hello, Hattie!'

Hattie spun around in surprise. He'd actually learnt to say it. 'Hello, Buddy!' she said.

She got up and walked over to the cage. Buddy was hopping along the branch, squawking, obviously happy to see her. They'd really bonded now; Buddy was part of her life.

'I don't know where we're going to live, Buddy,' she said. 'But I'll find somewhere nice and cosy, just for the two of us.'

She felt happier now, determined not to mope over Marcus. She had so much going for her. Thanks to Uncle Albert, she had enough money to get herself a nice home, her redundancy money had finally arrived in her bank account too, so she had plenty to live on for a while. She should be happy, not crying like a lovesick schoolgirl!

Jonathan phoned a little later to let her know the Bryants, the people who were buying the cottage, would like to pop in for another look around to check if there was anything urgent they needed to do as they were intending to let the cottage out this summer. 'They're trying to push the sale through by the end of July so that they can let it out in August and September and then refurbish during the winter months,' he said.

'That's fine,' she told him. She had to face facts. She couldn't stay in the cottage, much as she loved it, and Marcus didn't love her even though she loved him. Time to pull on her big-girl pants and move on.

She made herself another coffee and sat down with a notebook and pen to write down the pros and cons of her options, reminding herself that she was lucky to have options to choose from:

<u>Rent a place in Port Medden</u>

Pros

I love it and already have contacts for my photography business.

Cons

Living in the same village as Marcus and would probably keep bumping into him.

Business might be slow in the winter. It might be too quiet in the winter so I could find it boring.

Go over to France

Pros

It would be good to spend some time with Dad and my stepfamily.

Cons

Don't want to live over there so would still have to sort out a home when I came back. And what would I do with Buddy?

Go over to Portugal

Pros

Good to see Mum.

Cons

The same as going over to France.

Go to a completely new area

Pros

It would be a fresh new start.

Cons

I wouldn't know anyone and don't fancy starting right from scratch.

<u>Move back to Bristol</u>

Pros

I like and know Bristol. Mali and Lou are there. I could stay with them for a couple of weeks until I find a house to rent. I have contacts there and should be able to get work easily.

Cons

It isn't Port Medden.

She sipped her coffee as she studied the list. Then she made up her mind.

'We're going back to Bristol, Buddy,' she said. She picked up the phone to call Mali.

Mali almost whooped with delight.

'Of course you can stay with us for as long as you want!' she said.

'Thank you. Hopefully I'll find somewhere to rent quickly. And I'm sorry but the buyers want the sale to go through by the end of July so it means you and Lou won't be able to come down again for a holiday.'

'Don't you worry about that. Having you with us will be like a holiday. We can help you look for your new house, and settle in. It'll be fun.'

Mali was right. It was going to be fun, Hattie thought. This was a whole new chapter of her life. She'd soon forget Marcus and Port Medden once she was settled back in Bristol again.

Chapter Forty-One

The week whizzed by. The Bryants came to check over the cottage again on Thursday morning. 'You will leave it empty, won't you?' Mrs Bryant asked Hattie. 'We'll need to clean it all out and get some new furniture in before we let it.'

Hattie felt her heart sink. She hadn't thought about that. Of course they'd expect the cottage to be empty. 'Yes, unless there is anything you want me to leave?'

Mrs Bryant shook her head. 'No, it's all a bit . . . worn and dated.'

She was right, it was, Hattie acknowledged. Although, personally, she found the old sofa very comfy, and it looked cosy with the white throw she'd put over it. She loved the dresser too, with all of Uncle Albert's bits and pieces in it. The Bryants wanted it as a holiday let, she reminded herself.

'How soon can we push the sale through?' Mr Bryant asked Jonathan.

'Can we take some photos so we can show people?' Mrs Bryant asked. 'We've already got a couple who want to book August, and two more interested. There's someone who wants the last week in July too. I don't suppose we could get the sale through by the middle of July, could we, to give us time to tidy up and get new furniture in?'

That was only two weeks away! Hattie thought in panic.

'I don't think that's feasible. I'll check with my solicitor,' Hattie told them.

When she checked with her solicitor he said that three weeks was more feasible, so they settled on exchanging contracts on the Monday that week and completing on the Wednesday.

'We'll need your dad to come over and sign the papers for the exchange,' the solicitor said. 'I'll email him and let him know but I'm sure you'll be speaking to him.'

'I'll ring him this morning,' Hattie said.

'That's great love,' said her dad when she called him to tell him the news. 'I'll drive over in case there's anything I want to take back. Is it okay if I stay for the weekend?'

'Of course, it's your cottage too.' She'd be glad of the company and was looking forward to spending some time with her dad.

'I don't suppose I can persuade you to come back with me?'

'I'm going back to Bristol, Dad. Mali's putting me up until I find a place of my own. But I will come and see you soon, I promise.'

She decided to spend the afternoon sorting out the cupboards in the dresser. She guessed they held a lot of Uncle Albert's personal things; she'd put anything she thought her dad might like in a box to give to him.

She opened the cupboard doors and started to pull out the contents: old books, boxes of black-and-white photographs, another box of papers, some screwdrivers, a stapler. She sat down on the carpet and placed the box of photographs on her lap. Many of them were faded now, of people she didn't know and who probably weren't still alive. She peered at one photo of a little boy standing in front of a couple, a young man beside them. Was that Granny and Grandad? She turned the photo over: Albert, Mum, Roger and Owen it said. The date was 19 something but the last two figures were too faded for her to read. Her dad, his parents and Uncle Albert. It was the first time she'd seen a photo of them all. It really illustrated the age difference between her dad and Uncle Albert. No wonder they hadn't been very close.

Her dad had suggested she called a house-clearance firm to collect the furniture the week of the sale. She wondered whether to ask Winnie and Marcus if they wanted anything from the house, as they had both been fond of Uncle Albert. It would be a bit awkward, but Marcus had been kind to her uncle so she should at least ask if he wanted anything before everything was taken away. Besides, what did it matter about him and Estelle now? She wouldn't be here much longer to bother about anything he did. She'd been silly to get so worked up about it. She'd ask Winnie and Marcus if they had time to pop around now, it would make it easier for her to see Marcus if Winnie was there too.

She sent Marcus a quick text and then popped around to Primrose Cottage. Winnie answered on the first knock. 'Hello, my dear, how's the house sale going?' she asked cheerily.

'We're exchanging in three weeks,' Hattie told her.

'That soon? Well I'll miss you, and I'm sure Marcus will too. It's such a shame, you're a wonderful neighbour, but it is what it is.' Winnie rubbed her hands together briskly. 'Now, what can

I do for you? Or were you popping in for a cup of tea and a chat?'

'I'm organising a house-clearance company to come in and empty the cottage the day before we complete and was wondering if there was anything you wanted to remember Uncle Albert by? The furniture is quite old and worn, but maybe you'd like to have a look?'

'What a lovely idea. I will pop around, thank you. Did you want me to come now?'

'If you have time.' She heard a message ping and checked her phone. 'Marcus is on his way too.'

Her heart fluttered as she saw Marcus come out of his cottage as she and Winnie walked down the path to Fisherman's Rest.

'Afternoon, Marcus. I hope we don't want the same things,' Winnie said mischievously.

Marcus smiled. 'You can have first choice, Winnie.'

He glanced at Hattie and she threw him a brief smile to let him know that there was no awkwardness on her part. She was determined to be adult about this.

Once inside, Hattie put the kettle on and made tea for Winnie and coffee for her and Marcus while they both checked out the furniture. After much deliberating, Winnie decided upon a table lamp and a mantlepiece clock. 'I shall think of dear Albert whenever I look at them,' she said. Marcus took Albert's binoculars and the big ship he kept in the lounge window. 'If you're sure you don't want them?' he asked Hattie.

She shook her head. 'Please have them. Uncle Albert would want you to.'

'Have you saved anything to remember your uncle by, dear?' Winnie asked as they all sat sipping their drinks.

'I'm taking the painting over the fireplace.' That would remind her of her uncle and of Marcus. 'And I've got some photos. I'm going to look through them with my dad. Dad wants his pipe rack – he doesn't smoke but he said he always remembers Albert sitting in the rocking chair smoking. I'd like to keep the rocking chair too, but I don't think it will fit in my friend Mali's car. I'll be staying with her until I get myself a place in Bristol.'

'I'll be sad to see you go, Hattie. Do pop in and see us if you're ever down this way,' Winnie said.

'I will,' Hattie promised.

'What about Buddy?' Hattie felt Marcus's eyes upon her, he was waiting for her answer.

'Obviously, he's coming with me,' Hattie replied.

'Well, I must go now, dear, this has been lovely. And thank you so much for the mementos of Albert. I appreciate it.' Winnie got to her feet, picking up the bag that Hattie had put the table lamp and clock in.

'You're welcome.' Hattie stood up, expecting Marcus to go too but he remained seated.

What does he want? She thought as she let Winnie out and then came back in. He was standing now, hands in pockets, an earnest expression on his face.

'Hattie, I want to talk to you. Will you please hear me out?'

'What about?' she asked wearily.

'Monday. I did not sleep with Estelle and she tricked me into that kiss. Lady Thornwell came to pick up my painting for the exhibition. I overslept, quickly pulled on some shorts and went to answer the door to find her and Estelle on the doorstep.' He thrust his hand through his hair. 'They came in to look at the

282

painting and I helped them carry it out to the car. Then Estelle said she needed the loo so I let her back in. I had told her you would be home soon and I think she pretended she needed the loo to buy more time, saw you coming and quickly kissed me.' He looked genuinely remorseful. 'I'm sorry that you had to witness that.'

She bit her lip and averted her gaze. 'Well, thank you for explaining but it really doesn't matter. You're single. You can see who you want to.'

'It does matter. I've told you how she harasses me, and you came to the birthday party, pretended to be my girlfriend to put her off.'

'Didn't work though, did it?'

'No, it didn't. I promise you that I'm really not interested in her, whereas I . . . like you very much. You're leaving soon and I don't want us to part on bad terms.'

She liked him too. More than liked him. 'Neither do I. Let's forget all about it,' she said.

He held out his hand. 'Friends?'

She took it, trying not to notice the familiar tingle coursing around her body. 'Friends.'

'Will you let me help you sort all this out? You must still have such a lot to do.'

She did. Too much. 'The house clearance will take most of it, but I still need to sort through all the cupboards and drawers and make sure there's nothing important.' She sighed.

'So, you're going back to Bristol then?'

She nodded, too choked up to speak.

'And is that what you really want to do?'

She licked her lips, gulped and then she shook her head. 'No.

I know you won't believe this, but I'd like to stay here, in Fisherman's Rest. I love it in Port Medden and my photography business is picking up, but I've got no choice and I shouldn't be complaining. The money from the sale will help me start a new life.' She tilted her chin. 'But please don't assume that I'm walking away because I want to. I love it here.'

And I love you.

For a moment, she was scared that she had said the words aloud. He was looking at her, his eyes dark, his expression unfathomable. He nodded slowly. 'I understand. It must be difficult for you, but I'm sure you'll find somewhere nice to live and be happy.' His gaze flitted to the box of photos on the floor. 'I have to go to work soon so I'll leave you to look through the photos, but how about I come around tomorrow afternoon and help you sort out the rest of the cupboards?'

'Thanks. I'd love that.'

Chapter Forty-Two

'You're not looking very happy tonight,' Mandy remarked when Marcus walked in to do his evening shift. 'What's up? Is it because Hattie's leaving?'

Marcus looked at her miserably. 'So much for you and your intuition. The sale will be through in a couple of weeks and she's going back to Bristol.'

'Have you told her how you feel?'

'What's the point. It's quite clear she doesn't feel the same way. Besides, she has no choice. She has to leave.'

Mandy fixed him with a stern glance. 'There's always a choice. And even my intuition needs a helping hand sometimes. Tell her how you feel. And if she feels the same way you'll both sort something out.'

Marcus thought about Mandy's advice all evening but decided not to take it. It was obvious that Hattie only looked on him as a friend. She said she didn't want to leave Port Medden, or the cottage, but had said nothing about leaving him. And if she was *that* fond of Port Medden, or had any feelings for him, she could find somewhere to rent.

Or she could move in with him.

He'd been toying with the thought for a couple of weeks now, he was so desperate for Hattie not to leave. He had never even thought of living with one of his girlfriends before, he liked his own space, his independence. And hadn't thought enough of any of them to give that up for them. Hattie was different, though. Would she want to? Would it work? If it didn't, then he would have to ask her to leave and how horrible would that be?

He shook his head. No, it was all too much of a risk.

When he passed Fisherman's Rest later that evening, after finishing his shift, he saw that the light was on in the lounge. Hattie was still up. He stood at the gate, looking at the window, wondering whether to knock on the door. How had they gone from that easy friendship where he used to pop in on the way home from work to this?

He sighed and carried on to Curlew Cottage. He poured himself a glass of wine when he got inside and sipped it slowly, remembering making love with Hattie, her scent, the taste of her, the feel of her.

He was going to miss her.

The next morning, Hattie was up bright and early. She whisked open the curtains to look out at the sea over the rooftops. 'I'm going to make the most of the time I have left down here,' she decided. 'No more moping.'

So, straight after breakfast, she headed down to the beach for a swim in the sea. She'd promised herself she'd have a swim every morning but hadn't got around to it. Now, she was determined to find time for it. The beach was empty apart from a few surfers riding the waves. She looked out at them, wondering if one of them was Marcus, but they were too far out for her to see clearly. Well, it didn't matter if he was there, they had buried the hatchet and were both adult enough to be pleasant to each other for the short time she had left in Port Medden. She was pleased that Marcus was coming around that afternoon to help her sort through the cupboards. She was stupidly really looking forward to seeing him again and was determined to keep it light and pleasant.

She wriggled out of her shorts and vest top, stripping down to the brightly coloured bikini she was wearing underneath, and placed them in her beach bag, then put the bag by some rocks and covered it with a towel. Her phone and door keys were in the bag but there was no one about so they should be safe, she thought. She headed over to the sea, paddling until she got in deep enough to swim and plunged in.

The water was cool and refreshing. She swam for a while, making sure not to go out too far, feeling herself relax. When she'd finally had enough, she headed back for the beach and sat down on the sand, drying herself with her towel.

Then she lay down and closed her eyes, basking in the warmth of the sun on her skin.

'Morning. Have you been for a swim?'

She opened her eyes at the familiar voice. Marcus was standing in front of her, his wetsuit clinging to him like a second skin, his long hair pulled back into a low ponytail, his surfboard under his arm. He looked sensational. She felt her insides do a flip and sat up. 'Yes, I've been meaning to come for a morning swim for ages.' She tucked her still-wet hair behind her ears. 'I did wonder if you were one of the surfers out there.'

He sat down in the sand beside her, and lay the board beside him. 'Did you enjoy the swim?'

She turned her face towards him, then wished she hadn't as his gaze locked with hers, his eyes dark and mesmerising, and she felt her breath catch in her throat, her hands ache to reach out and touch his face, to feel her fingers on his skin. Damn, why did he always have this effect on her?

'I did. Thank you. Have you heard how your painting fared in the exhibition?' she asked, lowering her eyes as she brushed some sand off her legs, trying to give herself a chance to pull herself together.

'The exhibition ends today, so I should hear soon. Not that I'm expecting to get anywhere but Lady Thomwell said there's been quite a lot of interest in my paintings so who knows. I may get another commission.'

'Paintings?' she repeated, surprised. 'I thought you were only entering the painting of Buddy?'

'Er, yes, I was but Lady Thomwell came up to the attic with me to get it and spotted another painting she liked so took that too.'

'Really? That's great. When will you get your paintings back? I'd like to see the one of Buddy before I leave.' It sounded so final saying that. She'd be leaving Port Medden. Would never see Marcus again.

I'll be making a marvellous new life for myself.

'Lady Thomwell is bringing it back with her on Monday so I'll collect it then and you can see it.'

So, he was going over to Thomwell Manor to collect it? Would he be seeing Estelle too? If he was, it was none of her business.

'That'll be great. I look forward to it.' She scrambled to her feet and reached for her bag, then pulled her vest top over her head and wriggled into her shorts, feeling very self-conscious. 'I'm off now then. See you after lunch. If you still have time to come round?'

'One thirty be okay?'

'Perfect.' She picked up her bag and sandals. 'Bye.'

She walked back across the beach, forcing herself not to look over her shoulder to see if he was watching her. If he wasn't, she would be disappointed. And if he was, she would feel sad. There was no future for them, she had to accept that.

True to his word, Marcus knocked on the door at dead on one thirty. Hattie greeted him with a smile, determined to keep things light and friendly. And Marcus seemed of the same mind, holding out a foil-covered plate, saying, 'I come with cake.'

'Oh, yummy.' Hattie took the dish off him, and folded back the foil to take a peep as he stepped into the hall. 'Oh, carrot cake! Perfect.' One of her favourites.

'We had some left over last night, so I thought you might appreciate it.'

'Definitely. Want some now with a cuppa?' She opened the lounge door.

'Please.'

As soon as they walked in, Buddy started whistling and shouted, 'Where you been?' to Marcus.

'I think he's missed you after spending the weekend with you,' Hattie said, putting the cake down on the table and going into the kitchen to fill the kettle, leaving Marcus to talk to Buddy. Marcus must miss Buddy too, she thought. He'd been part of his life for years and soon he would be gone, with her.

'Please come and see him whenever you like. I'm sure you

miss him as much as he misses you,' she said, peering through the arch where she could see Marcus giving Buddy a grape.

'Thanks. I am going to miss the little fella.' He glanced at her. 'I know he will be fine with you, though. He's really taken to you now, hasn't he?'

She grinned. 'Yes and he actually says "Hello, Hattie" now. Listen.'

She stood by the cage. 'Hello, Buddy. Say "Hello Hattie".'

Buddy cocked his head at her. 'Hello, Hattie. Hello, Hattie.'

'See?' she said triumphantly. Marcus was smiling but he didn't look surprised. Then the penny dropped. 'You taught him last weekend, didn't you?'

'Yes. I thought it would be a nice surprise for you.'

Even though he'd been busy painting, he'd spent time over the weekend teaching Buddy to say 'Hello, Hattie' as a surprise for her. Did that mean he did care about her?

She suddenly realised that she was staring at him. She pulled herself together. 'That was lovely of you. Thank you. Now, how about we have this coffee and cake and get cracking?' she said, turning away to make the coffee and give her chance to compose herself.

It was a pleasant afternoon. Between the two of them, they sorted out the whole dresser, piling the things that had to be dumped in one box, the things her father might be interested in in another, and anything to go to charity shops in a third. Just like they had done when they were sorting out the wardrobes upstairs.

And ended up going to bed together.

She pushed the thought out of her mind and stood up, rubbing her legs. Sitting on the floor had made them ache. 'That's that sorted, then. Thanks for your help.'

'What about the ornaments in the dresser?' Marcus asked, getting to his feet too.

'I'll leave them for Dad to look through. What he doesn't want can go to the house clearance people.'

Marcus nodded. 'I'll be off, then. I'm at work tonight. Are you interested if there is any more cake leftover?'

'Absolutely! And Marcus?'

He looked at her questioningly.

'Thanks again for your help. And remember what I said, pop in and see Buddy any time.'

He nodded. 'Thanks.'

Well, she'd manged that okay, Hattie thought when Marcus had left. At least they were back to being friends. And that's the way she intended to keep it.

Chapter Forty-Three

Lady Thomwell phoned Marcus on Monday afternoon to say that his painting of Hattie had won first prize. 'It got a lot of attention. There are a couple of people wanting to buy it. I wasn't sure if you wanted to sell it, though.'

No he didn't. He had intended to frame it and hang it over his fireplace but now he didn't think he could bear to see it every day when Hattie had gone, taking his heart with her. He still didn't want to sell it, though. It was too personal. Perhaps he'd frame it and keep it in his attic.

'No, it isn't for sale,' he said.

'What about the painting of the parrot? I've got someone interested in that too.'

'No, that's not for sale either.' Perhaps he'd put the painting of Buddy over his fireplace.

He could hear Lady Thomwell's tuts down the phone. 'You're never going to have a lucrative career as an artist, Marcus, if you won't sell your paintings.'

'I will sell them. Just not those two.' They meant too much

to him. He didn't expect Lady Thomwell to understand; money was more important to her than it was to him.

Lady Thomwell told him that the exhibitors wanted to keep both paintings on display for another two weeks and wanted Marcus to come down to accept the prize money personally.

'Please come, the publicity will be good for you. Rupert is coming too. But don't worry, Estelle has gone back to Paris now, dear, so you don't have to worry about her pulling a trick like that again,' she said. 'I hope your girlfriend wasn't too upset.'

So, she had seen Estelle kiss him. 'No, she knows there was nothing in it.'

'Good. Now, congratulations on your win. You should be very proud. And please say you will come down to meet the exhibition team and to claim your prize at the end of the month. Bring your girlfriend too.'

Why not? The hotel would change his shifts if he gave them notice, and it would be a break. 'Yes, I'll come,' he said. 'I'm not sure about Hattie, she's moving soon.'

Lady Thomwell was delighted. 'You can travel with us, Rupert would be thrilled. We can all stay at the same hotel too and go out for dinner in the evening. There are a few people who want to meet you. Do try to get Hattie to come as well, after all she's the star of the show so to speak.'

He sighed. He hated stuff like this and Lady Thomwell knew it, but she was right – it was good for his career. So he agreed he'd try to talk Hattie into coming. Part of him wanted her to come too, it would give him chance to see her again. The trouble was, she had no idea that the painting existed.

When the phone call was finished, Marcus's thoughts drifted

to Hattie and how the hell he was going to tell her that he had secretly painted a portrait of her that had just won first prize and that Lady Thomwell wanted her to accompany him to collect it at the end of the month.

'Next week?' Hattie asked, her heart thumping. This was too soon. Much too soon.

'The buyers want to complete next week so they have chance to refurbish the cottage,' her solicitor told her. 'Everything is in place so there's nothing to stop you. I've already left a message for your father to see if he could come over this weekend and sign the necessary papers.'

'This weekend!' Hattie felt stupid repeating his words but she couldn't take them in. She hadn't expected this. The Bryants had always pushed for an earlier completion, though, and now there was nothing stopping them. Of course she could refuse.

'Would it be possible?' the solicitor asked.

She could hear beeps indicating an incoming call and guessed it was her dad. 'I think Dad's trying to get through, so let me talk to him and I'll call you back.'

She ended the call and accepted the incoming one. It was her dad.

'I've had a message from the solicitor, he wants to know if we will agree for the sale to go through next week,'.

'I know. I was talking to him when you were trying to get through,' she told him.

As she listened to the relief and excitement in her dad's voice as he said he couldn't believe the sale had gone through so quickly, that he could come over on Friday and stay for a few days, help Hattie finish clearing the house, she knew that she couldn't refuse. He needed this money and what difference did a week make? Mali would be fine with it. And Hattie had to leave anyway, why not get it over with. So she agreed.

When the phone call had ended, she had tears in her eyes. She wiped them on the back of her hand and went over to Buddy. 'Well, that's us out of here in just over a week, Buddy. What do you think of that, then?'

He fixed his beady eyes on her, opened his beak and squawked, 'Bloody Hell!'

'My sentiments exactly,' she agreed.

She pulled herself together and phoned Mali to tell her the news.

'Honey, are you sure about this? You're more than welcome here, but you love that cottage. I can hear the sadness in your voice. And what about Marcus?'

'I've told you there is no Marcus. We're just friends.'

'I still think you should tell your dad how you feel before the sale goes through. He might not be able to do anything about it, but he should know.'

'No, I can't. He needs the money and I don't want him to feel guilty,' Hattie replied. 'I'm fine about the sale. I always knew that I was only here temporarily. Are you sure that you're okay to put me up for a couple of weeks? I could get a B&B.'

'No way. We'd be delighted to have you, you know that. What day are you completing?'

'Tuesday. I have to be out by midday.'

'Then I'll book the day off and come down to help you. We can put your stuff in my car.'

'Thank you.' She was blessed to have a friend like Mali. Now, all she had to do was tell Marcus.

'Ah, Hattie, I was about to come round to see you,' he said when he opened the door and saw her standing there.

'The sale has gone through quicker than we expected. We're leaving next Tuesday. Dad's coming over at the weekend to sign the papers and is staying over to help me clear the house.'

'Next Tuesday?' Marcus repeated, stunned.

Hattie nodded, blinking back her tears.

'Look, do you want to come in, have a drink? You look a bit shaken up,' he said.

'I can't, there's so much to do. I can't believe it. I know it's only a week earlier than we planned. But next week! It's so final.'

God, he must think she was stupid standing on his doorstep babbling like this and on the point of tears too. 'Anyway, I thought I'd better let you know because of Buddy. And because there will be holidaymakers in the cottage from the end of this month. I'm sorry about that. I know that it's not what you wanted but . . .' She turned away before she burst into tears.

'Hattie, are you sure you don't want to come in for a drink?'

'No. Thanks but I've got lots to do,' she called, keeping her back to him so that he couldn't see the tears flowing down her face. She knew that he was watching her. *Go inside*, she thought. *Please, go inside*.

As she turned to go down her own path, she heard Marcus shut his door. *Thank goodness for that*. She hated being so abrupt, but knew that if she had gone into his house for a drink she would have ended up sobbing in his arms and making a complete fool of herself.

So, she lay on the sofa and sobbed instead.

It wasn't until much later that she remembered Marcus had said he had something to tell her. Well, whatever it was, it didn't matter now. She was leaving next week. She would never see Marcus again.

Sadness overwhelmed her. *Tomorrow, I'll pick myself up, put a smile on my face and get on with it,* she decided. *But tonight, tonight I'll allow myself to be sad.*

Chapter Forty-Four

Owen arrived midday on Friday.

'Hello, love.' He put down the overnight bag he was carrying and held out his arms, a big smile on his face. Hattie immediately stepped into them for a hug. A few months ago she would have hesitated, before quickly hugging her dad, but she'd got closer to him now and was really pleased to see him. She wanted to show him what she and Nick had done to the cottage and was glad he was here to help with the final packing. She felt so sad at leaving. She'd only been here just over two months but it seemed a lot longer and she felt as if she belonged here.

'The front garden looks amazing,' Owen said as he stepped into the hall, leaving his case by the front door and going into the lounge. 'And goodness, so does this!' His gaze swept the long room. 'I know you showed it all to me on WhatsApp but that didn't do it justice. It looks so fresh and bright and I love all the little nick-nacks you've got about. It's really cheerful and airy.'

'Thanks. I wanted it to look welcoming, and for anyone who came in to feel at home, as if they could live here.'

'Well, you've certainly achieved that. I popped in when I attended Albert's funeral and it was so dark and dingy. You've done wonders.'

'I should have come to the funeral with you. I'm sorry.'

'Don't you get beating yourself up about that. I expect you barely remember Albert.'

'I remember our holidays here, and I wish I had gone to the funeral now. Or at least met up with you afterwards,' she confessed.

'It's all water under the bridge now, love,' he said. 'Mind if I take a look around the rest of the cottage?'

'Of course. Wait until you see the bathroom. Do you want to bring your bag with you? I've put you in Uncle Albert's old room.'

'Good idea.' He picked up his bag and followed her out of the lounge, down the hall and up the first set of stairs, marvelling at the new bathroom suite and the fresh, bright bedroom with its matching bedspread and curtains. 'You've really worked hard on this, Hattie. I didn't expect you to do so much.'

'I've enjoyed doing it. It's a lovely cottage, I wanted to bring it back to life. Put your bag down, then come and see my room.'

He followed her up the staircase to the attic, nodding in approval as he walked in. 'You've certainly worked wonders with the entire cottage. But I expected you to have the bedroom downstairs, not this attic room.'

'I like this room. It reminds me of when we all came down on holiday when you and Mum were still together.' She felt awkward then, as if she was having a dig at him. She went over to the window and looked out. 'I like the view from this window too, over the rooftops and to the sea.'

'I'm so sorry, love.'

She turned around to face her Dad, about to ask what he was sorry for, then saw the look on his face, the clouding of his eyes, and the words stuck in her throat. She'd made him feel guilty.

'I didn't realise how hard the divorce would be for you. I should have made more time for you. Come to see you more.' His voice was heavy with regret.

'It's okay, Dad. I had a chat with Nick, and I can see things clearer now. I'm sorry I was so bolshie. I just felt . . . abandoned.'

'I was so busy, there was such a lot to do, and I thought you were happy with your mum. But I should have realised, made more of an effort.'

'It's fine, Dad. Really, it is.' She went over to him and gave him a hug. 'We made it in the end, didn't we? Thanks to Uncle Albert.'

Owen wrapped his arms around her. 'We did, love.'

'Come on, let me show you the back garden now. You'll love it,' Hattie said, easing herself out of the embrace.

Owen followed her downstairs and outside. His eyes widened as he stepped out into the back yard. 'It's incredible. You've transformed it, Hattie. No wonder the cottage was snapped up so quickly.'

'I like to sit out here and eat breakfast in the morning. The sun shines down and I can hear the seagulls squawking and smell the sea.' She sniffed. 'Can you smell it?'

Owen sniffed too. 'Yes, I can.'

He looked at the motorbike leaning against the shed wall. 'Is that yours?'

'Yes, it's so much easier to get about on a bike than in a car, although I'm thinking I might have to get myself a little car.'

'So, you've settled in here, then?' he asked, looking thoughtful.

Hattie nodded eagerly. 'I've had lots of commissions for photographs. Actually, I thought you might like to eat out tonight at Gwel Teg, the hotel where I photographed the wedding, and took the photos for the website. The people are so nice and friendly. Marcus next door is the chef there – he helped look after Uncle Albert a lot.'

'That sounds good,' Owen agreed. 'How about a cuppa first and then we'll make our way up there.'

Hattie went in to put the kettle on, pleased that her dad approved of all the changes she'd made to Fisherman's Rest. She could see he was really impressed.

'Now, tell me how the B&B is doing,' she asked as they sat down outside with their cups of tea. 'I bet Raina is busy without you to help this weekend.'

'Nick and Glenn are helping out. Business has picked up a bit, thank goodness.'

They both turned around as they heard the door open next door. It was Marcus, heading off for work. He glanced over the wall and waved.

Hattie waved back. 'This is my dad. Dad, this is Marcus.'

'I can see that; you've got the same features,' Marcus told her. He nodded at Owen. 'Pleased to meet you, Mr Rowland.'

'Owen, please. And thank you for looking after Albert, and helping Hattie,' Owen told him.

Marcus raised an eyebrow questioningly.

'I told Dad how you helped me with the decluttering,' Hattie told him.

'Ah, well, it was a pleasure. Now, you'll have to excuse me, I'm due in work soon.'

'We're coming up for a meal later. I want to show Dad the

hotel,' Hattie told him. 'Will you be able to join us afterwards in the bar?' What made her ask him that? An urge to see as much of him as she could before she left, she realised.

'I'll try to, but you'll have to hang about until just gone ten, I'm working until then.'

'That's no problem. We can have a leisurely meal and a drink while we're waiting,' Owen said.

'See you later, then.' Marcus nodded then dashed off.

'He seems a nice chap. He's a chef, you say?' Owen said.

'In the evenings. He's an artist too, so he paints in the day-time. He did a portrait for Lord Thomwell's birthday, he lives in a big Manor near Truro. And he had some paintings in an exhi-bition a couple of weeks ago,' she added, suddenly realising that she hadn't asked Marcus how he'd got on. She guessed he hadn't won or he would have told her. She must ask him to show her the portrait of Buddy before she left, though. She could take a photo of it and frame it.

'Very impressive,' Owen said. 'You two seem pretty friendly. I guess he's going to miss having you as a neighbour.'

'Maybe.' She was definitely going to miss him. 'Do you want to go for a walk along the harbour front then we can head to the hotel?'

'I'd love to. It was always one of my favourite places in Port Medden. I used to go with Albert on his boat, you know, when I was in my teens.'

'Did you really?' Hattie was fascinated. 'So you were really close at one time?' She grabbed her keys and they both walked out into the hall.

'We were,' Owen said. As they walked down to the harbour he told her about some of his fishing trips with Albert and

302

Hattie thought once again what a shame it was that he had lost touch with his older step-brother. Just as she had almost lost touch with her Dad.

Well now they were back on track. And she and Nick were on a better footing too. Thanks to Uncle Albert they were a reunited family.

They were looking over the harbour now. Hattie took a deep breath, inhaling the smell of sea air and fish. 'It's beautiful, isn't it?' she said. 'Uncle Albert was so lucky to live here. No wonder he never wanted to move.'

She felt her dad's eyes on her. 'You really love Port Medden, don't you?'

Damn, she hadn't meant to sound so enthusiastic. She didn't want him to feel guilty that she had to move out. 'Doesn't everyone love the seaside?' she said lightly.

Mandy greeted them enthusiastically when they arrived at the hotel, and Sue came out to say hello too, telling Owen how Hattie had saved Ellie and Reece's wedding day. 'She works magic with that camera,' she said.

'They seem to think a lot of you here,' Owen said as they tucked into their meal.

'They've been very kind to me. It really is a lovely place,' Hattie told him. She lowered her head as tears stung her eyes. What the heck was she doing, bursting into tears in front of her dad? Hopefully he hadn't noticed. It was because she was so sad at leaving Port Medden. It was suddenly hitting her that this was her last weekend here. She was actually going. And she so desperately didn't want to.

Grow up, you're just being sentimental. You knew this was only ever temporary. You'll soon find somewhere else just as nice to live.

303

She managed to pull herself together and they chatted easily through the meal. Owen asked to see some of the photos she'd taken, and Hattie showed him some of them on her phone. She showed him the board in the reception area with the photos of the members of staff that she'd taken. 'They're on the hotel Facebook page too,' she said. 'And Marcus did that painting over there.' She pointed to the painting of *The Storm*. 'I told you that he was talented.'

'He certainly is,' Owen agreed.

After dinner, they went for a drink in the hotel bar and Marcus joined them.

'Have you lived down here long, Marcus?' Owen asked.

Marcus told him he'd grown up there, and when his mum had remarried and moved away he'd missed Port Medden so much he'd moved in with his grandparents.

'And you wouldn't want to move away?' Owen asked. He seemed genuinely interested, Hattie thought in surprise.

Marcus took a sip of his lager before replying. 'No, I love it here. It's the sort of place that calls to you. Some people like the busyness of big cities, but me, I like quietness, stillness, to be by the sea. I like to ride the waves and walk barefoot along the shore.' He suddenly looked embarrassed. 'And I've gone on a bit there!'

'It's good to hear someone so enthusiastic about a place,' Owen told him. 'And I hear you're an artist too.'

'An award-winning artist,' Danny, the barman, said, collecting their empty glasses. 'He likes to keep it quiet, though. I wouldn't have known, if I didn't read it in the paper. You must be proud,' he said to Hattie.

'What?' Hattie looked from Marcus to the barman in astonishment. 'You mean that you won that exhibition?'

'Danny,' Marcus said but Danny did no more than pick up the local paper from off the coffee table and open it to the second page.

'There. Didn't you know?'

Hattie stared at the article in front of her. It announced that local artist Marcus Wilson had won top prize in an exhibition in London. Below it was a photo of the award-winning painting. And it wasn't Buddy. It was Hattie in her black leathers astride her motorbike.

Chapter Forty-Five

Hattie was staring incredulously at the photo. She looked stunned. Speechless. Hell, he hadn't wanted her to find out like that, he'd been trying to tell her but how do you tell someone that you've done a secret painting of them and entered it into an exhibition? It sounded a bit stalkerish.

'That is a marvellous painting, you've really caught Hattie's spirit,' Owen said admiringly. 'I'd love to see the original.'

'It's still at the exhibition at the moment,' Marcus told him, his eyes on Hattie. Her gaze was on him now, her eyes wide, her expression hard to read.

'When did you do this? Why didn't you tell me?' she demanded.

'I was going to, I only heard that I won last week, then you had the news that the house sale was going through quicker than you thought and, well, it never seemed the right time.'

'How much are you selling the painting for?' Owen asked.

Marcus shook his head. 'It isn't for sale.'

He wished he could read Hattie's expression. Was she angry? Pleased? It was hard to tell.

He could feel Owen's eyes on him, scrutinising him. He was probably thinking that it was a creepy thing to do, to paint someone and not tell them. He'd be right too. Whatever had possessed him to do it?

Because I wanted a memento of her, something to remember her by when she had gone.

Owen glanced from Marcus to Hattie, then got to his feet. 'Well, excuse me while I go to the loo.'

He was giving them time to talk, Marcus realised. He leaned over the table. 'I'm sorry. I should have told you but you were so busy with the move.' He paused. 'Do you mind?'

'You painted it from that photo you took of me at Lord Thomwell's birthday, ,' she said, her voice little more than a whisper.

He nodded, trying to figure out whether she was pleased or upset. 'You looked so alive . . .' And sexy and gorgeous.

'Why did you paint a picture of me and enter it into an exhibition without telling me?'

Why indeed. He frowned, trying to find the words to explain. 'I didn't intend to enter it in the exhibition, but Lady Thomwell saw it and talked me into it. She took it down to London herself.'

'You showed it to Lady Thomwell – and probably Estelle – but not to me?'

Okay, so she wasn't pleased, she was upset.

'I didn't mean them to see it, they followed me up to the attic instead of waiting outside for me to bring the painting of Buddy down.' He rested his elbows on the table and leaned across. 'I've been trying to find the right time to tell you. I was going to tell you today but then I saw your dad was here and, well, I wanted to catch you on your own.'

'Dad's signing the sale papers for the cottage, we're exchanging on Monday and completing on Tuesday. When exactly did you plan on telling me? The day I left?'

'I'm sorry if you're upset . . .'

'Upset? You blasted me for taking a photo of you surfing without your permission, remember? Yet you think it's okay to paint my portrait and put it in an exhibition without telling me?'

She looked furious. And she was right to be. He should have told her. How could he explain? *Just tell her, she's leaving anyway so what does it matter?*

'I told you, I didn't mean to put the painting in an exhibition, that was Lady Thomwell's idea,' he blurted out. 'I painted it for myself, as something to remember you by.'

Hattie was stunned. Why did Marcus want something to remember her by? Could he possibly have feelings for her like she did for him? If so, why hadn't he said before, instead of leaving it until now, when she was leaving?

And the painting, it was beautiful. It made her look sexy, exciting . . . is that how he saw her?

He was looking at her now, and she was sure that was love she saw in his eyes. She couldn't tear her gaze from him, she wanted to reach out and touch him, to feel his skin against hers.

God, this was hopeless. Why now?

'Hattie . . .' his voice seemed to come from deep within his throat.

She pushed her chair back and stood up. 'I can't do this. Not now.'

Fighting back tears, she ran out of the bar into the reception, where her dad was talking to Mandy.

'All right, love?' he asked as she desperately tried to pull herself together.

She nodded, not trusting herself to speak. 'Do you mind if we go home now?'

'Of course we can.'

'Remember to come and say goodbye to us before you leave,' Mandy told her.

'I will.' Her voice sounded wobbly and she was sure she was going to burst into tears right there.

Her father followed her out of the hotel and they walked down the hill in silence, neither of them saying a word until they were back at Fisherman's Rest. Still struggling to compose herself, Hattie put the kettle on.

'Are you all right, love? Did the painting upset you?'

She tried to find the words to express how she felt without letting her dad know she was in love with Marcus. 'It was a bit of a shock, that's all. It's the last thing I expected him to do. And to not tell me . . .' Her voice trailed off and she stared down into her drink.

'He must think a lot of you.'

Startled, she raised her head, her eyes flicking to her father's face, then away again. 'Why do you say that?'

'It's obvious. He painted it in secret, and the painting is so personal to him that he won't sell it. And as it's the winning painting in the exhibition, I bet there are collectors who would pay a lot of money for it.'

Hattie bit her lip. She couldn't cope with this now, thinking that Marcus might love her as she loved him.

'Do you . . . think a lot of him too?' Her father's voice was quiet.

'We're friends, that's all.'

'Is that because you're selling this cottage and moving away, so you both don't want to take things any further?'

We have taken things further and it was wonderful. She forced herself to meet his scrutinising gaze. She didn't want him feeling guilty about selling the cottage, he needed the money. 'It just wouldn't work between us, Dad. It's a good job I am moving away,' she told him.

'If you're sure?'

'Absolutely.'

So why did she end up crying into her pillow that night, not able to hold back her tears at the thought of never seeing Marcus again?

The next morning, she pulled herself together, washed her face in cold water to ease her swollen eyes, and smoothed on a layer of foundation to try and reduce the redness. She looked at her reflection in the mirror. Passable. Then she pasted a big smile on her face and went downstairs, where her dad was already up, sitting out in the back yard drinking a coffee.

'You're an early bird,' she told him, pulling up the chair next to him and sitting on it. 'Couldn't you sleep? I know the seagulls are a bit noisy.'

He took a gulp of his coffee before replying. 'It wasn't the seagulls, it was my thoughts that kept me awake. I was thinking of all the holidays we had down here with Albert. They were good times, weren't they?'

She nodded, surprised to hear that her dad had been reminiscing.

310

'Albert loved this cottage. And I can see that you do too. You've transformed it, but still kept its character. You've made it your home instead of Albert's home.'

That's how she thought of the cottage, as her home. But it wasn't, it was soon going to be home to a string of holidaymakers. 'I made it nice so we could sell it quicker,' she said, not wanting her dad to feel guilty about having to sell.

Owen drained his coffee and put the mug down on the table, then turned to her. He took both her hands in his, his gaze on her face. 'Hattie, I want you to answer something truthfully for me. Will you do that?'

Uh-oh, was he going to ask her if she was in love with Marcus? She nodded slowly, bracing herself for the question.

'If you could stay in this cottage, live here in Port Medden, would you want to?'

What should she say? She couldn't live here and she didn't want him to feel bad about selling but she had promised to tell the truth.

'Well, I do like it here, but don't worry, I'll soon find somewhere else I like just as much,' she told him. 'Don't feel bad about us having to sell. I always knew I was only here for a little while, and it's done me good. I know what I want to do with my life now.'

'Be a self-employed photographer, you mean?'

'Yes, you'd be amazed how many commissions I've had, Dad. I really think I can make a go of it.'

He was still holding her hands. 'Then let's not sell the cottage. You stay here. You can buy me out, paying so much a month. What do you say?'

For a moment, she thought she hadn't heard right. She stared

311

at him and he smiled and nodded. She swallowed. Was he serious? 'You need the money though, don't you? For the B&B? Nick said you were desperate for it.'

'I need ten thousand now to pay off the one loan that moves to high interest next month, the rest of the loans are low interest so if you could pay me back enough each month to cover them that would be fine. I thought maybe we could raise the ten thousand against the house then take it off what you owe me.'

'We don't need to. I have that. I've got my redundancy money. I can give you ten thousand out of that and still have enough to live on while I set my business up.' She couldn't believe this was really happening.

'That's brilliant. And I don't want the full asking price for the cottage, not off my own daughter.' He mentioned a much lower sum and a monthly payment that Hattie could manage easily. Even if her photography business didn't take off as well as she hoped, a part-time job would easily cover the cottage payment and food.

'Are you sure, Dad?'

'I'm positive. I can see how much you love the cottage and I'd like to keep it in the family. I reckon Albert would approve too.'

Hattie clapped her hands in delight. 'Thank you so much.'

'Right, well, now that's settled, I'll phone the solicitor and tell him the sale is off.'

'I should feel guilty about that but I don't,' Hattie said. 'The Bryants just wanted the place as a holiday home. They'll soon find another one. I don't think Jonathan will be pleased, though.'

'That can't be helped,' Owen said, picking up his phone.

Hattie listened as her Dad told the solicitor that they had changed their mind about selling Fisherman's Rest, Hattie would be buying him out and living in it. Then he asked him to draw up all the necessary paperwork for Hattie to buy his half of the cottage. After that, he phoned Jonathan to let him know the sale was off. 'Now, how about we go out for lunch to celebrate you being the owner of Fisherman's Rest,' he said.

'Thank you, Dad!' Hattie threw her arms around his neck and gave him a big hug.

Chapter Forty-Six

It had been a wonderful weekend. Hattie and her dad had talked a lot, built a lot of bridges, and she was really looking forward to visiting him at Christmas.

'Bring a friend if you want,' he said as he hugged her goodbye on Monday.

She glanced at him. 'That's very kind of you.' She didn't ask him which friend; she knew who he meant. Her dad had got this idea in his head that Marcus was in love with her. He was wrong. If he was in love with her, he would have told her, asked her not to leave. He didn't even know now that she wasn't leaving anymore, and she wasn't going to knock on his door and tell him. She wasn't staying for him. She was staying because she loved the cottage and Port Medden. Because this was the place she wanted to live.

She felt a bit sad as she waved her father goodbye. For the first time since she was a child, she felt close to him again, and had really enjoyed his company. He'd been so kind and understanding, and she was overwhelmed at the fact that Fisherman's Rest was now her home. Forever. She closed the door and went back into the lounge, looking around happily.

'This is our home, Buddy,' she said to the parrot who was cheerfully nibbling at a piece of apple. He lifted his head and stared at Hattie, then squawked, 'Bloody hell!'

She grinned. She could hardly believe it too. Fisherman's Rest belonged to her. She didn't have to move. She could stay here in Port Medden, the little town she had come to love. Living next door to Marcus.

Would he be pleased? she wondered.

She'd just made herself a cup of frothy coffee and was tucking into a slice of chocolate cake when there was a knock on the door. She sighed, hoping it wasn't Jonathan come to try and talk her into changing her mind. He hadn't been very happy when Owen had phoned that morning to say that they weren't going ahead with the sale. Perhaps if she ignored it he might think that she was out and go away. She took another bite of her cake.

There was another knock on the door. Whoever it was, wasn't going to give up.

She swallowed down the cake in her mouth and got up and went to answer the door. To her surprise, it was Marcus standing on the doorstep, not Jonathan.

'I saw your dad go out and, well, I wanted to talk to you. Can I come in for a few minutes?'

He looked a bit awkward. She wondered if this was about the painting again. Maybe he'd got it back and was going to show it to her. She had said she wanted to see it.

'Sure.' She turned back towards the lounge, leaving Marcus to close the front door behind him and follow her through.

As soon as he saw Marcus, Buddy started hopping on his perch and whistling. 'Where you been? Where you been?'

Marcus grinned and walked over to the cage. 'Working, mate,' he said. He dug around in his pocket, pulled out a grape and handed it to the parrot, who took it with great delight.

'I'm going to miss him.' Marcus turned around to Hattie. 'And you. That's what I came to say, really. That I'm going to miss you. Lots. I wish I hadn't wasted so much of the short time we had together being so disapproving and snarky. I wish we hadn't had that stupid mix-up with Estelle. I wish we had longer together. And –' he gazed at her – 'I wanted to ask you if we could maybe go out for a goodbye meal tonight?'

Was he saying that he didn't want her to go? 'No,' she said simply.

She saw his face cloud over. He nodded briskly. 'Okay. I understand. Sorry if I got it wrong.'

He went to march past her, his face tightly set, but she grabbed his hand. 'No, because I'm not going anywhere. I'm staying right here. Dad's selling the cottage to me. I'm paying him so much a month.'

Marcus's eyes held hers. 'You're not leaving?'

She shook her head, hardly daring to breathe. Was he pleased? He looked stunned. Did he love her? Had she got it all wrong?

Then Marcus's face broke into a wide smile and he held out his arms. 'That is the best news ever.'

She went into his arms and nestled against his chest. Was he pleased as a friend? Because he could still see Buddy?

Marcus wrapped his arms around her and hugged her tightly. Then he said softly, 'Hattie . . .'

She eased herself out of the embrace a bit to look at him. 'Yes . . . ?'

'I love you.'

He was gazing down at her, with such tenderness in his eyes that she knew he meant it.

'I love you too.'

'Really?'

She nodded. 'Really.'

He pulled her closer, his mouth seeking hers, and then she was lost in the passion of his embrace.

Much, much later, as they lay entwined on the sofa, their clothes a tangled heap on the floor where they had discarded them before making love, Hattie thought that she had never felt happier. She was home.

'I think I fell in love with you the first time I set eyes on you,' Marcus whispered in her ear. 'Only I didn't know it then.'

'When you walked in on me naked in the kitchen, you mean?' she said.

'Well, you did look incredibly gorgeous. Then you glared at me with fire flashing in your eyes, swiped the tablecloth of the table and wrapped yourself in it while you stood your ground and argued with me. How could I resist?'

She groaned. 'I must have looked ridiculous.'

'You looked incredibly sexy, and feisty. I don't think I've ever met anyone like you, Hattie. You're so natural, so warm and easy-going.' He pulled her closer to him and kissed her on the forehead. 'I tried so hard to fight it because I knew you were leaving, and in my experience long-distance relationships don't work out. But I couldn't bear you to leave with us at logger-heads. That's why I came around today.'

She snuggled into him. 'I felt the same. I didn't want to admit I loved you because it would complicate things. I knew we had to sell the cottage, but Dad saw how much it meant to me, and

I think he realised how much we meant to each other too, so he said he wanted me to have Fisherman's Rest, to keep it in the family. He's sold his half to me really cheap and letting me pay it monthly.'

'That's brilliant.' He smiled down at her. 'Mandy could see that we loved each other too. She told me that you were meant to stay in Port Medden. Her intuition told her that you wouldn't leave. It seems that she was right.'

'I'm glad. I don't want to leave,' Hattie murmured as she nestled into his chest. 'This is exactly where I want to be.'

Marcus lowered his head and kissed her. 'And this is exactly where I want to be too.'

'Night, night!' Buddy squawked. 'Time for bed!'

'I think Buddy is right. Shall we go up?' Marcus asked.

'That sounds like a very good idea,' Hattie agreed.

Chapter Forty-Seven

Two weeks later

Hattie's breath caught in her throat as she stared up at the painting of Buddy. It was so lifelike, the colours so vibrant. Marcus had caught the cheeky parrot's personality so well. She couldn't believe that this one hadn't won first prize. Marcus really was talented.

'It's brilliant,' she told Marcus, who was standing by her side. 'I can almost feel the feathers. I expect Buddy to open his beak and squawk "Bugger off!" any minute.'

'It is spectacular, and I'm sure it would have won a prize, but an artist is only allowed one award no matter how many paintings they enter, and the one of you is absolutely stunning,' said Lady Thomwell, who was standing on the other side of her.

Hattie felt her cheeks flush. She felt a bit uncomfortable being the centre of such attention, and still hardly believed that Marcus had secretly painted a portrait of her and entered it into this competition.

'You must be dying to see it?' Lady Thomwell said, turning to look at her.

She was. Yet she felt self-conscious too. She nodded. 'I am curious.'

They carried on walking along the room. Marcus held her hand as they gazed at the different paintings on the wall. There had been so many talented entries, what had made them choose Marcus's painting of her? Hattie wondered.

'Here we are, my dear,' Lady Thomwell said.

Hattie looked up at the wall, then gasped at the woman who almost leapt out of the frame at her. Black-leather clad Hattie, straddling her motorbike, the zip of her jacket undone enough to reveal the top of her sun-kissed breasts, her unruly blond hair blowing behind her in the wind, her ruby-red lips parted in a half-smile, her sapphire-blue eyes twinkling with mischief. She looked sexy, wild, exciting. And anyone who looked at this painting would have no doubt that the artist loved the woman in it. Love was there in every stroke of the brush, every tiny detail, breathing so much life into the painting that it looked as if the rider might rev up the bike any moment and come racing out of the picture. It took her breath away looking at it and knowing that Marcus had painted it in secret. That he had refused to sell it because this was his memento of her. His declaration of love, even if maybe he hadn't realised that at the time. She couldn't tear her eyes away from it. Then she realised that Marcus and Lady Thomwell were waiting for her reaction.

'It's . . .' She sought around for an adequate word to describe it. 'Amazing,' she plumped for, even though that sounded so lame. She turned to Marcus. 'I can't believe it's me. It's so . . . alive.'

'Which is how I see you. Alive. Free.' He squeezed her hand. 'And incredibly sexy.'

She felt her cheeks flush again.

'It's an arresting portrait. The judges were apparently unanimous in their decision to award it first prize,' Lady Thomwell said. 'And it's this portrait that made Estelle realise that she didn't stand a chance with you.' She was talking to Marcus now. 'The love for the subject is so evident. It leaps out at you.'

So, she wasn't the only one who had seen that. Marcus had painted her out of love. He had secretly loved her all those weeks. Just as she had secretly loved him.

'Can we have a photo of the artist and the woman in the painting together?' a photographer asked.

Hattie and Marcus obliged, standing hand in hand in front of the painting. Then they were both interviewed, the reporters wanting to know how Hattie had felt when she realised Marcus's secret painting of her had won first prize. 'Astonished, proud ... honoured,' she said, smiling at him.

Much later, when they got back to the hotel they were staying in for the night, Marcus wrapped her in his arms and kissed her. 'Do you like the painting?'

'I love it!' she nestled into him.

'I'm sorry I did it in secret, I should have told you, but that would have meant ...'

'Telling me how you feel?' she asked gently.

He nodded. 'And I wasn't ready to confess that yet, not even to myself.'

'Neither was I,' she admitted. 'I needed time to get used to Port Medden, to fall in love with this place first, before I admitted I loved you. I had to make sure that I was staying here for me, not for you, that I would be happy to still live here if you didn't love me.'

321

'And would you?' he asked softly.

She nodded. 'Yes. I feel like it's my home, I never want to move.' She looked up at him, suddenly serious. 'But I am glad that you love me. It would have been so hard to see you every day, otherwise, and to see you with someone else.'

'That will never happen,' he promised. And then they were kissing again. And then the kissing deepened and they were making love.

The next morning, they set off for the journey back to Cornwall in Lady Thomwell's chauffeur-driven Rolls-Royce. The two paintings were in the boot.

'Let me know if you ever want to sell one of those paintings, Marcus,' Lady Thomwell said when they had pulled up at the back of the cottages and Marcus and Hattie were taking the paintings out of the boot. She smiled as her eyes rested on Hattie. 'Although, I doubt if you ever will.'

'I won't,' he told her. 'They are absolutely not for sale.'

They waved as Lady Thomwell drove off, then looked at each other. 'What are you going to do with the paintings?' Hattie asked him.

'Well, I was going to hang them up in my lounge to remind me of you and Buddy when you'd left,' he said.

'But now we're not going . . .'

'I'm going to put the one of you in my bedroom, so that you're the first thing I see when I open my eyes every morning,' he said, kissing her.

'And the one of Buddy?'

'I thought you might like that. You could do with a couple more paintings on your walls.'

She smiled. 'I would love it. If you're sure.'

'Absolutely sure. Now, how about I take my painting in, then come and hang yours up for you?'

'I'll leave the catch on the door for you and put the kettle on,' she told him.

Buddy was pleased to see her when she walked in, squawking, 'Hello, Hattie!' and dancing along his perch. Seeing how happy he was to have company again gave Hattie an idea. When Marcus arrived a few minutes later with the painting of Buddy, she asked him to put it up on the wall opposite the cage, so that Buddy could see it. As she had thought, the parrot was fascinated with the painting. He cocked his head on one side, whistled, then started talking to it.

Marcus grinned. 'I think you've found the perfect solution to Buddy being lonely when you're out.'

'It's so realistic, it's incredible,' she told him.

She looked around the cottage and breathed out a sigh of happiness. 'I can't believe this is my home. I'm so glad I don't have to leave it.'

'So am I.' Marcus wound his arms around her and kissed her. 'I can't imagine my life without you.'

'I don't even want to think of mine without you,' she replied. Then they were in each other's arms again, their kisses deepening, their caresses getting more urgent, and the coffee went cold.

Much, much later, they made fresh coffee, and a sandwich, then went for a walk along the beach, hand in hand. As she gazed out across the shimmering ocean, Marcus's arm around her shoulder, Hattie thought that this was exactly where she wanted to be, by Marcus's side. Forever.

Acknowledgements

Firstly I'd like to thank the publishing team at Headline for allowing me to revisit Port Medden, the Cornish town where my bestselling romance, *The Cornish Hotel by the Sea*, is set. I really enjoyed meeting Ellie, Reece, Sue and Mandy again, bringing Marcus out of the kitchen and introducing new characters to my readers. Writing about Cornwall always brings back happy memories of the summer holidays spent there when my children were young, and the years I lived there. It will always remain one of my favourite places.

I'd especially like to thank my fabulous editor Katie Sunley, copy editor Eloise Wood and proof-reader Kay Gale for their expertise and support. Thanks also to talented artist Emily Cordelle for designing both this beautiful cover, and the gorgeous new cover for *The Cornish Hotel by the Sea*.

I am indebted to the bloggers and authors who support me by hosting me on their blogs, reviewing my books and sharing my posts. Particular thanks to the members of the Romantic Novelists' Association who are always willing to share their writing experience and advice. Also thanks to Rob Tysall of Tysall's

Photography for answering my questions on photography – any mistakes are my own. And of course, my thanks to the readers who buy my books, allowing me to live the dream of being an author. Thank you all so much.

Finally, last but not least, everlasting thanks to my lovely Dave, the wind beneath my wings, and my family and friends who all encourage me and support me so much. I love you all. x

Read more from
Karen King …

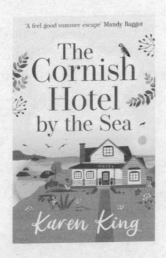

'A feel-good summer escape' Mandy Baggot

The
Cornish Hotel
by the Sea

Karen King

Ellie Truman's mum has been struggling to keep the family
hotel in Cornwall afloat since Ellie's dad passed away.
Ellie is determined to help her mum, even if that means
moving back to the sleepy Cornish village of Port Medden
she fled from broken-hearted a few years ago.

Running the hotel isn't easy and Ellie is grateful for the
help from charming guest, Reece Mitchell. Ellie feels
herself falling for Reece but should she trust him and
risk getting her heart broken again? And will their
hard work be enough to save the hotel?

ACCENT